The unexp

gaze jump t mirror. Instantly, his startled look jumped to the side mirror. By God, the guy was passing him *again*. Mann turned his head to scowl at the leviathan form as it drifted by. He tried to see into the cab but couldn't because of its height. What's with him, anyway? he wondered. What the hell are we having here, a contest? See which vehicle can stay ahead the longer?

He thought of speeding up to stay ahead but changed his mind. When the truck and trailer started back into the west-bound lane, he let up on the pedal, voicing a newly incredulous sound as he saw that if he hadn't slowed down, he would have been prematurely cut off again. Jesus Christ, he thought. What's with this guy?

DUEL

and other horror stories of the road

Edited by
WILLIAM PATTRICK

A STAR BOOK
published by
the Paperback Division of
W. H. Allen & Co. Plc

A Star Book
Published in 1987
by The Paperback Division of
W. H. Allen & Co. Plc
44 Hill Street, London W1X 8LB

First published in Great Britain by
W. H. Allen & Co. Plc in 1987

Printed and bound in Great Britain by
Anchor Brendon Ltd, Tiptree, Essex

ISBN 0 352 32164 4

Contents

INTRODUCTION 7
THE CAR WITH THE GREEN LIGHTS
William Le Queux 11
THE DUST-CLOUD *E. F. Benson* 29
HOW IT HAPPENED
Sir Arthur Conan Doyle 43
THE LAST TRIP *Archie Binns* 49
THE DEMON LOVER *Elizabeth Bowen* 59
JAY WALKERS *H. Russell Wakefield* 69
THE GHOST OF THE MODEL T
Betsy Emmons 83
THE GHOST CAR *Ken Batten* 91
NEW CORNER *L. T. C. Rolt* 109
'JUST LIKE WILD BOB' *William F. Nolan* 123
AUTO SUGGESTION *Charles Beaumont* 133
DUEL *Richard Matheson* 149
SECOND CHANCE *Jack Finney* 175
TRUCKS *Stephen King* 193
THE HITCH-HIKER *Roald Dahl* 211
ACKNOWLEDGEMENTS 224

For

BILL WAGLAND

– here's to life on the open road!

Introduction

It is just about one hundred years since the invention of the motor car. I say 'just about', because one of the biggest mysteries of all about the car is precisely when it was first made. There are several claimants to the honour, and indeed many attempts had been made at building a petrol-powered, passenger-carrying vehicle before two Germans, Karl Benz and Gottlieb Daimler, produced the first genuine motor vehicles in the middle 1880s. Motoring historians are still divided on the facts, but it seems most probable that Benz's three-wheel, internal-combustion-engined vehicle underwent its tests in 1885, while Daimler's pioneer four-wheeler took to the road only a few months later in 1886. What is beyond dispute, though, is that the two companies later merged and settled on the year 1986 to celebrate the centenary.

Just to complicate the issue, the Austrians have claimed that a certain Siegfried Markus ran a car of sorts in Vienna as early as 1875, while the French maintain that a textile manufacturer called Edouard Delamare-Deboutteville invented a two-cylinder 4.4-litre engine and fitted it to an old horse-carriage in 1884. (They even had a special three-month exhibition in Paris in 1984 to mark the occasion!) The Italians, too, have put forward a contender, Enrico Bernardi, a professor of agricultural machinery at Padua, who designed a vehicle with a tiny 122-cc single-cylinder engine that same year, while in Britain, a certain Thomas Rickett was said to have been making steam 'cars' long before any of these Europeans – way back in 1859, in fact.

Only the Americans are seemingly content to remain out of serious contention, though there are still those who think Henry Ford was the first manufacturer, but he did not actually make his first vehicle until 1893.

The fact of the matter is that the motor car – like many great inventions – was never really 'invented'. Instead it underwent a gradual process of refinement from the early steam-powered 'horseless carriage' until it became the fully-fledged item of about one hundred years ago – catching on with the public with a speed matched only by that of the microchip. It is beyond doubt one of the half-dozen most important creations to have affected twentieth-century life.

It comes as no surprise when considering the mystery which surrounds the birth of the motor car to discover that mystery has remained in close attendance to it ever since. There have, indeed, been all manner of mysterious incidents in which cars have been involved – ranging from inexplicable accidents to haunted roads and even phantom cars. You need only consult one of the many histories of motoring to see what I mean, or else take a selection of cuttings from the files of any great newspaper.

In the *Sunday Express* of December 1983, for instance, there is a story of the ghost that haunts the A40 near London and has dashed across the road so many times to be 'struck' by horrified motorists that it can be nothing other than a phantom. Equally well documented are stories of the figure of a man who has appeared repeatedly on a highway on Long Island near New York and was described by a *New York Times* reporter in May 1979 as being thought to be 'the victim of a hit-and-run motorist twenty years earlier'. Other newspapers have reported ghostly drivers and even phantom vehicles such as cars and buses. An account was written by the famous ghost hunter Elliott O'Donnell in 1933 says: 'Phantom coaches are a very common form of family haunting, and now phantom motor cars are joining this ghostly throng. A man I met recently in London told me that, on three occasions, before a death in his family, a motor car had been heard to come up the drive of their country house and stop at their front door. Yet, on each occasion, when they went to see who their visitor was, no one and no car was there. The phenomenon occurred one winter when the snow lay thick on the ground, but the mysterious car left no imprint.'

From these few examples, it is plain to see that there is mystery aplenty to be found in the annals of motoring. And this fact has also attracted the attention of some of the finest short story writers of the past century – as the contributions which form this collection will now bear testimony. They are, in fact, only the tip of the iceberg, but they do represent more than adequately the many different types of mysterious motoring story which can be found in the pages of hundreds of books, magazines and journals. It has been my pleasure to sift the best for your entertainment. May your journey now be an exciting and enthralling one – but no after-sale service is offered, I regret. Nor any redress for unexpected accidents, unforeseen shocks or even breakdowns. For you are travelling from hereon entirely at your own risk!

WILLIAM PATTRICK,
Suffolk, 1986.

THE CAR WITH THE GREEN LIGHTS

William Le Queux

One of the earliest writers to become captivated by the joys of motoring was William Le Queux (1864–1927) who was described on his hugely popular books as 'The Master of Mystery'. Le Queux was initially a special correspondent for several London newspapers, travelling all over Europe and Africa, before he gave this up to turn his many vivid first-hand experiences into novels. He had a special interest in spies and spying and this is reflected in several of his best-selling titles such as The Invasion of 1910 *(1906) which accurately predicted the First World War, and* The Zeppelin Destroyer *(1916).*

Le Queux had an abiding interest in things mechanical, too, and his biographer, N. St. Barbe Sladen, records in The Real Le Queux *(1938) how the novelist came to be one of the earliest motorists in Britain: 'The first motor car that arrived in England was shown one evening at the Imperial Institute in London, and a dinner followed. The public were astounded at the new marvel. Le Queux attended the dinner with the late Lord Northcliffe, who almost immediately afterwards ordered one of the new "road vehicles", and Le Queux was his companion on many of his early runs, both in England and abroad. Le Queux soon followed suit and bought his own motor car and was one of the first to travel across France to Monte Carlo. The breakdowns en route were apparently both numerous and unpleasant!' Not surprisingly, Le Queux later wrote a couple of novels about motoring,* The Mystery of a Motor Car *(1906) and* The Lady in the Car *(1908), both of which drew on his experiences of the hazardous open road! He also wrote the following short mystery story for the* Premier Magazine *in February 1916 which makes an ideal opening tale for the collection. I have a particular fondness for it because it is set in my native East Anglia (one of two such tales in the book: E. F. Benson's contribution is the other); and because of its evocative description of night-time motoring back in the early years of the century. The ideal setting for a fine mystery tale!*

A curious leaf from the Diary of Villiers Beethom-Saunders, Doctor of Medicine, of Harley Street, London – known to his intimates as 'Cinders' – revealed by his friend and executor, Charles Barrington Mayne, Esquire, Barrister-at-Law, of Fig Tree Court, Temple, and edited by William Le Queux.

This, and the few following pages of these confessions of mine, will, I believe, my dear Mayne, strike you as perhaps interesting, certainly surprising.

They will, I trust, reveal to you that, after all, my heart has not always been quite so black as my written words have already shown you, and that, though I have now passed away to the land which lies beyond the human ken and though my memory may be detested, it is only hated by those guilty of their own evil works.

As you will have already gathered from the foregoing strange narratives which I have here set down, it has been my keen spirit of patriotism and my stern determination to combat evil and annihilate my country's enemies which led me to the commission of those crimes of which I here openly confess I only reveal the truth – and the absolute truth. In this page of what you, and no doubt others, will term my disgraceful history, I think you will give me credit for being at least an honest and patriotic Briton, with 'Britain for the British' as my motto.

You recollect Ralph Hicks, our mutual friend – 'Pom-Pom Hicks,' as we used to call him, the nick-name he was known by out in South Africa, because of the quick execution he did among the Boers? Before the present war he lived, as you know, in rooms in Chelsea, where you and I have often smoked with him, and we used to meet over a drink in a certain small hotel in Jermyn Street.

A thin, wiry man, with hair slightly tinged with grey, he was, in the pre-war days, a constant traveller on the Continent, more often than not moving about rapidly from place to place, without any apparent reason or motive. He would write to me from the Grand at Rome one week, from Athens or from the Pera Palace in Constantinople the next, and then, as suddenly, he would ring me up from Chelsea, and ask me to come over for a smoke, and tell me of his rapid journeys and the curious people he had met. He was one of London's enigmas.

As you well know, he was once lost to us entirely for quite nine months, and his man Simms began to grow very anxious about him, and to fear that he might have died unidentified in some foreign hotel. Yet, of a sudden, late one night he turned up at my place in Harley Street, expecting to find me. Lettice was at home, and he left word with her that he had gone home feeling rather queer, and asked if I would run over and see him.

I did so, and I found him with a high temperature. He seemed very nervy and unstrung, yet he would reveal nothing to me, except that he said: 'I was in Madrid three months ago, and I believe I was poisoned, Cinders. I've never felt really well since. I wonder what it can be?'

For a week I treated him, and he recovered entirely, though he would never disclose where he had been all those months, except for his first reference to Madrid, or why he had not sent word of his existence to anyone. You, my dear Mayne, used, I remember, to remark upon the curious mystery surrounding him, and his reluctance to tell us why he so often flew abroad without any apparent motive. It certainly was not for his own pleasure, for he would go to the Riviera, or Southern Italy, in the full blaze of the summer months, to Paris when everyone was away in the mountains, or at the sea; or to the Meuse or to the Moselle in the depths of winter.

One clear June night in 1914 – before the outbreak of war – 'Pom-Pom' came to me at the moment when I was about to turn in after a very heavy day at the hospital, and as we smoked together he grew serious and looked very straight into my face, saying:

'Look here, Cinders, old chap, I think I can trust you with a secret, can't I?'

'I really hope so!' was my reply.

'Well,' he added, not without some slight hesitation, I noticed, 'I'm wondering if I could really trust you.'

'My dear Pom-Pom,' I said, 'as a professional man of some standing, I am often entrusted with a good many curious secrets – secrets which, if revealed, would, I believe, cause many scandals in Society homes.'

'I know – yes, I know!' he said, with slight irritation. 'It isn't that. No, no! I have no interest in domestic scandal, either in the castle or the cottage. My outlook upon life has for years been far wider. Now, tell me, Cinders, have you not regarded me for the past three years or so as something of a mystery?'

I hesitated.

'Well, if you really want to know – yes,' was my frank reply.

'I knew it. I've watched you and your lawyer friend, Mayne,' he said. 'I know how you have put your heads together and whispered when I have shaken your hands and left you.' Then, after a pause, he took a big gulp of the Scotch whisky-and-soda at his elbow, and, leaning back, blew a whiff from the fragrant Corona he was smoking. Then deliberately he exclaimed: 'Well, trusting that you will ever respect my confidence, dear old Cinders, I will now tell you the truth, because afterwards I want you to help me – if you will.'

'If I can, I certainly will do so,' I replied, somewhat surprised.

'The fact is, my dear fellow, that I'm about to leave London – perhaps early tomorrow morning – upon a journey that must be long and dangerous. The end of it I can't see. Indeed, I may perhaps never return. But while I am absent I beg of you to remain my friend. Will you?'

'Why, certainly!' I exclaimed, staring at him in surprise. 'But I hardly follow you. Why should this journey of yours be so dangerous?'

'Ah! That's a secret which, for the present, I'm not permitted to divulge,' was his slow, curious reply. 'Today I am sadly in need of a real, true friend, and I feel that I could not do better than seek your aid, Cinders. You've always been so decent to me – even though I know you have more than once suspected me of not playing the game. Well, I've not told you the whole truth,' he declared, with a faint, mysterious smile, 'simply because the seal of silence has been set upon my own lips – so I cannot betray a confidence placed in me. Do you blame me?'

'Of course not,' I said. 'But in what way do you need my assistance? What can I do?'

He paused for a moment. Then he replied. 'Simply this. I'm going away. Soon after I have gone you may hear of some amazing happenings – events that will startle the civilised world,' he said, speaking quite calmly, his eyes fixed upon mine. 'Today all is peace; tomorrow – next week – or next month there may be war – Great Britain may be at war. Who knows?'

I looked at him, wondering whether he had taken leave of his senses, for all was so peaceful.

'Ah!' he laughed. 'I quite see that you are startled, Cinders! You, and all the world, little dream of the terrible truth – of the terrors shortly in store for Europe and for our own dear land.'

'How do you know?' I demanded.

'Never mind how I know, Cinders,' was his answer, speaking very coolly and slowly. 'I only tell you to watch carefully the course of events, and to ask yourself whether this prophecy, made to you on this night in June, is not fulfilled. As soon as it is you will know that I shall be in gravest peril. And it is you alone who will be able to help me.'

'How?' I inquired eagerly.

Rising, he took a scrap of paper from my writing-table, and with the pencil attached to his watch-chain, scribbled an address – that of a certain George Clutterbuck, living in Lamington Mansions, that big block of flats at Westminster overlooking St James's Park.

'Keep that carefully,' he urged. Then, a moment later, he said, 'You once told me that you could read Swedish – is that so?'

'Well, just a bit,' was my reply. 'Long ago I spent a couple of years at the Royal Hospital in Gothenburg.'

'Good! I shall send you regularly the *Aftonbladet*, the Stockholm newspaper. They will despatch it daily from the office. Here is a copy,' and he drew one from his pocket, and, opening it in the centre, placed his finger upon the head of the second advertisement column, saying: 'What I want you to do is to glance at the head of this column every day, in order to find any message from me. Be sure and never miss a single day, will you? So very much depends upon it. When you get the message, will you act exactly as it directs?'

'Certainly, my dear Pom-Pom,' was my reply. 'But all this sounds awfully mysterious. What does it mean?'

He paused, and looked seriously into my eyes – very seriously.

'It means much more than you can ever dream, Cinders,' was his reply. 'If you will promise faithfully to carry out any request you find in the paper, then I shall leave London with a contented mind, feeling that at least I possess one good and true friend.'

'I have promised,' I said, much mystified at his words. 'When do you expect to send me the message?'

He shrugged his shoulders, that habit of his you will well remember.

'Ah! I don't know. It may be weeks – or months. Exactly

when, I cannot tell you,' was his answer.

'Where will you be? Can't I write to you, or you to me? Why advertise in a Swedish paper?'

'Because – well, I shall be unable to write,' was his mysterious answer.

I confess that by his attitude and his words I was much puzzled. I copied the address he had given me into my address book, and it was late into that balmy June night before he rose and gripped my hand hard in farewell.

'Well, good-bye, Cinders, I trust in you to help me,' he said. 'In anybody I send to you you may place implicit confidence. He will mention one word to you, a variation of your own name – "Ashes." By that you will know that he is my messenger. You'll remember that, won't you?'

'Yes,' I said. 'Good-bye, Pom-Pom – and good luck on your mysterious journey.'

Then I opened the door, and he passed down the steps into the moonlit streets and out of sight.

Three weeks slipped by. You will remember how, more than once, you expressed to me wonder as to where Pom-Pom Hicks had gone. I, too, often wondered.

Then one night, that of August 4, a thunderbolt fell upon the world – the event which our friend had so mysteriously forecasted – the Empires of Great Britain and Germany were at war. It was you, my dear Mayne, who rang me up at one o'clock, I being at the time in bed, and told me the fateful news.

I then remembered those words of the man who had gone down my steps and disappeared that night in June. I said not a word, neither to you nor to Lettice, for I regarded his confidence as sacred. Yet how was it possible that he should have had secret knowledge of that disaster that was to befall the world? His record as a gallant and fearless soldier had indeed been a brilliant one. Many men had praised his wonderful exploits in South Africa, where he had won the D.S.O. I had heard men who had seen his work declare that Pom-Pom led a charmed life, and that no enemy bullet could ever wound him. And this was the man who knew that war was intended by Germany, and who had warned me against the terrors that were to overshadow Europe!

As that night I rose and went out into the London streets, where the excitement had risen to fever-heat, I suddenly recollected his promise to send me the Stockholm *Aftonbladet*, and wondered why I had not received it.

Then weeks and months went on – dark months for our dear country. The hospitals soon became filled with the maimed from the front, and I, with the whole of Harley Street, was kept busy night and day. Poor fellows! Only the doctor who tends them knows the pluck, the dogged sternness, and the deep gratitude of the British 'Tommy.' The Briton only shows himself in his true and sterling colours in the trenches or on the sick-bed, a statement with which every medical man in the land will, I feel confident, agree.

In vain I waited for the promised newspaper. Christmas passed; the New Year came. Belgium had been occupied, and the Franco-British forces had presented a bold front against the invasion of France by an enemy whose character and mode of warfare not only put to shame the methods of barbarians, but would be handed down in the history of the world as satanic.

One night – the night of May 26 – two hundred and ninety-six days after war had broken out – the evening papers contained the report of the unfortunate loss of the Triumph. I had dined with you at the club, and on my return to Harley Street I found among my letters the first copy of the *Aftonbladet*.

Pom-Pom Hicks had not forgotten me, after all!

I tore off the wrapper and searched the column he had indicated, but could discover no message.

Then copies of the paper began to arrive with great regularity, two or three by each mail from Sweden, despatched from the office of the journal in Stockholm.

I recollected how he had urged me to keep a careful eye upon that column; therefore, after examining the papers, I carefully arranged them and filed them, so as to see if I had missed any copy.

All went regularly, until one day I was dismayed to find that copies for Monday, July 19, Tuesday, July 20, and Friday, July 23 had not been sent to me. Had a secret message, intended for my eye alone, appeared? Had I missed it? This thought worried me considerably. That Pom-Pom had some very real and serious motive in the curious arrangement he had come to with me there could be no doubt, for Europe was now at war, and he was living in secrecy somewhere across the North Sea – where, no one could tell.

More than once I had been half inclined to call upon his friend

Clutterbuck, but I recollected that he had given me express instructions not to do so until I heard from him. Therefore, having made a promise to him, I could not well break it.

The summer days and weeks still went on. I wrote to the office of the *Aftonbladet* in Stockholm, and, after much delay, received the three missing copies of the journal, through which I eagerly glanced, being much relieved to find no message.

September was passing, and still by each mail from Scandinavia came the Stockholm newspaper, which I examined with as much care as I would examine a patient in my consulting-room.

One morning, while at breakfast with Lettice, I opened the paper dated October 2, and turning mechanically to the column which I so often examined in vain, an advertisement paragraph caught my eye, beginning 'Ashes.'

In Swedish, it ran:

Dear Loved One, – Do you recollect how we strolled upon the beach at Morsey, on the night of the ninth, and how two men from a Dutch trawler came ashore and chatted with us? They brought us a little present. If you do not, please go and see – and act. With all affection,
Pom-Pom.

I read and re-read that curious message. At last our old friend had broken silence. What could he mean?

As I sat reflectively, I saw that his instructions were to go to some place called Morsey on the night of the ninth, and there await somebody who would land on the beach from a Dutch trawler.

Morsey? I had never heard of it, and wondered where it could be.

Saying nothing to Lettice, I left the table after breakfast and looked it up in the 'Postal Guide,' finding that Morsey possessed a telegraph-office, and that it was somewhere in the vicinity of Great Yarmouth.

Then I got out my motor-map, and found that Morsey Gap – which, no doubt, was the spot on the beach referred to – was on the North Sea, midway between Winterton and Raxham, north of the wireless station at Caister, and some distance from Morsey village. Inland lay the Norfolk Broads, Hickling and Potter Heigham.

From the map I also saw that Morsey Gap must be at a lonely, unfrequented spot, for even the roads there over the marsh were uncertain and not at all inviting.

Four poor ailing patients were already in my waiting-room. Phew! The Harley Street doctor had but little time for thought after war had broken out. Yet I fear that I disregarded those patients with whom my secretary had made appointments while I carefully reflected upon the facts.

The 'ninth' was mentioned. That morning was the eighth. The appointment was for the following night. Should I drive the two-seater alone to Morsey, or should I take somebody to bear me company?

I thought of Lettice. She was a good driver, and a fine specimen of the go-ahead, athletic English girl. Should I reveal to her the whole truth, and take her as my companion?

I decided to do so, and after I had seen my patients – two of whom were, alas! too far gone to save from the grave – I called her in, made her sit in the patients' chair, and there revealed to her all that I have now written here.

She heard me to the end, her big, dark eyes opening wider and wider as I unfolded the mysterious circumstances of Pom-Pom's life and movements, as far as I knew them.

'Certainly, dad!' she exclaimed at last. 'Let's go down to Morsey together tomorrow. It's quite evident that he is sending over some messenger to you secretly. How awfully exciting! I shall love it! Do let me go with you, won't you?' she implored.

So, after some hesitation, I was compelled to accede to the girl's suggestion – for she could always twist me round her finger, as you know, Mayne – and, on the long motor-drive from London to the Norfolk coast and back, I felt that I wanted the companionship of somebody I could trust.

If you look up your diary, my dear fellow, you will find that on the night of the ninth you and I had arranged to dine with the Englefields, in Sussex Place. Don't you remember that early in the morning I 'phoned to you, excusing myself, as I had to go and see a patient in the country – the same old Harley Street excuse to evade an appointment?

Well, in the morning I, with Lettice at my side, set out on the Chelmsford Road, and at twilight we found ourselves leaving Yarmouth by the Caister Road, skirting the bleak shore to Great Ormesby, where, leaving the main highway, we turned off through sleepy little villages and on by a series of puzzling and narrow by-roads close to the sea, passing a small collection of houses which a labourer told us, in his broad Norfolk, was West

Tomerton, whence we found a straight, narrow lane which led us down to the sea to the spot known as Morsey Gap.

We took the car as far as we could, almost on to the actual beach, and, having switched off our headlights, got out to reconnoitre.

Though yet early in the evening, it was already dark and cloudy. Upon the shingle the long, cold waves beat with regular cadence, for the sea was unusually calm for that time of year, there being but a light south-easterly wind. The spot was, indeed, dismal and lonely; perhaps one of the most unfrequented points on the whole East Coast.

Not a light could be seen anywhere, and the only sound was the distant chime of a church clock somewhere in the distance far inland.

'What a quiet place, dad!' my girl exclaimed as, wrapped in her big motor-coat and muffler, she stood beside me while I lit my pipe. 'I wonder if anybody will really meet us?'

'Perhaps,' was my reply. 'Who knows? That cryptic message was certainly meant to convey an appointment, and, at any rate, I have fulfilled my promise.'

'You don't think that it may be some trap or other?' my daughter asked, with some apprehension. 'That somebody intends to do you some harm?'

I laughed, and, drawing my automatic pistol from my pocket, said: 'Well, if they do, I shall die game, dear. But I don't think that. Pom-Pom was a good fellow and our friend.'

Then we both lapsed into silence, having seated ourselves upon a rock to listen and to wait as to our nostrils came the odour of the wide, open sea.

Again and again that distant church clock chimed. Time went on; the darkness became more intense, and with the advancing tide the waves seemed to increase, and the wind became stronger, the howl of a dog being borne upon it.

I knew that Lettice was cold after our long drive, but she never murmured. Now and then, after listening intently, our eyes alert for the least speck of light, we would converse in whispers. Away over that dark, rolling sea, where lurked the enemy's submarines, and where, in secret, mines were so often sown, a thousand eyes were watching and guarding Britain's shore, while unseen were patrol-boats and coast-watchers, ready at any instant to raise the alarm and tap forth a wireless call in case of the least suspicion.

Though we strained our eyes, we could not discern the least speck of light at sea. All was cavernous blackness right away to the indistinct horizon on the starless sky. Truly, our vigil was one of eager breathlessness and of chilling inactivity.

'Hark!' gasped Lettice suddenly, just before eight o'clock. 'Listen! What was that? Did you hear it, dad?'

I did. It was a low, grating sound – that of a boat's keel striking the shingle.

A moment later, in the darkness, there could be heard heavy footsteps coming along the beach. They halted for a moment, and then in the darkness we heard a low whistle.

Thrice it was repeated, and then I replied to it.

That moment was one of the weirdest I have spent in my life.

As soon as I had acknowledged the call a small flash-lamp was shown, while I, on my part, showed mine; and then the stranger advanced to where we were standing.

My light showed him to be a big, broad-shouldered man in heavy sea-boots and yellow oilskins, a man with shaggy brows, high cheek-bones, and a scraggy, pointed beard.

'I look for Ashes. Do I find, eh?' asked the stranger, in a deep, guttural voice, speaking in broken English.

'Yes,' I replied. 'You are from my friend Hicks, I suppose?'

'Ja! Meester Heecks, he send dis for me gif Ashes. Hein?'

And from beneath his oilskin he produced a small, square brown paper parcel, tied up strongly with thick string. Its size I judged to be about twelve inches long by five wide and four inches deep.

'Thank you!' I replied, taking it. 'But to whom am I indebted for its conveyance here? I mean, who are you, sir?' I asked of this stranger of the night, who had come so mysteriously up from the sea.

'Me? Oh, me name Jan Hangest, master of der trawler *Alkemade*, of Koog, in Texel! Me frent of Meester Heecks, frent of England.'

And he laughed broadly.

Then, apparently having been warned by Pom-Pom against telling me anything if a third party were present, he suddenly asked: 'May I speek you all alone?'

Lettice realised the situation in an instant, and exclaimed: 'I'll walk along, dad, while you speak to Mr Hangest!'

Then, as soon as she had left us, the skipper of the Dutch trawler, who had run the gauntlet of mines and patrol-boats in order to meet me, began to tell me, in a low voice, one or two interesting facts.

After I had listened to them, I began to fully understand the true importance of the Dutchman's mysterious mission.

'An' Meester Heecks 'e ask you to still look in der journal for 'ee's news. You understand, eh?' said the burly Dutchman.

'Quite,' was my reply.

And then he seemed in great eagerness to get away, telling me, with a light laugh, that if caught there by the patrol his presence would necessitate so much unpleasant explanation.

From his conversation I gathered that his trawler was lying about two miles out, and that he was keen to get away again out of the territorial limit, and back to the island of Texel, whence he had sailed.

Of him I could obtain no direct news of Pom-Pom's whereabouts.

'I see Meester Heecks in Maasluis one week ago. He go away. I not know 'ees address.'

Then, having thanked him for the packet he had brought me, we gripped hands, and he disappeared again into the cavernous darkness, where at the water's edge, his men were waiting with the boat.

'What did that man tell you?' asked Lettice, with all a woman's natural curiosity, as she approached me. 'Do tell me, dad! Isn't it really exciting, eh? What a fine specimen of a North Sea fisherman he was, wasn't he?'

'Yes, dear. But let us get along,' I said, feverishly anxious to be back in London at the earliest moment.

'But what's in the packet?' she asked, as we returned to the car and again switched on the lights.

'Only a box of cigars,' I replied. 'I think I'll try one: they are certain to be of a choice brand.'

Therefore, with my penknife, I cut the string, and, taking off the outer brown cover, found that the box, in order to preserve it from wet, was further wrapped up in an old newspaper, green in colour – an old copy of a London evening journal I saw it to be.

Then I prised open Pom-Pom's present, and took out an excellent cigar, rewrapping the box in its coverings and placing it on the seat beside us.

Lettice, having watched me bite off the end of the weed and slowly light it, exclaimed: 'Well, is that all, dad? There seems a lot of unnecessary mystery regarding the present of a mere box of cigars.' Then she added, 'I do wish you'd tell me the truth.'

'I have, my child,' was my reply. 'Mr Hicks has sent me a present of a box of very choice cigars – and very choice they are, I can assure you.'

And I blew a cloud of smoke in appreciation.

With that I restarted the engine, and when Lettice had settled herself beside me and tucked up the rug around her, we turned, and went forth out upon the road again with a run of a hundred and forty miles or so before us back to Harley Street.

It was then half-past ten, and I judged, having come over the same road and therefore knowing it, that, if we spent half an hour over a snack of supper in Yarmouth, we might be at our own door by six in the morning, or perhaps before.

This I told Lettice, who, chilled to the bone, was huddled up beside me, and who later on, when we drew up at the old-fashioned Stag Hotel, appreciated to the full a plate of palatable hot soup.

When, on starting off again up the London road, the heavy clouds had lifted and the moon was shining, I was able to see the road, and keep up a good pace. The regulations regarding headlights on cars were very strict. Just at that time, owing to Zeppelin raids, somebody had advanced a theory in the House of Commons that enemy airships were being directed by motor-cars with swivel searchlights, and all motorists conformed willingly to the regulations – under the drastic penalties of the Defence of the Realm Act, of course – except out on the open country roads, where I, for one, switched on my big electric headlights, and trusted to luck not to be hauled before the local Justice of the Peace.

Lettice had had her soup and a cup of hot coffee to follow, while I had had a good stiff 'peg', for I confess that I was dead cold that night after those hours on the dark, wind-swept beach, and both of us felt 'game' as we sped southward, passing the landmarks we had noted on our northward journey – a turning here, a farmhouse there, and a double bend elsewhere, with a steep hill and a long, uphill road.

I could follow the workings of Lettice's mind. Full well she knew that I had not told her the truth, that I had not explained what the heavy-booted Dutch fisherman had really revealed to me. But it was a secret. Pom-Pom had told the man Hangest to impart it to me, and to me alone.

Few secrets have I ever had from Lettice, as you well know, my dear fellow. She's a good girl, honest, open, and true; but if secrecy were imposed upon me, as it was so often in my professional capacity, I made it a rule never to betray a confidence. So it was in this case.

Through Saxmundham, Wickham Market, and Roodbridge, through those long, dark, narrow streets of Ipswich, past the Great White Horse and the town hall, and out again, we sped to Colchester, making good time, with the engine going like clockwork. At starting I had had rather a fierce clutch, but it had now dropped down to normal, and nothing troubled me except to get to London at the earliest possible moment with my precious box of cigars.

The road from Ipswich to Colchester is, as all motorists know, a flat, open one, past the railway line at Chapel Station, on by that sharp turn just on entering Stratford St Mary, and then straight away into Colchester.

Before we entered the latter town I shut off the strong electric headlights, leaving only the oil side-lights burning, for we found the place in total darkness as slowly we passed through it, and then out upon the road – the ancient Stane Street – through Coggeshall to Chelmsford. Having passed through the latter town, I again switched on the headlights, and went on through Ingatestone, now approaching London. Just at a double bend of the lonely road, which ran beneath a railway arch, I was, however, compelled to slow up, for I saw before me a flash-lamp being waved – the sign of danger.

I heard voices shouting, and at once pulled up, to find two men – special constables, no doubt – in the road barring my progress.

'Your lights are too strong,' I heard a voice say. 'Where's your licence?'

I produced it, and he examined it under his lamp, whereupon a third man came up and looked over his shoulder. One of the men scribbled something in a notebook, but, to my surprise, I saw that he was only making pretence of taking the details of my licence.

This at once struck me as curious.

'I'm sorry, Doctor,' said one of the men, who appeared to be in authority, though he was not wearing the armlet of the special constabulary, 'but we have orders to search all cars proceeding to London by this road.'

'Why?' I protested. 'I'm not a German spy, man! Don't be foolish! You're frightening my daughter here.'

'Can't help that,' declared another, in a low, guttural voice which struck me as possessing an undoubted foreign accent.

Then the speaker opened the door of the car, and with one of his companions began to investigate inside. With Lettice I got out. They felt in the deep pockets, taking out my guide-books and maps, the little basket containing some food and a flask, my flash-lamp, a shawl of my daughter's, as well as my box of cigars with its wrappings, which they examined, and all of which they placed on the roadside.

'Look here,' I cried, anxiously watching them empty the car. 'By what right do you make this search? Where is your authority?'

In a second the barrels of three big automatic pistols were pointed at us, a man who spoke with a German accent saying:

'Our authority is dis! You are Doktor Saunders, and you hav' been to der coast. Those cigars are Dutch – a new box. Ve shall keep them. Now you can go – and if you or your daughter tell a soul of how you haf been stopped it will not go well with you. You understand?' he added threateningly.

I did most certainly understand that we had run into a trap evidently set for us, without any loophole for escape. I saw that poor Lettice was terribly frightened at the determined attitude of the men.

'Well, gentlemen,' I said, with a forced laugh, trying to remain cool. 'I give you best this time, and I'll get along, if you don't object. I hope you'll enjoy the cigars.'

I was wondering whether they were expecting to find any message concealed in one of those excellent Upmanns?

The man grinned.

'If you promise secrecy, then dis incident may be at once dismissed,' he said, in a hard voice next moment. 'But if not, den you may expect to hear of us again. Our fatherland has many good and powerful frients here in your country.'

'Oh, that's all right,' I said cheerily. 'But as my lights are perhaps a little too bright, as you say, I may be stopped again. So I'd better dim them, hadn't I?'

And, stooping, I picked up the green newspaper in which the cigar-box had been wrapped, and which I saw lay discarded in the road, and taking off its outside sheet, I tore it in halves and placed one within each of the head-lamps, thus reducing their glare to a pale green.

Then, having given us back our basket, rug, and shawl, they retired, carrying away with them Pom-Pom's mysterious present of cigars, much to my bitter chagrin.

'Who are those men?' whispered Lettice in terror, as we moved off again.

'Secret agents of Germany, dear, without a doubt,' was my hard reply. 'They must somehow have learnt of our journey, and of the visit to Pom-Pom's messenger. But,' I added, 'don't let us discuss the affair until we get home. They waited here for us, evidently determined that those cigars should not reach London.'

And then I drove on as hard as ever I could, perhaps even recklessly, until at last we began to enter the eastern suburbs of London, and on until we passed through the City streets, silent and deserted at that early hour of the morning.

And as we flew along both our minds were, I think, full of the loss of that mysterious present from Pom-Pom.

'I expect that, hidden in one of those cigars, was some secret message – information gathered by Mr Hicks in the enemy's camp,' Lettice remarked as presently we turned from Whitehall and crossed into Westminster.

'Who knows?' I said. 'But before I go home I want to find that Mr Clutterbuck who lives in Lamington Mansions.'

Dawn had not broken, for we travelled through the night at as high a speed as I dared, and had not paused, save for that strange adventure near Ingatestone; therefore it was still dark when – with our green lights shining – we passed the Houses of Parliament, and afterwards I drew up before the door of that palatial block of flats overlooking St James's Park.

When I got down I switched off the headlights, and taking out the pieces of newspaper, folded them together, saying to Lettice: 'I think these have now served their purpose.'

Five minutes later, while Lettice waited in the car, I stood in a small, cosy sitting-room on the third floor, when a tall, dark-eyed, grey-haired, rather military-looking man, in a silk dressing-gown, entered.

For a second he glanced at me inquiringly, and then, in a tone of interrogation, uttered the single word: 'Ashes?'

'Yes,' I replied.

Briefly I told him of the advertisement in the *Aftonbladet*, of my journey, of my adventure on the way home, and of how I had dimmed my headlights with the outside pages of the green-tinted newspaper.

Upon hearing this, and at sight of the two pieces of discarded newspaper, the man Clutterbuck laughed heartily, and at once became intensely interested in them as I smoothed them upon the table before him.

Then, for the first time, I noticed that in the blank half-column reserved for 'stop-press' news was printed what appeared to be a quantity of Stock Exchange quotations.

'By Jove! Rather a neat idea of our friend Hicks, isn't it?' remarked my companion, whom I afterwards found was the assistant director of the British Secret Service. 'He evidently got hold of this old newspaper somewhere in Germany, and had his message printed by a hand press in the "stop-press" column, so as to evade detection. Gad! Quite a good idea!' he went on as, taking a pencil, he bent and began to rapidly decipher the figure-code in which the secret message was printed. 'And it is information of most vital importance to us, Doctor,' he said, with suppressed excitement, a few moments later, 'details of a desperate and unsuspected German plot against us in the United States. We never dreamt that such a plot existed! I must lose no time in going round to Whitehall with it. On behalf of the Director of Intelligence, I thank you very, very much, Doctor. It was most fortunate that that Dutch skipper, when he got you alone, told you to smoke the cigars, but to look after the newspaper, wasn't it, eh?'

And he laughed contentedly as he gripped my hand, and I wished him good-morning.

Afterwards, when I met him in Bond Street a week later, he told me, in confidence, that the prompt information sent from Berlin by our friend Pom-Pom had been the means of preventing the loss of thousands of valuable lives which would otherwise have been sacrificed, by great explosions intended to take place at certain great works making munitions for Great Britain and her Allies.

THE DUST-CLOUD

E. F. Benson

Motoring in the pioneer days was not only uncertain because of the possibility of break-downs far from assistance, or hazardous because of the condition of the roads, but also because the motor cars were, of course, deadly pieces of machinery in themselves. They may not have travelled at such speeds as we are used to today, but they were just as capable of crashing and injuring and even killing the passengers as well as colliding with unwary pedestrians. It was not long, in fact, before certain localities began to gain the reputation of needing special care by motorists. Some – a few – were even said to be haunted by the victims of motoring accidents and thereby began a tradition which has continued to this day. Such stories were ideal material for the writers of supernatural fiction and my next selection is one of the earliest tales of this kind I have been able to trace.

'The Dust-Cloud' is just one of many fine ghost stories written by Edward Frederic Benson *(1867–1940), son of an Archbishop of Canterbury, and author of the 'Lucia' series of light Edwardian society novels which have recently been so successfully adapted for television. After an early involvement in archaeological studies which took him to Greece and Egypt, Benson returned to England, settled in Sussex, and became a successful writer of novels, biographies and short stories. In these stories he demonstrated a skill with the supernatural which has resulted in the best of these tales remaining readable and genuinely spine-tingling to the present time. As E. F. Benson was also an enthusiastic motorist it comes as no surprise to find cars in several of his stories, but in none of them is the vehicle quite such a memorable one as the reader will find emerging from 'The Dust-Cloud' . . .*

The big French windows were open on to the lawn, and, dinner being over, two or three of the party who were staying for the week at the end of August with the Combe-Martins had strolled out on to the terrace to look at the sea, over which the moon, large and low, was just rising and tracing a path of pale gold from horizon to shore, while others, less lunar of inclination, had gone in search of bridge or billiards. Coffee had come round immediately after dessert, and the end of dinner, according to the delectable custom of the house, was as informal as the end of breakfast. Every one, that is to say, remained or went away, smoked, drank port or abstained, according to his personal tastes. Thus, on this particular evening it so happened that Harry Combe-Martin and I were very soon left alone in the dining-room, because we were talking unmitigated motor 'shop', and the rest of the party (small wonder) were bored with it, and had left us. The shop was home-shop, so to speak, for it was almost entirely concerned with the manifold perfections of the new six-cylinder Clarence which my host in a moment of extravagance, which he did not in the least regret, had just purchased; in which, too, he proposed to take me over to lunch at a friend's house near Hunstanton on the following day. He observed with legitimate pride that an early start would be unnecessary as the distance was only eighty miles and there were no police traps.

'Queer things these big motors are,' he said, relapsing into generalities as we rose to go. 'Often I can scarcely believe that my new car is merely a machine. It seems to me to possess an independent life of its own. It is really much more like a thoroughbred with a wonderfully fine mouth.'

'And the moods of a thoroughbred?' I asked.

'No; it's got an excellent temper, I'm glad to say. It doesn't mind being checked, or even stopped, when it's going its best. Some of these big cars can't stand that. They get sulky – I assure you it is literally true – if they are checked too often.'

He paused on his way to ring the bell. 'Guy Elphinstone's car, for instance,' he said: 'it was a bad-tempered brute, a violent, vicious beast of a car.'

'What make?' I asked.

'Twenty-five horse-power Amédée. They are a fretful strain of car; too thin, not enough bone – and bone is very good for the nerves. The brute liked running over a chicken or a rabbit, though perhaps it was less the car's ill-temper than Guy's, poor chap. Well, he paid for it – he paid to the uttermost farthing. Did you know him?'

'No; but surely I have heard the name. Ah, yes he ran over a child, did he not?'

'Yes,' said Harry, 'and then smashed up against his own park gates.'

'Killed, wasn't he?'

'Oh, yes, killed instantly, and the car just a heap of splinters. There's an odd story about it, I'm told, in the village: rather in your line.'

'Ghosts?' I asked.

'Yes, the ghost of his motor car. Seems almost too up-to-date, doesn't it?'

'And what's the story?' I demanded.

'Why, just this. His place was outside the village of Bircham, ten miles out from Norwich; and there's a long straight bit of road there – that's where he ran over the child – and a couple of hundred yards farther on, a rather awkward turn into the park gates. Well, a month or two ago, soon after the accident, one old gaffer in the village swore he had seen a motor there coming full tilt along the road, but without a sound, and it disappeared at the lodge gates of the park, which were shut. Soon after another said he had heard a motor whirl by him at the same place, followed by a hideous scream, but he saw nothing.'

'The scream is rather horrible,' said I.

'Ah, I see what you mean! I only thought of his siren. Guy had a siren on his exhaust, same as I have. His had a dreadful frightened sort of wail, and always made me feel creepy.'

'And is that all the story?' I asked; 'that one old man thought he saw a noiseless motor, and another thought he heard an invisible one?'

Harry flicked the ash off his cigarette into the grate. 'Oh, dear no!' he said. 'Half-a-dozen of them have seen something or heard something. It is quite a heavily authenticated yarn.'

'Yes, and talked over and edited in the public-house,' I said.

'Well, not a man of them will go there after dark. Also the lodge-keeper gave notice a week or two after the accident. He said he was always hearing a motor stop and hoot outside the lodge, and he was kept running out at all hours of the night to see what it was.'

'And what was it?'

'It wasn't anything. Simply nothing there. He thought it

rather uncanny, anyhow, and threw up a good post. Besides, his wife was always hearing a child scream, and while her man toddled out to the gate she would go and see whether the kids were all right. And the kids themselves . . .'

'Ah, what of them?' I asked.

'They kept coming to their mother, asking who the little girl was who walked up and down the road and would not speak to them or play with them.'

'It's a many-sided story,' I said. 'All the witnesses seem to have heard and seen different things.'

'Yes, that is just what to my mind makes the yarn so good,' he said. 'Personally I don't take much stock in spooks at all. But given that there are such things as spooks, and given that the death of the child and the death of Guy have caused spooks to play about there, it seems to me a very good point that different people should be aware of different phenomena. One hears the car, another sees it, one hears the child scream, another sees the child. How does that strike you?'

This, I am bound to say, was a new view to me, and the more I thought of it the more reasonable it appeared. For the vast majority of mankind have all those occult senses by which is perceived the spiritual world (which, I hold, is thick and populous around us), sealed up, as it were; in other words, the majority of mankind never hear or see a ghost at all. Is it not, then, very probable that of the remainder – those, in fact, to whom occult experiences have happened or can happen – few should have every sense unsealed, but that some should have the unsealed ear, others the unsealed eye – that some should be clairaudient, others clairvoyant?

'Yes, it strikes me as reasonable,' I said. 'Can't you take me over there?'

'Certainly! If you will stop till Friday I'll take you over on Thursday. The others all go that day, so that we can get there after dark.'

I shook my head. 'I can't stop till Friday, I'm afraid,' I said. 'I must leave on Thursday. But how about tomorrow? Can't we take it on the way to or from Hunstanton?'

'No; it's thirty miles out of our way. Besides, to be at Bircham after dark means that we shouldn't get back here till midnight. And as host to my guests . . .'

'Ah! things are only heard and seen after dark, are they?' I asked. 'That makes it so much less interesting. It is like a séance where all lights are put out.'

'Well, the accident happened at night,' he said. 'I don't know the rules, but that may have some bearing on it, I should think.'

I had one question more in the back of my mind, but I did not like to ask it. At least, I wanted information on this subject without appearing to ask for it.

'Neither do I know the rules of motors,' I said; 'and I don't understand you when you say that Guy Elphinstone's machine was an irritable, cross-grained brute, that liked running over chickens and rabbits. But I think you subsequently said that the irritability may have been the irritability of its owner. Did he mind being checked?'

'It made him blind-mad if it happened often,' said Harry. 'I shall never forget a drive I had with him once: there were hay-carts and perambulators every hundred yards. It was perfectly ghastly; it was like being with a madman. And when we got inside his gate, his dog came running out to meet him. He did not go an inch out of his course: it was worse than that – he went for it, just grinding his teeth with rage. I never drove with him again.'

He stopped a moment, guessing what might be in my mind. 'I say, you mustn't think – you mustn't think . . .' he began.

'No, of course not,' said I.

Harry Combe-Martin's house stood close to the weather-eaten, sandy cliffs of the Suffolk shore, which are being incessantly gnawed away by the hunger of the insatiable sea. Fathoms deep below it, and now many hundred yards out, lies what was once the second port in England; but now of the ancient town of Dunwich, and of its seven great churches, nothing remains but one, and that ruinous and already half destroyed by the falling cliff and the encroachments of the sea. Foot by foot, it too is disappearing, and of the graveyard which surrounded it more than half is gone, so that from the face of the sandy cliff on which it stands there stick out like straws in glass, as Dante says, the bones of those who were once committed there to the kindly and stable earth.

Whether it was the remembrance of this rather grim spectacle as I had seen it that afternoon, or whether Harry's story had caused some trouble in my brain, or whether it was merely that the keen bracing air of this place, to one who had just come from the sleepy languor of the Norfolk Broads, kept me sleepless, I do not know; but anyhow, the moment I put out my light that night and got into bed, I felt that all the footlights and gas-jets in the internal theatre of my mind sprang into flame, and that I was very vividly and alertly awake. It was in vain that I counted a hundred forwards and a hundred backwards, that I pictured to myself a flock of visionary sheep coming singly through a gap in an imaginary hedge, and tried to number their monotonous and uniform countenances, that I played noughts and crosses with myself, that I marked out scores of double lawn-tennis courts – for which each repetition of these supposedly soporific exercises I only became more intensely wakeful. It was not in remote hope of sleep that I continued to repeat these weary performances long after their inefficacy was proved to the hilt, but because I was strangely unwilling in this timeless hour of the night to think about those protruding relics of humanity; also I quite distinctly did not desire to think about that subject with regard to which I had, a few hours ago, promised Harry that I would not make it the subject of reflection. For these reasons I continued during the black hours to practise these narcotic exercises of the mind, knowing well that if I paused on the tedious treadmill my thoughts, like some released spring, would fly back to rather gruesome subjects. I kept my mind, in fact, talking loud to itself, so that it should not hear what other voices were saying.

Then by degrees these absurd mental occupations became impossible; my mind simply refused to occupy itself with them any longer; and next moment I was thinking intently and eagerly, not about the bones protruding from the gnawed section of sandcliff, but about the subject I had said I would not dwell upon. And like a flash it came upon me why Harry had bidden me not think about it. Surely in order that I should not come to the same conclusion as he had come to.

Now the whole question of 'haunt' – haunted spots, haunted houses, and so forth – has always seemed to me to be utterly unsolved, and to be neither proved nor disproved to a satisfactory degree. From the earliest times, certainly from the earliest known Egyptian records, there has been a belief that the scene of a crime is often revisited, sometimes by the spirit of him who has committed it – seeking rest, we must suppose, and finding none; sometimes, and more inexplicably, by the spirit of his victim, crying perhaps, like the blood of Abel, for vengeance. And though the stories of these village gossips in the alehouse about noiseless visions and invisible noises were all as yet unsifted and unreliable, yet I could not help wondering if they (such as they were) pointed to something authentic and to be classed under this head of appearances. But more striking than the yarns of the gaffers seemed to me the questions of the lodge-keeper's children. How should children have imagined the figure of a child that would not speak to them or play with them? Perhaps it was a real child, a sulky child. Yes – perhaps. But perhaps not. Then after this preliminary skirmish I found myself settling down to the question that I had said I would not think about; in other words, the possible origin of these phenomena interested me more than the phenomena themselves. For what exactly had Guy Elphinstone, that savage driver, done? Had or had not the death of the child been entirely an accident, a thing (given he drove a motor at all) outside his own control? Or had he, irritated beyond endurance at the checks and delays of the day, not pulled up when it was just possible he might have, but had run over the child as he would have run over a rabbit or a hen, or even his own dog? And what, in any case, poor wretched brute, must have been his thoughts in that terrible instant that intervened between the child's death and his own, when a moment later he smashed into the closed gates of his own lodge? Was remorse his – bitter, despairing contrition? That could hardly have been so; or else surely, knowing only for certain that he had knocked a child down, he would have stopped; he would have done his best, whatever that might be, to repair the irreparable harm. But he had not stopped; he had gone on, it seemed, at full speed, for on the collision the car had been smashed into matchwood and steel shavings. Again, with double force, had this dreadful thing been a complete accident, he would have stopped. So then – most terrible question of all – had he, after making murder, rushed on to what proved to be his own death, filled with some hellish glee at what he had done? Indeed, as in the churchyard on the cliff, bones of the buried stuck starkly out into the night.

The pale tired light of earliest morning had turned the window-blinds into glimmering squares before I slept; and when I woke, the servant who called me was already rattling them briskly up on their rollers, and letting the calm serenity of the August day stream into the room. Through the open windows poured in sunlight and sea-wind, the scent of flowers and the song of birds; and each and all were wonderfully reassuring, banishing the hooded forms that had haunted the night, and I thought of the disquietude of the dark hours as a traveller may think of the billows and tempests of the ocean over which he has safely journeyed, unable, now that they belong to the limbo of the past, to recall his qualms and tossings with any vivid uneasiness. Not without a feeling of relief, too, did I dwell on the knowledge that I was definitely not going to visit this equivocal spot. Our drive today, as Harry had said, would not take us within thirty miles of it, and tomorrow I but went to the station and away. Though a thorough-paced seeker after truth might, no doubt, have regretted that the laws of time and space did not permit him to visit Bircham after the sinister dark had fallen, and test whether for him there was visible or audible truth in the tales of the village gossips, I was conscious of no such regret. Bircham and its fables had given me a very bad night, and I was perfectly aware that I did not in the least want to go near it, though yesterday I had quite truthfully said I should like to do so. In this brightness, too, of sun and sea-wind I felt none of the *malaise* at my waking moments which a sleepless night usually gives me; I felt particularly well, particularly pleased to be alive, and also, as I have said, particularly content not to be going to Bircham. I was quite satisfied to leave my curiosity unsatisfied.

The motor came round about eleven, and we started at once, Harry and Mrs Morrison, a cousin of his, sitting behind in the big back seat, large enough to hold a comfortable three, and I on the left of the driver, in a sort of trance – I am not ashamed to confess it – of expectancy and delight. For this was in the early days of motors, when there was still the sense of romance and adventure round them. I did not want to drive, any more than Harry wanted to; for driving, so I hold, is too absorbing; it takes the attention in too firm a grip: the mania of the true motorist is not consciously enjoyed. For the passion for motors is a taste – I had almost said a gift – as distinct and as keenly individual as the passion for music or mathematics. Those who use motors most (merely as a means of getting rapidly from one place to another) are often entirely without it, while those whom adverse circumstances (over which they have no control) compel to use them least may have it to a supreme degree. To those who have it, analysis of their passion is perhaps superfluous; to those who have it not, explanation is almost unintelligible. Pace, however, and the control of pace, and above all the sensuous consciousness of pace, is at the root of it; and pleasure in pace is common to most people, whether it be in the form of a galloping horse, or the pace of the skate hissing over smooth ice, or the pace of a free-wheel bicycle humming down-hill, or, more impersonally, the pace of a smashed ball at lawn-tennis, the driven ball at golf, or the low boundary hit at cricket. But the sensuous consciousness of pace, as I have said, is needful: one might experience it seated in front of the engine of an express train, though not in a wadded, shut-windowed carriage, where the wind of movement is not felt. Then add to this rapture of the rush through riven air the knowledge that huge relentless force is controlled by a little lever, and directed by a little wheel on which the hands of the driver seem to lie so negligently. A great untamed devil has there his bridle, and he answers to it, as Harry had said, like a horse with a fine mouth. He has hunger and thirst, too, unslakeable, and greedily he laps of his soup of petrol which turns to fire in his mouth: electricity, the force that rends clouds asunder, and causes towers to totter, is the spoon with which he feeds himself; and as he eats he races onward, and the road opens like torn linen in front of him. Yet how obedient, how amenable is he! – for with a touch on his snaffle his speed is redoubled, or melts into thin air, so that before you know you have touched the rein he has exchanged his swallow-flight for a mere saunter through the lanes. But he ever loves to run; and knowing this, you will bid him lift up his voice and tell those who are in his path that he is coming, so that he will not need the touch that checks. Hoarse and jovial is his voice, hooting to the wayfarer; and if his hooting be not heard he has a great guttural falsetto scream that leaps from octave to octave, and echoes from the hedges that are passing in blurred lines of hanging green. And, as you go, the romantic isolation of divers in deep seas is yours; masked and hooded companions may be near you also, in their driving-dress for this plunge through the swift tides of air; but you, like them, are alone and isolated, conscious only of the ripped riband of road, the two great lantern-eyes of the wonderful monster that look through drooped eyelids by day, but gleam with fire by night, the two ear-laps of splash-boards, and the long lean bonnet in front which is the skull and brain-case of that swift, untiring energy that feeds on fire, and whirls its two tons of weight up hill and down dale, as if some new law as everlasting as gravity, and like gravity making it go ever swifter, was its sole control.

For the first hour the essence of these joys, any description of which compared to the real thing is but as a stagnant pond compared to the bright rushing of a mountain stream, was mine. A straight switchback road lay in front of us, and the monster plunged silently down hill, and said below his breath, 'Ha-ha – ha-ha – ha-ha,' as, without diminution of speed, he breasted the opposing slope. In my control were his great vocal cords (for in those days hooter and siren were on the driver's left, and lay convenient to the hand of him who occupied the next seat), and it rejoiced me to let him hoot to a pony-cart, three hundred yards ahead, with a hand on his falsetto scream if his ordinary tones of conversation were unheard or disregarded. Then came a road crossing ours at right-angles, and the dear monster seemed to say, 'Yes, yes – see how obedient and careful I am. I stroll with my hands in my pockets.' Then again a puppy from a farmhouse staggered warlike into the road, and the monster said, 'Poor little chap! get home to your mother, or I'll talk to you in earnest.' The poor little chap did not take the hint, so the monster slackened speed and just said, 'Whoof!' Then it chuckled to itself as the puppy scuttled into the hedge, seriously alarmed; the next moment our self-made wind screeched and whistled round us again.

Napoleon, I believe, said that the power of an army lay in its feet: that is true also of the monster. There was a loud bang, and in thirty seconds we were at a standstill. The monster's off forefoot troubled it, and the chauffeur said, 'Yes, sir – burst.'

So the burst boot was taken off and a new one put on, a boot that had never been on foot before. The foot in question was held up on a jack during this operation, and the new boot laced up with a pump. This took exactly twenty-five minutes. Then the monster got his spoon going again, and said, 'Let me run: oh, let me run!' And for fifteen miles on a straight and empty road it ran. I timed the miles, but shall not produce their chronology for the benefit of a forsworn constabulary.

But there were no more dithrambics that morning. We should have reached Hunstanton in time for lunch. Instead, we waited to repair our fourth puncture at 1.45 p.m., twenty-five miles short of our destination. This fourth puncture was caused by a spicule of flint three-quarters of an inch long – sharp, it is true, but weighing perhaps two pennyweights, while we weighed two tons. It seemed an impertinence. So we lunched at a wayside inn, and during lunch the pundits held a consultation, of which the upshot was this:

We had no more boots for our monster, for his off fore-foot had burst once, and punctured once (thus necessitating two socks and one boot). Similarly, but more so, his off hind-foot had burst twice (thus necessitating two boots and two socks). Now, there was no certain shoemaker's shop at Hunstanton, as far as we knew, but there was a regular universal store at King's Lynn, which was about equidistant.

And, so said the chauffeur, there was something wrong with the monster's spoon (ignition), and he didn't rightly know what, and therefore it seemed the prudent part not to go to Hunstanton (lunch, a thing of the preterite, having been the object), but to the well-supplied King's Lynn. And we all breathed a pious hope that we might get there.

Whizz: hoot: purr! The last boot held, the spoon went busily to the monster's mouth, and we just flowed into King's Lynn. The return journey, so I vaguely gathered, would be made by other roads; but, personally, intoxicated with air and movement, I neither asked nor desired to know what those roads would be. This one small but rather salient fact is necessary to record here, that as we waited at King's Lynn, and as we buzzed homewards afterwards, no thought of Bircham entered my head at all. The subsequent hallucination, if hallucination it was, was not, as far as I know, self-suggested. That we had gone out of our way for the sake of the garage, I knew, and that was all. Harry also told me that he did not know where our road would take us.

The rest that follows is the baldest possible narrative of what actually occurred. But it seems to me, a humble student of the occult, to be curious.

While we waited we had tea in a hotel looking on to a big empty square of houses, and after tea we waited a very long time for our monster to pick us up. Then the telephone from the garage inquired for 'the gentleman of the motor,' and since Harry had strolled out to get a local evening paper with news of the last Test Match, I applied ear and month to that elusive instrument. What I heard was not encouraging: the ignition had gone very wrong indeed, and 'perhaps' in an hour we should be able to start. It was then about half-past six, and we were just seventy-eight miles from Dunwich.

Harry came back soon after this, and I told him what the message from the garage had been. What he said was this: 'Then we shan't get back till long after dinner. We might just as well have camped out to see your ghost.'

As I have already said, no notion of Bircham was in my mind, and I mention this as evidence that, even if it had been, Harry's remark would have implied that we were not going through Bircham.

The hour lengthened itself into an hour and a half. Then the monster, quite well again, came hooting round the corner, and we got in.

'Whack her up, Jack,' said Harry to the chauffeur. 'The roads will be empty. You had better light up at once.'

The monster, with its eyes agleam, was whacked up, and never in my life have I been carried so cautiously and yet so swiftly. Jack never took a risk or the possibility of a risk, but when the road was clear and open he let the monster run just as fast as it was able. Its eyes made day of the road fifty yards ahead, and the romance of night was fairyland round us. Hares started from the roadside, and raced in front of us for a hundred yards, then just wheeled in time to avoid the ear-flaps of the great triumphant brute that carried us. Moths flitted across, struck sometimes by the lenses of its eyes, and the miles peeled over our shoulders. When It occurred we were going top-speed. And this was It – quite unsensational, but to us quite inexplicable unless my midnight imaginings happened to be true.

As I have said, I was in command of the hooter and of the siren. We were flying along on a straight down-grade, as fast as ever we could go, for the engines were working, though the decline was considerable. Then quite suddenly I saw in front of us a thick cloud of dust, and knew instinctively and on the instant, without thought or reasoning, what that must mean. Evidently something going very fast (or else so large a cloud could not have been raised) was in front of us, and going in the same direction as ourselves. Had it been something on the road coming to meet us, we should of course have seen the vehicle first and run into the dust-cloud afterwards. Had it, again, been something of low speed – a horse and dog-cart, for instance – no such dust could have been raised. But, as it was, I knew at once that there was a motor travelling swiftly just ahead of us, also that it was not going as fast as we were, or we should have run into its dust much more gradually. But we went into it as into a suddenly lowered curtain.

Then I shouted to Jack. 'Slow down, and put on the brake,' I shrieked. 'There's something just ahead of us.'

As I spoke I wrought a wild concerto on the hooter, and with my right hand groped for the siren, but did not find it. Simultaneously I heard a wild, frightened shriek, just as if I had sounded the siren myself. Jack had felt for it too, and our hands fingered each other. Then we entered the dust-cloud.

We slowed down with extraordinary rapidity, and still peering ahead we went dead-slow through it. I had not put on my goggles after leaving King's Lynn, and the dust stung and smarted in my eyes. It was not, therefore, a belt of fog, but real road-dust. And at the moment we crept through it I felt Harry's hands on my shoulder.

'There's something just ahead,' he said. 'Look! don't you see the tail light?'

As a matter of fact, I did not; and, still going very slow, we came out of that dust-cloud. The broad empty road stretched in front of us; a hedge was on each side, and there was no turning either to right or left. Only, on the right, was a lodge, and gates which were closed. The lodge had no lights in any window.

Then we came to a standstill; the air was dead-calm, not a leaf in the hedgerow trees was moving, not a grain of dust was lifted from the road. But, behind, the dust-cloud still hung in the air, and stopped dead-short at the closed lodge-gates. We had moved very slowly for the last hundred yards: it was difficult to suppose that it was of our making. Then Jack spoke, with a curious crack in his voice.

'It must have been a motor, sir,' he said. 'But where is it?'

I had no reply to this, and from behind another voice, Harry's voice, spoke. For the moment I did not recognise it, for it was strained and faltering.

'Did you open the siren?' he asked. 'It didn't sound like your siren. It sounded like, like . . .'

'I didn't open the siren,' said I.

Then we went on again. Soon we came to scattered lights in houses by the wayside.

'What's this place?' I asked Jack.

'Bircham, sir,' said he.

HOW IT HAPPENED

Sir Arthur Conan Doyle

Few readers will need me to remind them that Sir Arthur Conan Doyle was the creator of the great Sherlock Holmes who now ranks among the immortal characters of literature. Holmes has, though, tended to obscure both Conan Doyle's own reputation as well as his very considerable number of other books and stories on subjects far removed from crime and detection. Indeed, he several times regretted that work such as his historical and supernatural fiction was not judged other than in comparison to the adventures of the Great Detective.

Sir Arthur Conan Doyle (1859–1930) trained to be a doctor and only turned to writing to fill in the bleak hours in his surgery awaiting patients. Early in his literary career he showed a particular interest in the supernatural – especially Spiritualism – and later in his life devoted much time and energy to investigating such phenomena as ghosts, spirits and even fairies. He was very intrigued with the idea of contact with the dead and attended a great many séances at which mediums attempted to make contact with spirits 'on the other side'. From one such séance in the spring of 1913 came the idea for the following story about a motoring accident and its unexpected finale. His own knowledge of motoring enabled him to add just the right touches of authenticity to the narrative. It is, in truth, a tale as ingenious and clever as any Sherlock Holmes case – though the events might seem perhaps a little more fantastic than that most down-to-earth of investigators would have countenanced. But judge for yourself . . .

She was a writing medium. This is what she wrote:

I can remember some things upon that evening most distinctly, and others are like some vague, broken dreams. That is what makes it so difficult to tell a connected story. I have no idea now what it was that had taken me to London and brought me back so late. It just merges into all my other visits to London. But from the time that I got out at the little country station everything is extraordinarily clear. I can live it again – every instant of it.

I remember so well walking down the platform and looking at the illuminated clock at the end which told me that it was half-past eleven. I remember also my wondering whether I could get home before midnight. Then I remember the big motor, with its glaring head-lights and glitter of polished brass, waiting for me outside. It was my new thirty-horse-power Robur, which had only been delivered that day. I remember also asking Perkins, my chauffeur, how she had gone, and his saying that he thought she was excellent.

'I'll try her myself,' said I, and I climbed into the driver's seat.

'The gears are not the same,' said he. 'Perhaps, sir, I had better drive.'

'No; I should like to try her,' said I.

And so we started on the five-mile drive for home.

My old car had the gears as they used always to be in notches on a bar. In this car you passed the gear-lever through a gate to get on the higher ones. It was not difficult to master, and soon I thought that I understood it. It was foolish, no doubt, to begin to learn a new system in the dark, but one often does foolish things, and one has not always to pay the full price for them. I got along very well until I came to Claystall Hill. It is one of the worst hills in England, a mile and a half long and one in six in places, with three fairly sharp curves. My park gate stands at the very foot of it upon the main London road.

We were just over the brow of this hill, where the grade is steepest, when the trouble began. I had been on the top speed, and wanted to get her on the free; but she stuck between gears, and I had to get her back on the top again. By this time she was going at a great rate, so I clapped on both brakes, and one after the other they gave way. I didn't mind so much when I felt my footbrake snap, but when I put all my weight on my side-brake, and the lever clanged to its full limit without a catch, it brought a cold sweat out of me. By this time we were fairly tearing down the slope. The lights were brilliant, and I brought her round the first curve all right. Then we did the second one, though it was a close shave for the ditch. There was a mile of straight then with the third curve beneath it, and after that the gate of the park. If I could shoot into that harbour all would be well, for the slope up to the house would bring her to a stand.

Perkins behaved splendidly. I should like that to be known. He was perfectly cool and alert. I had thought at the very beginning of taking the bank, and he read my intention.

'I wouldn't do it, sir,' said he. 'At this pace it must go over and we should have it on the top of us.'

Of course he was right. He got to the electric switch and had it off, so we were in the free; but we were still running at a fearful pace. He laid his hands on the wheel.

'I'll keep her steady,' said he, 'if you care to jump and chance it. We can never get round that curve. Better jump, sir.'

'No,' said I; 'I'll stick it out. You can jump if you like.'

'I'll stick it with you, sir,' said he.

If it had been the old car I should have jammed the gear-lever into the reverse, and seen what would happen. I expect she would have stripped her gears or smashed up somehow, but it would have been a chance. As it was, I was helpless. Perkins tried to climb across, but you couldn't do it going at that pace. The wheels were whirring like a high wind and the big body creaking and groaning with the strain. But the lights were brilliant, and one could steer to an inch. I remember thinking what an awful and yet majestic sight we should appear to anyone who met us. It was a narrow road, and we were just a great, roaring, golden death to anyone who came in our path.

We got round the corner with one wheel three feet high upon the bank. I thought we were surely over, but after staggering for a moment she righted and darted onwards. That was the third corner and the last one. There was only the park gate now. It was facing us, but, as luck would have it, not facing us directly. It was about twenty yards to the left up the main road into which we ran. Perhaps I could have done it, but I expect that the steering-gear had been jarred when we ran on the bank. The wheel did not turn easily. We shot out of the lane. I saw the open gate on the left. I whirled round my wheel with all the strength of my wrists. Perkins and I threw our bodies across, and then the next instant, going at fifty miles an hour, my right wheel struck full on the right-hand pillar of my own gate. I heard the crash. I was conscious of flying through the air, and then – and then . . .!

When I became aware of my own existence once more I was among some brushwood in the shadow of the oaks upon the lodge side of the drive. A man was standing beside me. I imagined at first that it was Perkins, but when I looked again I saw that it was Stanley, a man whom I had known at college some years before, and for whom I had a really genuine affection. There was always something peculiarly sympathetic to me in Stanley's personality; and I was proud to think that I had some similar influence upon him. At the present moment I was surprised to see him, but I was like a man in a dream, giddy and shaken and quite prepared to take things as I found them without questioning them.

'What a smash!' I said. 'Good Lord, what an awful smash!'

He nodded his head, and even in the gloom I could see that he was smiling the gentle, wistful smile which I connected with him.

I was quite unable to move. Indeed, I had not any desire to try to move. But my senses were exceedingly alert. I saw the wreck of the motor lit up by the moving lanterns. I saw the little group of people and heard the hushed voices. There were the lodge-keeper and his wife, and one or two more. They were taking no notice of me, but were very busy round the car. Then suddenly I heard a cry of pain.

'The weight is on him. Lift it easy,' cried a voice.

'It's only my leg!' said another one, which I recognised as Perkins's. 'Where's master?' he cried.

'Here I am,' I answered, but they did not seem to hear me. They were all bending over something which lay in front of the car.

Stanley laid his hand upon my shoulder, and his touch was inexpressibly soothing. I felt light and happy, in spite of all.

'No pain, of course?' said he.

'None,' said I.

'There never is,' said he.

And then suddenly a wave of amazement passed over me. Stanley! Stanley! Why, Stanley had surely died of enteric at Bloemfontein in the Boer War!

'Stanley!' I cried, and the words seemed to choke my throat – 'Stanley, you are dead.'

He looked at me with the same old gentle, wistful smile.

'So are you,' he answered.

THE LAST TRIP

Archie Binns

Before the arrival of the internal-combustion engine, people had been transported from town to town by coach and horses, and over the years numerous legends had developed – particularly in the remoter parts of Britain – about 'Phantom Coaches' which galloped the old highways during the dark reaches of the night. It was invariably believed to be an omen of bad luck to see one of these vehicles with its sweat-stained black horses, skeleton driver and unearthly passengers – and the theme has proved to be a popular one with generations of writers of fantasy fiction. A classic example is Amelia Edwards' blood-curdling tale, 'The Phantom Coach' written over one hundred years ago and rarely equalled.

The bus which is the featured vehicle in this next story is by no means a phantom, but the passengers its driver picks up are certainly an unearthly lot. Archie Binns (1899–1971) was a much-travelled American writer who specialised in 'off-trail' stories as well as novels of mystery and horror. His updating of the old phantom coach legend in this story which first appeared in 1925, is as good a version as any I have come across. Indeed, memories of it sometimes flash unnervingly into my mind on the rare occasions when I find myself sharing a late-night bus ride with a group of passengers I have never met before . . .

The driver congratulated himself on having only one more trip to make that night. It was nearly 11.30 when he brought the long-backed car up to the bus station on Pacific Street and let his passengers out. When he got back to Lewis he would turn in for the night. And it was high time.

A group of men stood waiting at the edge of the kerb, and almost as soon as the bus had been emptied it was full again. Butler looked around. Eight men occupied the eight places in the tonneau.

'One more for the emergency seat, and we're off,' he thought. And while he was thinking it, the ninth man came to the kerb and took the seat beside him.

'That's the way to get passengers,' he told himself as he took up the fares. 'Just the right number and no waiting.' It was something that had never happened before in his long experience as a driver.

In less than a minute after arriving, he was jockeying the long-backed bus out through the traffic. He climbed the H Street hill, gathered speed on the lever and slipped into the overdrive without disturbing the clutch.

It was a dark, windless night and there was nothing to see but the pool of headlights on the road. In the darkened tonneau eight passengers sat like shadows without speaking, nodding slightly with the motion of the car. Beside the driver the ninth man looked steadily and silently into the darkness. Butler was annoyed.

'Anyone would say that I was driving them to a funeral,' he thought.

The light of the last house slipped by and they rushed on between the dark walls of scrub pines that bordered the road. And no one had spoken a word.

'What a gang of passengers!' he breathed to himself.

Suddenly the buzzer vibrated through the silence. And for some reason the man at the wheel started.

'Driver, I want to get out here,' a voice called from the darkness of the tonneau.

Obediently he put his feet on the pedals and brought the bus to a full stop with the handbrake. A man climbed out and disappeared into the blackness.

'The devil,' the driver thought as he started on; 'I never saw a cross-road here!'

Again the big car whined along in the overdrive. And not a word had been spoken except by the man who had got out. A nice party!

Three minutes later the buzzer broke through the silence.

'Driver.'

Again his feet reached for the pedals.

'I want to get out here.'

The car came to a stop, a man got out, closed the door; and they rolled on.

'Is there any place for that man to go?' Butler wondered. 'Anyway, it was too dark for him to see where we were.'

A small car, travelling rapidly, hummed by. And in some way it gave him a feeling of relief. He glanced back. In the moment of light he saw six remaining passengers in the tonneau, sitting like so many shadows, nodding slightly with the motion of the bus. When the other car had passed, the night and the road seemed darker and uglier than before.

Hardly a minute later he started again at the harsh noise of the buzzer.

'Driver, I want to get out here.'

The same voice, and the same blackness of scrub pines. As the man got out, the driver put his head into the darkness and looked about. There might or might not have been some trail through the woods. He could not see.

He used the throttle a little more.

'It may be some game that they are up to,' he told himself. 'But if they want to rob me, why do they get out before they have their money's worth out of their fares?'

Now the bus was fairly swallowing up the road.

'Half-an-hour more of this and we're . . .'

B-r-r-! The buzzer again.

'Driver, I want to get out here!'

Butler did not put out his head to look this time. It seemed safer not to. Besides, he knew that there was no crossroad of any kind. Out of the corner of his eye he glanced at the man beside him in the emergency seat.

'Is he in this, too?' the driver wondered. 'Why can't he say something?'

But the fellow was still looking out into the darkness, without ever having moved his head.

'What a cursed, black road,' he muttered inside his chest. When the buzzer growled again he started violently because he had been listening tensely.

'Driver, I want to get out here,' he mimicked to himself. And his skin prickled all over when the words were repeated, in exactly the same tone, from the darkened tonneau.

The fifth man got out. Butler drove on and did not look around. Without being fully conscious of it, he was driving faster than he had ever driven before. The lightened car rocked as it plunged on over the road.

'Why is it that the fewer there are, the more scared I am?' he wondered.

He listened intently for the buzzer, nearly starting out of his seat at the first harsh vibration.

'Driver, I want to get out here.'

And the sixth man disappeared into the blackness of the pines, where there was neither house nor trail. The two remaining men in the back of the car were silent as shadows. In the emergency seat the other man had never moved nor turned his head.

'I wish we could meet some more cars,' the driver thought. He put on the brakes as the buzzer snarled again.

'Driver, I want to get out here.'

The repeated sound of the buzzer and the voice was maddening. Again he stopped between the ugly walls of the darkness, letting the seventh passenger out.

'Seven from nine makes two,' he told himself as the bus lunged on. 'If they start anything, I might be able to handle the two of them. If only the one beside me would turn around, or get out, or say something!'

And the long car shot rocking through the darkness, with only the driver and the one shadow in the great tonneau, and the man who was looking intently into the blackness of pines and the night. Butler gripped the wheel and felt his hair prickling on his head. The one in the back was moving about. Perhaps he was reaching for the . . .

B-r-r-r-!

The buzzer seemed attached to his nerves, racking them with its harsh vibrations.

'Driver, I want to get out here.'

It was spoken in the same tone that the others had used. But each time it was repeated it became more hateful and uncanny.

He let the eighth man out.

'Good-night.'

'What!' the driver exclaimed. The two words had startled him unbelievably.

The door had no sooner closed on the empty tonneau than the car was in motion again. Why had he started so when the man said 'good-night'? Passengers often did that. But spoken by the last of the eight, the words seemed to have a strange meaning.

'Eight from nine makes one,' he reassured himself, slipping into the overdrive again. 'But who is the one, and what is he up to?'

As if in answer, the man in the emergency seat took a deep breath, like a sigh, and turned from studying the darkness. It was a face that the driver had never seen before, smooth and pale, with dark, luminous eyes. The man folded his arms over his breast and spoke for the first time.

'How far is it to the Woodland Cemetery?'

Butler started violently and pressed the throttle.

'Five miles.' Then he added, 'We're having a nice ride, aren't we?'

The passenger laughed.

'Ha, ha! You are driving fast, Mr Butler.'

He flinched at the weird sound of the laughter mingled with the rush of the car; and the mention of his name made him tremble, because he felt that he must do or say something. 'Well, better introduce yourself, since we are riding together.'

'If you wish,' was the cool reply. 'My name is Death.'

'I didn't quite get it.'

'Death!'

The bus driver put his feet on the pedals.

'This has gone far enough to suit me,' he thought.

'Better not,' the man beside him remarked. 'Do you see anything under my elbow!'

In the dim light that was shed from the instrument board he made out the muzzle of an automatic pistol, protruding slightly from under folded arms.

'As you like,' he agreed. 'Where were we? Your name is Death, I believe. I suppose that is why you are going to the cemetery.'

'Exactly, that is why we are going to the cemetery.'

The driver felt a horrible chill coming over him.

'*We?* I didn't know I was invited.'

'You were invited when I planned this ride.'

'So you planned it, eh, with the others getting out along the road?'

'Exactly, so that we could go alone.'

The passenger began tapping on the foot-boards with his feet, keeping time with the swaying car. Butler tightened his grip on the wheel, shivering and snarling like an animal in a cage.

'If you are Mister Death, then it's the cemetery for you. But you might tell me what's the idea of taking me along. By God!' he burst out; 'if you carried a scythe, as you are supposed to, instead of that pistol, I would take a chance on seeing if we both went there!'

'Death has tricked people before,' the passenger observed coolly. 'And hadn't you better think a minute and see if there isn't a reason for your going there?'

'What the devil are you driving at? What have I done?'

'You should remember.'

'Remember what?'

The driver's heart pounded so that he could hear it above the roar of the motor; and the car that raced over the road seemed to be standing still in the horrible darkness.

'So you don't remember?'

'No. What is it?'

'How far is it to the cemetery now?'

'About three miles. Why?'

'And still you don't remember?'

'No. Who the devil are you?'

'You have forgotten!' the passenger cried, his eyes shining like those of a cat. 'God, I wish I could forget! And you don't even remember!'

'But what is it I don't remember?'

'Listen. When you were a bus driver here in 1918, did you once crowd a woman's car into a ditch?'

'What is that to you?'

'So you did?'

'Yes,' the driver admitted sullenly. 'What is that to you?'

'What happened to the woman?'

'The car turned over and she died. But who – what was she to you?'

'Everything!'

The passenger stared with mad intentness. Then he continued.

'I would have died long ago if it hadn't been for her. I was blown up and shot to pieces. But I wouldn't die. Then, when I was ready to come home, I heard that you had killed her.'

'But it wasn't my fault! I had to keep on schedule. That day . . .'

He turned his face away from the wild, unnatural light in the man's eyes. Before him there rose the scene that he had never let himself think of since the day it happened; the crowded bus tearing over the road to make up time, the grey roadster pushed to the edge of the ditch by the heavier vehicle, the gasp of the passengers, followed by a shriek that went up and up, as the small car turned over and crumpled, the bus sliding to a stop with smoking brakes, the white-faced passengers crowding round, the delicate, drooping face of the girl, and the blood – blood all over her white dress! The driver pressed the throttle as far down as it would go, trying to get away from the fearful picture.

'So you killed us both. It was too much to stand. They brought back what was left of me, and put me away. I waited my chance until tonight, when I came to find you.'

Still the picture floated before his eyes, while the shrieking pierced him through. And this madman or ghost was making him remember every detail.

'How far is it to the cemetery now?'

'A mile,' Butler said between chattering teeth.

'Good, we shall be in time!'

The bus lumbered swiftly down the hill, through the valley, and roared up the other slope, with the passenger beating time to its rhythm. As he neared the crest, the driver saw a faint light in the sky. Soon they would be on the open flat, in sight of the cemetery . . .

'Quick, how far is it now?'

'A quarter of a mile.'

His staring eyes were ready to burst and the hair bristled on his head. The drooping face, the blood all over the white dress, and the shrieking, filled his eyes and ears.

'If I can only get past without stopping,' he repeated to himself.

The black iron fence came in sight; the dim gravestones flitted by like ghosts. Just ahead, at the bend in the highway, the dark gateway of the cemetery rose against the sky. If he kept on the road at that turn, he would be safe in sight of the lights of the town.

Butler winced fearfully as the car rocked over an unevenness of the road. The dark arch of the gateway seemed to draw his eyes towards it, like a magnet.

'We are here!' the passenger cried, rising in his seat.

The wheel twisted in the driver's hands, and the long-backed car careered and banked sharply. Then it plunged towards the cemetery, where the white gravestones stood waiting, row after row, like ghosts, to welcome his arrival.

One side of the stone entrance leapt up before the car. And at the moment of the crash that sounded to the sky, there was a wild, triumphant burst of laughter, either from the mad passenger – or the dead who were waiting.

THE DEMON LOVER

Elizabeth Bowen

From one form of public transport, the bus, we turn to another, the taxi, that eponymous vehicle which is always on the streets when you don't want one and disappears the instant you do. There have, in fact, been quite a number of mysterious short stories about taxis – John Metcalfe's 'The Grey House' comes to mind, as does Nell Kay's curious and allegedly true story of 'Our Haunted Taxi Ride' – but my favourite has long been this next item which also happens to be something of a macabre classic.

Elizabeth Bowen (1899–1973) lived for many years in London and doubtless took innumerable taxi rides. And perhaps one gave her the idea for 'The Demon Lover'? Although famous as one of the leading novelists of this century, Mrs Bowen wrote a number of highly regarded weird tales, some of the best collected in The Cat Jumps *(1934) and the volume named after the story here which first appeared in 1945. It is a disquieting tale which might well cause you to look very carefully the next time you are thinking of hailing a cab . . .*

Towards the end of her day in London Mrs Drover went round to her shut-up house to look for several things she wanted to take away. Some belonged to herself, some to her family, who were by now used to their country life. It was late August; it had been a steamy, showery day: at the moment the trees down the pavement glittered in an escape of humid yellow afternoon sun. Against the next batch of clouds, already piling up ink-dark, broken chimneys and parapets stood out. In her once familiar street, as in any unused channel, an unfamiliar queerness had silted up; a cat wove itself in and out of railings, but no human eye watched Mrs Drover's return. Shifting some parcels under her arm, she slowly forced round her latchkey in an unwilling lock, then gave the door, which had warped, a push with her knee. Dead air came out to meet her as she went in.

The staircase window having been boarded up, no light came down into the hall. But one door, she could just see, stood ajar, so she went quickly through into the room and unshuttered the big window in there. Now the prosaic woman, looking about her, was more perplexed than she knew by everything that she saw, by traces of her long former habit of life – the yellow smoke-stain up the white marble mantelpiece, the ring left by a vase on the top of the escritoire; the bruise in the wallpaper where, on the door being thrown open widely, the china handle had always hit the wall. The piano, having gone away to be stored, had left what looked like claw-marks on its part of the parquet. Though not much dust had seeped in, each object wore a film of another kind; and, the only ventilation being the chimney, the whole drawing-room smelled of the cold hearth. Mrs Drover put down her parcels on the escritoire and left the room to proceed upstairs; the things she wanted were in a bedroom chest.

She had been anxious to see how the house was – the part-time caretaker she shared with some neighbours was away this week on his holiday, known to be not yet back. At the best of times he did not look in often, and she was never sure that she trusted him. There were some cracks in the structure, left by the last bombing, on which she was anxious to keep an eye. Not that one could do anything . . .

A shaft of refracted daylight now lay across the hall. She stopped dead and stared at the hall table – on this lay a letter addressed to her.

She thought first – then the caretaker *must* be back. All the same, who, seeing the house shuttered, would have dropped a letter in at the box? It was not a circular, it was not a bill. And the post office redirected, to the address in the country, everything for her that came through the post. The caretaker (even if he *were* back) did not know she was due in London today – her call here had been planned to be a surprise – so his negligence in the matter of this letter, leaving it to wait in the dusk and the dust, annoyed her. Annoyed, she picked up the letter, which bore no stamp. But it cannot be important, or they would know . . . She took the letter rapidly upstairs with her, without a stop to look at the writing till she reached what had been her bedroom, where she let in light. The room looked over the garden and other gardens: the sun had gone in; as the clouds sharpened and lowered, the trees and rank lawns seemed already to smoke with dark. Her reluctance to look again at the letter came from the fact that she felt intruded upon – and by someone contemptuous of her ways. However, in the tenseness preceding the fall of rain she read it: it was a few lines.

Dear Kathleen,

You will not have forgotten that today is our anniversary, and the day we said. The years have gone by at once slowly and fast. In view of the fact that nothing has changed, I shall rely upon you to keep your promise. I was sorry to see you leave London, but was satisfied that you would be back in time. You may expect me, therefore, at the hour arranged.

Until then . . .

K.

Mrs Drover looked for the date: it was today's. She dropped the letter on to the bed-springs, then picked it up to see the writing again – her lips, beneath the remains of lipstick, beginning to go white. She felt so much the change in her own face that she went to the mirror, polished a clear patch in it and looked at once urgently and stealthily in. She was confronted by a woman of forty-four, with eyes starting out under a hat-brim that had been rather carelessly pulled down. She had not put on any more powder since she left the shop where she ate her solitary tea. The pearls her husband had given her on their marriage hung loose round her now rather thinner throat, slipping into the V of the pink wool jumper her sister knitted last autumn as they sat round the fire. Mrs Drover's most normal expression was one of controlled worry, but of assent. Since the birth of the third of her little boys, attended by a quite serious illness, she had had an intermittent muscular flicker to the left of her mouth, but in spite of this she could always sustain a manner that was at once energetic and calm.

Turning from her own face as precipitately as she had gone to meet it, she went to the chest where the things were, unlocked it, threw up the lid and knelt to search. But as rain began to come crashing down she could not keep from looking over her shoulder at the stripped bed on which the letter lay. Behind the blanket of rain the clock of the church that still stood struck six – with rapidly heightening apprehension she counted each of the slow strokes. 'The hour arranged . . . My God,' she said, '*what* hour? How should I . . .? after twenty-five years. . . .'

The young girl talking to the soldier in the garden had not ever completely seen his face. It was dark; they were saying goodbye under a tree. Now and then – for it felt, from not seeing him at this intense moment, as though she had never seen him at all – she verified his presence for these few moments longer by putting out a hand, which he each time pressed, without very much kindness, and painfully, on to one of the breast buttons of his uniform. That cut of the button on the palm of her hand was, principally, what she was to carry away. This was so near the end of a leave from France that she could only wish him already gone. It was August 1916. Being not kissed, being drawn away from and looked at intimidated Kathleen till she imagined spectral glitters in the place of his eyes. Turning away and looking back up the lawn she saw, through branches of trees, the drawing-room window alight: she caught a breath for the moment when she could go running back there into the safe arms of her mother and sister, and cry: 'What shall I do, what shall I do? He has gone.'

Hearing her catch her breath, her fiancé said, without feeling: 'Cold?'

'You're going away such a long way.'

'Not so far as you think.'

'I don't understand?'

'You don't have to,' he said. 'You will. You know what we said.'

'But that was – suppose you – I mean, suppose.'

'I shall be with you,' he said, 'sooner or later. You won't forget that. You need do nothing but wait.'

Only a little more than a minute later she was free to run up the silent lawn. Looking in through the window at her mother and sister, who did not for the moment perceive her, she already felt that unnatural promise drive down between her and the rest of all human kind. No other way of having given herself could have made her feel so apart, lost and forsworn. She could not have plighted a more sinister troth.

Kathleen behaved well when, some months later, her fiancé was reported missing, presumed killed. Her family not only supported her but were able to praise her courage without stint because they could not regret, as a husband for her, the man they knew almost nothing about. They hoped she would, in a year or two, console herself – and had it been only a question of consolation things might have gone much straighter ahead. But her trouble, behind just a little grief, was a complete dislocation from everything. She did not reject other lovers, for these failed to appear: for years she failed to attract men – and with the approach of her thirties it became natural enough to share her family's anxiousness on this score. She began to put herself out, to wonder; and at thirty-two she was very greatly relieved to find herself being courted by William Drover. She married him, and the two of them settled down in this quiet, arboreal part of Kensington: in this house the years piled up, her children were born and they all lived till they were driven out by the bombs of the next war. Her movements as Mrs Drover were circumscribed, and she dismissed any idea that they were still watched.

As things were – dead or living the letter-writer sent her only a threat. Unable, for some minutes, to go on kneeling with her back exposed to the empty room, Mrs Drover rose from the chest to sit on an upright chair whose back was firmly against the wall. The desuetude of her former bedroom, her married London home's whole air of being a cracked cup from which memory, with its reassuring power, had either evaporated or leaked away, made a crisis – and at just this crisis the letter-writer had, knowledgeably, struck.

The hollowness of the house this evening cancelled years on years of voices, habits and steps. Through the shut windows she only heard rain fall on the roofs around. To rally herself, she said she was in a mood – and, for two or three seconds shutting her eyes, told herself that she had imagined the letter. But she opened them – there it lay on the bed.

On the supernatural side of the letter's entrance she was not permitting her mind to dwell. Who, in London, knew she meant to call at the house today? Evidently, however, this had been known. The caretaker, *had* he come back, had had no cause to expect her: he would have taken the letter in his pocket, to forward it, at his own time, through the post. There was no other sign that the caretaker had been in – but, if not? Letters dropped in at doors of deserted houses do not fly or walk to tables in halls. They do not sit on the dust of empty tables with the air of certainty that they will be found. There is needed some human hand – but nobody but the caretaker had a key. Under circumstances she did not care to consider, a house can be entered without a key. It was possible that she was not alone now. She might be being waited for, downstairs. Waited for – until when? Until 'the hour arranged'. At least that was not six o'clock: six had struck.

She rose from the chair and went over and locked the door.

The thing was, to get out. To fly? No, not that: she had to catch her train. As a woman whose utter dependability was the keystone of her family life she was not willing to return to the country, to her husband, her little boys and her sister, without the objects she had come up to fetch. Resuming work at the chest she set about making up a number of parcels in a rapid, fumbling-decisive way. These, with her shopping parcels, would be too much to carry; these meant a taxi – at the thought of the taxi her heart went up and her normal breathing resumed. I will ring up the taxi now; the taxi cannot come too soon: I shall hear the taxi out there running its engine, till I walk calmly down to it through the hall. I'll ring up – But no: the telephone is cut off . . . She tugged at a knot she had tied wrong.

The idea of flight . . . He was never kind to me, not really. I don't remember him kind at all. Mother said he never considered me. He was set on me, that was what it was – not love. Not love, not meaning a person well. What did he do, to make me promise like that? I can't remember – but she found that she could.

She remembered with such dreadful acuteness that the twenty-five years since then dissolved like smoke and she instinctively looked for the weal left by the button on the palm of her hand. She remembered not only all that he said and did but the complete suspension of *her* existence during that August week. I was not myself – they all told me so at the time.

She remembered – but with one white burning blank as where acid has dropped on a photograph: *under no conditions* could she remember his face.

So, wherever he may be waiting, I shall not know him. You have no time to run from a face you do not expect.

The thing was to get to the taxi before any clock struck what could be the hour. She would slip down the street and round the side of the square to where the square gave on the main road. She would return in the taxi, safe, to her own door, and bring the solid driver into the house with her to pick up the parcels from room to room. The idea of the taxi driver made her decisive, bold: she unlocked her door, went to the top of the staircase and listened down.

She heard nothing – but while she was hearing nothing the *passé* air of the staircase was disturbed by a draught that travelled up to her face. It emanated from the basement: down there a door or window was being opened by someone who chose this moment to leave the house.

The rain had stopped; the pavements steamily shone as Mrs Drover let herself out by inches from her own front door into the empty street. The unoccupied houses opposite continued to meet her look with their damaged stare. Making towards the thoroughfare and the taxi, she tried not to keep looking behind. Indeed, the silence was so intense – one of those creeks of London silence exaggerated this summer by the damage of war – that no tread could have gained on hers unheard. Where her street debouched on the square where people went on living, she grew conscious of, and checked, her unnatural pace. Across the open end of the square two buses impassively passed each other: women, a perambulator, cyclists, a man wheeling a barrow signalised, once again, the ordinary flow of life. At the square's most populous corner should be – and was – the short taxi rank. This evening, only one taxi – but this, although it presented its black rump, appeared already to be alertly waiting for her. Indeed, without looking round the driver started his engine as she panted up from behind and put her hand on the door. As she did so, the clock struck seven. The taxi faced the main road: to make the trip back to her house it would have to turn – she had settled back on the seat and the taxi *had* turned before she, surprised by its knowing movement, recollected that she had not 'said where'. She leaned forward to scratch at the glass panel that divided the driver's head from her own.

The driver braked to what was almost a stop, turned round and slid the glass panel back: the jolt of this flung Mrs Drover forwards till her face was almost into the glass. Through the aperture driver and passenger, not six inches between them, remained for an eternity eye to eye. Mrs Drover's mouth hung open for some seconds before she could issue her first scream. After that she continued to scream freely and to beat with her gloved hands on the glass all round as the taxi, accelerating without mercy, made off with her into the hinterland of deserted streets.

JAY WALKERS

H. Russell Wakefield

The idea of a stretch of road being haunted by a phantom motor car has been explored in the earlier story, 'The Dust-Cloud'. In this next contribution we encounter a specific locality which has been the scene of six mysterious and fatal motor accidents – all of which occurred on the same date in different years and at the same time. It is a fascinating story for two reasons: firstly, because the author, H. Russell Wakefield, was himself involved in an inexplicable motoring accident in 1936; and, secondly, because the event occurred on the Ledbury to Hereford road in Herefordshire where the story is set. What, therefore, is fact and what is fiction in what follows is open to conjecture!

Herbert Russell Wakefield (1888–1964) is one of England's premier ghost-story writers of this century, an author to be bracketed with M. R. James and Robert Aickman. As a young man he was strongly sceptical about the supernatural, but after experiencing some very strange sensations in an old house in which he stayed, he became fascinated by ghosts and began to write stories on these themes, beginning with 'The Red Lodge' about the house which had prompted his interest. He was a keen motorist, too, with a special interest in vintage cars, and this is to be found reflected in other of his tales such as 'Used Car' and 'Or Persons Unknown'. But surpassing all these, I think, is 'Jay Walkers' – with its fascinating background and unexpected climax.

Those who possess an eye for oddities and enigmas may recall an item of news which was recorded at varying lengths – from half a column upwards – in several of the London 'dailies' about the middle of September three years ago. The 'story,' as I believe it is termed in press circles, was headed 'A Haunted Road' – or words to that effect – and it stated that another fatal accident, this time to a travelling salesman, had occurred on a stretch of road in Herefordshire. The victim had been discovered underneath his overturned car about 9 p.m. and he had been dead about half an hour. This, it was said, was the sixth motor fatality within ten years at this precise spot – or very near it – on this same date, and very much at this same time. Apparently the representative of the agency who sent in this story had made some rather cursory inquiries in the neighbourhood, particularly in the village of M——, which is situated about two miles from the scene of these accidents, and gathered from the local people that this piece of road was 'haunted', by what or whom he did not state. And that, if you please, was the beginning and end of the information these journals deigned to grant their readers; the 'story' was not 'followed up' even to the extent of a paragraph, but left in its pregnant strangeness, disparate and bare. And this is typical of many press tales. I suppose it is due to 'pressure on our space', but the fact is there are only two topics which a popular newspaper ever seems consistently to explore and exploit: its own merits and those of British Womanhood. Perhaps it is because my father, a much-travelled man, considered British women the dullest in the world, that I have never been able to see eye to eye with the press that these assumptions are unchangeable, but this is a digression. Now for many years I have interested myself in Metapsychics, the science – if it can so be termed – of supernormal and occult phenomena, and I flatter myself I have investigated the history and credentials of more specimens of this genre than any other living Englishman. It is my hobby, my craving if you like, and fortunately I possess the means and the leisure to devote myself to it thoroughly and conscientiously. Therefore, when I read that 'intriguing' (I dislike the word but there is no other that precisely does its work) item of news and realised I should be vouchsafed no more information from the same source, I made up my mind to clear the matter up. Quite possibly, I knew, it was just one of the many tales of its type, consisting far more of embroidery than stuff: but somehow it had an air about it which persuaded me it was worth investigation. So I took train to Ledbury, which was distant some eight miles from the village of M——. (I have resolved to maintain a certain reticence regarding place and personal names for a reason which I shall later explain.) I may say also that I have some reputation for pedantry amongst my friends; probably my enemies – if I have any – for I possess too neutral a temperament to have many, describe me as a bore; but I prefer pedantry to inaccuracy; I would sooner be a bore than a bluffer.

At Ledbury I installed myself at a hotel, and set out the next morning to consult the files of the local paper which bottles and dispenses the usual small beer of the regions round about. At the end of eight hours' laborious search I had verified the following facts: there *had* been six fatal automobile accidents on the Ledbury–M—— Road within the last decade, always roughly at the same spot on the same date, September 10th, and each of these fatalities had occurred between 8 and 9 p.m. – the exact time was not known in three instances as the crash had not been discovered till an uncertain period after its occurrence.

In 1926 a Ledbury doctor was found dead in his car which had left the road and telescoped against a telegraph pole.

In 1929 a local publican was driving his wife and daughter back from Malvern, when he apparently lost control, and his car ran into a ditch. All three were killed instantly, but the crash was heard and the time of its occurrence verified as 8.35.

In 1931 a local parson, driving alone, was killed when his car overturned. His body was discovered at 8.50.

In 1933 a Birmingham business man, touring the locality with his wife and two young sons, drove his saloon obliquely off the road into a field where it fell on its side and burst into flames. All four were burnt to death. This accident took place about 8.30.

In 1935 a Hereford building contractor, driving back from Ledbury, was found dying in the middle of the road having been hurled through the windscreen of his car, which had crashed into the hedge. Just before he died in hospital, he said, 'Did I hit them?' The accident happened about 8.30.

Finally in 1936 this salesman had met his fate as stated. He was found at 8.45 by a passing car, and a doctor testified at the inquest he had been dead for a very short time.

Now it will occur to the reader to ask why, if there was some casual link between these accidents, was there no record of any such previous to 1926. Naturally I turned my attention to this problem and got this much enlightenment. Before the War the road was notoriously bad and practically unused by motor traffic. In 1923 the local authorities found the pressure on the neighbouring highways becoming heavy and it was decided to improve this secondary road by relaying it, trimming hedges, and so on. It was not re-opened till December, 1925. Furthermore, I found a small paragraph recording the inquest on a local labourer's daughter who was found dead beside her cycle on this same stretch on September 10th, 1921. The theory was she had been thrown off on to her head when her cycle struck a stone. She was discovered about nine and had been dead a short time.

My next step was, of course, to visit the scene of these happenings to see if there was anything in this piece of road to encourage disaster, though I had gathered from the various inquests that such was not the case, and that the weather had been fine and the surface dry on every occasion. I hired a car and went there the next day. My driver was a stolid, unresponsive fellow who took no interest in my errand; but he knew the place by repute. 'Here we are,' he announced, after half and hour's drive. I found myself at the bottom of a shallow valley which pierced the road at this point, and from which it ran up pretty steeply due north and south. Consequently I judged the speed of cars at this point would tend to be high as they were 'opened-out' to take the rise, otherwise there was nothing whatsoever to justify its malign record. My stolid chauffeur agreed with me in this, declaring he had driven it countless times in all weathers and found no perils or snares appertaining to it. His adequate imagination, however, seemed to find the axiom that ninety per cent of motorists were congenital idiots, quite adequate explanation of the spate of blood on this, as on every other, stretch of road in the United Kingdom.

But I was not so easily satisfied: in fact, I found it impossible to write off this strange sequence as one of the vagaries of coincidence, many and fantastic though these can be. In fact, I knew again that sense of leashed elation which comes to me when I am, as I believe sportsmen put it, 'on a good thing'.

My next move was clearly indicated, to delve into this alleged 'haunting'. After dinner that night I invited Mine Host to share a pint of port with me in the smoking-room. After an exchange of rather flaccid civilities I brought the conversation round to what I was after, using the newspaper story as an introduction to the topic. This landlord was somewhat narrow-eyed and mundane-minded, and I received no very sympathetic response. He seemed to share the view of my chauffeur that most motorists abrogated their senses when they slipped in their clutches. 'They've got to crash somewhere,' he laughed, 'besides, half-past eight is just the time when they're hurrying home after stoking-up at pubs, and then take the hill too hard. I don't say the parson was tight, but parsons and old women are the worst drivers on the roads. Anyway they've got to put something in the papers.'

'Then you've heard nothing of any story or legend in connection with that piece of road?' I asked.

'No, sir, and I'll bet my boots there's no such; but,' he said, 'there's a gentleman who comes in here most nights who can tell you if there's any such yarn. He's an authority on these parts, he writes on 'em. He's a rich gentleman who lives at Metling Manor, two miles out of the town.'

He looked at the clock. 'It's near his usual time; I'll let you know if he comes in.'

Presently he returned in company with an elderly man of robust, genial and intelligent appearance. He introduced us and departed.

'Well, sir,' said my new acquaintance, accepting a glass of port. 'I did not gather from Curtis very clearly what you wished to ask me about, but I am at your service.'

Whereupon I gave him a précis of my reasons for being in the vicinity, and I could see he was somewhat impressed.

'Very interesting occupation, yours,' he said, 'as unusual as interesting. My hobby is peering at the heavens through a small telescope; so we are both of us preoccupied with an enigma. I may say I am no great expert; in fact, I could do with a course at the Academy of Professor William Hay, no doubt.' (I think this is what he remarked, but the allusion quite escapes me.)

'As for your "ghosts," I am quite open-minded. Understanding, as we do, nothing of the purpose, and precious little of the content of creation, one more mystery makes little difference. And I'll give you this; it *is* a very suggestive sequence, a great straining of one's belief in coincidence. And, appropriately enough that mile of road has a history, if one can so describe it.'

'It has!' I said eagerly.

'Yes; though the fact must be known to very few I dare say

there's some vague oral tradition in the neighbourhood, but I don't advise you to go in search of it. Those you might interrogate would merely put you down as another reporter, though, if I may say so, you in no way resemble one, and they mistrust the breed. Probably you would be palmed off with a catalogue of lies by the local Pint-Scrounger, and that would be the beginning and end of your gleanings there.' He spoke with great vivacity and gusto, and was palpably a man of superior character and parts. I thanked him for this timely advice and waited for his further pleasure.

'I'm not sure,' he continued, 'I can tell you anything very illuminating. Did you ever hear of a Victorian Q.C. called W—— M——?' (I am again observing a necessary reticence.)

'Remotely so, I think,' I replied.

'He was a lamentably dull dog,' continued my companion, 'but he had a very large criminal practice during the last quarter of the century. In an ill-omened moment he decided to write his reminiscences, which in their soporific potency are about equivalent to a lethal dose of chloral. However, he devotes what seems a disproportionate amount of this drowsy stuff to a case which was connected with that very mile of road, though he had merely a watching brief in a coroner's court. I have a copy of the book which I will gladly lend you.'

I thanked him sincerely for his courtesy.

'The person whose interests he was watching,' he continued, 'was a certain H—— B——, a man of thirty who lived with his mother in a house just at the top of the hill on the Ledbury side of the valley. He had some money of his own and led the life of a small country gentleman. This house has since been pulled down, and I believe, for your satisfaction, had the reputation of being haunted. In 1888 this H—— B—— was engaged to be married to a Miss L——, a young woman of great beauty, but beneath him in station, according to the world's values, being the daughter of a Birmingham tanner in a very small way of business. This maiden he had seduced, or been seduced by – it is of no consequence – and he had promised to marry her, a promise which his mother, a woman of strong character and principles, insisted he should keep. The wedding was fixed for some time in October. One evening in September – it may have been your tenth, I do not recall – when the girl was staying with the mother, she and this H—— B—— went for a walk and arrived back later in the evening. The girl was taken ill that night and died the next day. That is all I remember about the case, save that H—— B——, who was absolved of all suspicion married soon after an American millionairess and went to live in the States. I know nothing of his subsequent history. The details of the affair you will find in W—— M——'s book.'

I thanked him again but added, 'I an not proposing to go against your advice, but that account in the papers suggested that there *was* some local tradition the road was suspect in some way – in the vaguest of terms I grant you, but . . .'

'Excuse me interrupting,' he said, 'but I quite get your point. If that scribe wasn't merely adorning his tale with an appropriate fiction, he must have heard something. Leave that to me: I know the countrymen round here like the back of my hand, and I'll do a little ferreting around and let you know. Don't thank me, I'm highly interested. I'm supposed to be somewhat of an authority on Herefordshire history and customs, and this is quite within my province. When are you leaving here?'

'Tomorrow morning.'

'Then I will send the book to your home address if you will give it me, and I will make these inquiries at once and write you of any information I can glean.'

I told him how delighted I was to have found such an accomplished and courteous helper. Whereupon we finished the bottle, and Mr Thomas Tusker, as he was named, drove off home.

He was as good as his word, and thirty-six hours later the book was delivered at my home in Belgrave Square. I opened it eagerly as no doubt many others had done; but unlike them, at least so I fancy, I was not disappointed. It was a well-produced crown 8vo, published in 1898, with a lengthy and ponderous dedication to some unnamed female; and this, I found, was a characteristic and ominous introduction. Certainly he was a master of tepid verbosity, but this was all to the good from my point of view. It did not take me long to reach the year 1888 and the chapter dealing with the events antecedent and subsequent to the death of Miss L——. (I may say the author exercised the same discretionary powers as myself, and refers to the characters concerned by their initials only. It is quite conceivable H—— B—— is still alive.)

It appears – to use his own jargon – that on September 20th, 1888, he received an urgent request from a firm of Hereford solicitors and the offer of a substantial fee for representing this

H—— B—— at an adjourned inquest in Ledbury. On calling upon the firm he was informed of the following circumstances: the doctor who attended Miss L—— had refused to give a death certificate and a post-mortem had been ordered. The experts who performed this gave it as their opinion that Miss L—— had died as the result of poisoning by some vegetable alkaloid, probably atropine or aconitine. Apparently – I may say I know little of such matters – the tests for the presence of such poisons in the human body were, in those days, indirect and rudimentary, but experiments had been made on some small rodents which reinforced this hypothesis; and that her symptoms were consistent with it. The author had 'mugged-up' some information about these vegetable alkaloids in connection with a murder case in which he had acted for the defence, and which was the chief cause of his being briefed for Mr H—— B——. The solicitors informed him that local feeling was running high against his client, more on general principles than from definite grounds of suspicion; he being haughty, high-minded, and boorish. It is clear, too, that his counsel took a strong dislike to him, though he never suggests he doubted his innocence. When the inquest was resumed, Mr H—— B—— was to all intents and purposes in the dock. However, our author, according to his own complacent account, had little difficulty in relieving his anxiety. Firstly, there appeared to be no motive. The marriage was arranged, and the parties to it on terms of great affection – Mr H—— B—— fully repenting of his amorous indiscretion and anxious to make reparation. Again no evidence whatsoever of his purchase, or otherwise procuring, of any poison, could be produced, though it is clear the fullest investigation had been covertly made. Our author – who has no small opinion of himself – is not backward in pointing out how he belaboured and pulverised the medical experts, thus leaving the jury in a great state of uncertainty as to whether death had been due to poison and not natural causes – heart trouble, 'idiopathic convulsions' – whatever they may be – or possibly a surfeit of bliss. If there were any traces of an alkaloid in the body, argued our author, it was probably a cadaveric alkaloid – whatever *that* may be. So the verdict was Death from Natural Causes, and our author pocketed his fee and went back to London.

But although, as I have stated, he professed to believe in his client's innocence, his chapter leaves the impression that Mr H—— B—— was in serious jeopardy, and it required the talents of Mr W—— M—— to get him safely out of it. And since he never knew that his client subsequently married an American heiress – well, in any case that could never have concerned him. He writes in conclusion:

I have devoted considerable space to what may seem a case of little interest and minor importance, but there were elements of strangeness and, from my point of view, difficulty about it. The girl was in robust health at eight o'clock one morning and dead by eight o'clock the next. Until I pressed them hard, the medical witnesses were very positive that the symptoms: high temperature, double vision, delirium, and the changes immediately preceding death, were consistent and consistent only, with poisoning by a vegetable alkaloid; and though I shook them, I think they remained of the same opinion still. Could any convincing degree of motive have been urged, far more if any procuring of poison been traced to my client, it must have gone hard with him. It is not one of the defences – for it amounted to that – on which I look back with least satisfaction. I may add the finding of the jury was received with murmurs of anger and disapproval.

Speaking purely for myself, I should say that the impression left on the untutored is that the one thing Miss L—— did *not* die from was a natural cause, but that may have been due to humanity's passionate preference for believing the worst if it is inhumanly possible.

A week later I received the following letter.

Dear Sir Anstruther,

'Well, I have "snooped around" and you were certainly right. There is a very strong and adhesive local tradition that one is liable to encounter unexpected pedestrians on that piece of road on the evening of September 10th. In fact, those living in the vicinity give the area a wide berth on that anniversary. They attribute these crashes unhesitatingly to such encounters. There is another queer little belief. My informant, an astonishingly well-preserved nonagenarian, told me that the girl is supposed to have been singing as she walked through M—— with her lover. "A song about doing her hair," declared my Ancient. I wondered if it conceivably might be Haydn's

"My Mother bids me Bind my Hair" – one of the supreme delicacies of all time – and hummed the first ten bars. "Yes, that was the tune, and you might hear her singing it still," he declared after his third pint, "if you were near to Pix Hill around eight-thirty on September tenth." While the spell was on me I felt somehow as though I had strayed for a moment over the frontier of fairyland. This haunting business is a slippery half-concept. If one spot is haunted, why not all? If at one hour, why not always? Should not every battlefield be awake with the grapplings and loud with the cries of those who fought there? But they are not. Anyway it's your line of country, not mine, and I hope this is some use to you. And don't forget to advise me if your further researches lead you anywhere. This is a nice fragment of peasant legend; so comparatively recent in origin. It has moved me somewhat. Keep me informed.

Yours sincerely,
Thomas Tusker

The hand-writing was very characteristic, lithe, 'extempore,' vigorous, and careless.

Well, this was satisfactory verification, so far as it went, though there was no palpable connection between Pix Hill and the events which had occurred here. However, there was nothing to be done but wait the best part of eleven months, till September 10th came round again. Meanwhile I devoted my time chiefly to putting into shape another 50,000 words of my opuscula on Modern Metapsychics, which I hope to have published – no doubt at my own expense – about the year 1948. I also bought a bicycle, and had some exercise I had not enjoyed – or suffered – for more than twenty years.

On September 9th, I took my cycle down to Ledbury and put up at the same hotel. I had previously informed Mr Tusker of my coming and he dined with me that night. We discussed the case for a time, but nothing of our talk is worth repeating here.

At six o'clock the following evening I set out on my cycle and an hour and a half later reached Pix Hill. I decided to take up my position at the bottom of the switchback where the valley crossed the road, and sat down there in the hedge as though merely resting for a while. And, indeed, I felt the need of it. No doubt you, my readers, are smiling at the picture of me squatting in a dusty hedge and waiting for some occult manifestation. Maybe you think I was feeling an old fool! It was not so. I have had sufficient successes to fortify me against failure, and impatience is not one of my vices – or virtues.

It was an exquisite evening with hardly a hint of autumn to be discerned. Benignly warm, the sun climbing down through delicate ribbons of cloud and a gentle breeze blowing from the south. Rooks cawed, small birds rolled in the dust and I could just see through the hedge a company of rabbits feeding and playing in the field opposite. In these placid circumstances I began to feel drowsy, but the occasional passing of a car kept me awake. Apart from these, there were no signs of the presence of man.

Then suddenly it came. Now I have little descriptive power. I can catalogue and marshall facts as well as another, but I lack the range of vocabulary or flexibility of phrase to convey in any vivid manner how the world changed for me at that moment. It was not a new sensation – I have had it several times, but it never loses its strangeness and its shock. First there came, as always, that curious anticipatory sign. You know, the sharp twitch or flicker shown by an electric bulb that is about to break. Imagine that vastly intensified, painfully, distressingly so, a vicious flash that seems to generate in the brain and escape through the eyes. Some such sensation is the invariable prelude to these transmissions, if I may so term them. Then, to employ a bathetic comparison, it is rather as though one were suddenly encased in a gas helmet and peering out through its cloudy eyeslots. There is the same sense of oppression and slight suffocation, and the appearance of everything is changed, toned down, losing its quality, as it were. Again it is as if one were projected into another psychic dimension, a region where complete soundlessness reigns, and so far as the *setting* for these manifestations is concerned, stillness. Every seen thing is fixed and rigid, like soldiers at attention; every tree stands as stark and idle as a painted cypress in a painted graveyard. (And these were not the trees I had seen bending to the breeze a moment before.) There is a dread sense of suspense as though the stage was set, and some dim thing about to be performed. One feels isolated, enclosed, almost imprisoned. One waits for one knows not what. My eyes focused themselves to this lost landscape, and then I saw them, slipping on to the screen of my consciousness. They had their backs to me. He was garbed in light, tight trousers, tight short coat and straw hat. She was wearing a frock of muslin, or some such stuff, tight-backed, tiny-waisted with a long full skirt; and fallen back from her head and swinging by a ribbon was a large bonnet or hat. (I can revisualise them as I write with the most precise definition.) They were pacing slowly up the hill, he on a grass verge (no longer existing), she beside him on the road. Every now and again he turned into the hedge and plucked at the bushes, and then, placing his right hand round the girl's waist, fed her, as it were, with his left. As she turned her head to take the berries, as I suppose they were, in her mouth, I could see her face was smiling and radiant with happiness. He had done this perhaps six times when he glanced furtively around and behind him. I can see that evil face, its expression one of great agitation combined with hard resolve. He dropped back a pace or two, and unobserved by her, pulled a branch or twig towards him and broke it off. Then, with his hands concealed behind him, he picked stealthily at the branch. A moment later he regained her side, and taking her waist as before, he brought his left hand across her face and held it there. I saw her draw back her head as though taken by surprise and glance across at him as though puzzled and perplexed. And then they walked on side by side. At that moment there came a jangling roar and something hurtled by me, so close I leaped aside. Twenty yards ahead of me the car swerved violently over to its right side and I could see the driver struggling to regain control. It was too late; the long bonnet struck a telegraph pole, splintered it in halves and drove on into the hedge. I could see a figure hurled straight up from it like a man tossed in a blanket. For a second it sprawled suspended against a breeze-blown tree. . . .

I stayed on for the inquest; this time the Press seemed genuinely stirred, and I went about with eager reporters in my train like the Belle of the Ball. In answer to their almost menacing entreaties I told them that if I had anything to impart to the world on the affair, apart from my evidence at the inquest which was purely perfunctory, it would be available in my *Modern Metapsychics*, the probable publication date of which was 1948. This pronouncement did not seem to appease them.

I dined with Tusker on the night before the inquest and gave him the 'story' these disgruntled pests had sought. 'Well,' he said, 'it is a strange and somehow disturbing business, but I cannot see it explains anything at all.'

'No,' I replied doubtfully, 'and, of course, there is no reason why it should. These apparitions often have no apparent *raison d'être*, no teleological purpose; and yet for some reason I feel I have missed the significance of something that I saw.'

What that something might be suddenly occurred to me in the train going home. On arrival I at once sat down and wrote to Tusker. Four days later I received the following reply –

Dear Sir Anstruther,

'I think I see what you're getting at. Curiously enough Atropa Belladonna used to flourish abnormally in this part of Herefordshire, but about fifteen years ago a number of brats were poisoned by the berries and an edict went forth that it was to be laid low as much as possible. Furthermore I paid a visit to Pix Hill on Monday and had a chat with an old hedger I found at work. He told me there was plenty of the muck there at one time, and on searching together we found a small plant not so far from where you had your adventure, which we yanked up.

As a result of all this I have come to regard you with considerable awe, as one who, if you will forgive the expression, is true to the sinister traditions of British Baronets. In spite of which I am enormously looking forward to visiting you in November.

Yours very sincerely,
Thomas Tusker.

THE GHOST OF THE MODEL T

Betsy Emmons

Any motoring enthusiast asked to name the two most famous types of motor car in the world would almost certainly plump for the British-made Rolls-Royce and the American Model T Ford. Appropriately, therefore, I have selected stories featuring both these cars for inclusion in this collection. As Henry Ford was in business just before Mr Rolls and Mr Royce, the Model T will appear first.

Henry Ford (1863–1947) produced his first petrol-driven car in 1893, founded the company that bears his name in Detroit in 1899, and then in 1908 pioneered the modern 'assembly-line' mass-production techniques for the Model T. In the years up to 1928, 15 million of these unmistakable vehicles were made, making it by far the most popular American car. The success of the Model T also made it something of a legend – a legend which has survived to this day.

The Ford Model T has, in fact, cropped up in a large number of books and short stories, but in no other case in a tale quite so bizarre as the one which follows. 'The Ghost of the Model T' suitably made its debut in print in 1942 in a magazine which has also become a legend, Weird Tales, *now the most sought-after of all fantasy publications. Author Betsy Emmons (1910–1979) had worked for a time in the American automobile industry as a publication relations officer, and several of the stories she contributed to* Weird Tales *featured motor cars. None, though, is quite so evocative of a great motor than this strange tale . . .*

Nobody would ever have expected Phil Barnes to be haunted, because Phil wasn't the type. Phil was strictly Mr Average, a nice enough guy, but no imagination. That's why I've had to decide that his story was the real thing. He couldn't have made it up, and it wasn't the kind of yarn you find in anthologies of spook stories. Besides, I saw the ending myself.

Phil and I were on our way up one Sunday morning to the cabin in the Catskills we share with a couple of other guys, using it now and then for hunting or fishing or just to have a man's party, away from our wives. It was warm enough to have the top down, and we were thinking about catching a nice mess of brook trout and broiling them over an open fire. Phil was driving his new car, a cream-coloured convertible Flash roadster, with a black top.

We stopped in a roadside diner for ham and eggs, and when we came out we saw that another car had bumped into the Flash from behind. The other car was about the worst-looking I ever saw, a Model T, around fifteen years old. There was a peculiarly rakish curl to the front fender, and a star-shaped breakage in the windshield. The Flash hadn't suffered much – just a dented bumper and a few scratches.

'Isn't that too bad!' I said. 'But I don't suppose you could collect from the owner of a jalopy like that, even if it were worth the trouble of suing.'

Then I saw Phil's face. It was crumpled up in a way I couldn't describe, and it was a colour I don't like to remember. 'Calm down, old man!' I told him. 'Why get upset about a scratch or two? You look as if you'd seen a ghost.'

Phil gave me an awful look. 'Don't say that!' he gurgled. And he hurried me into the Flash, glancing back over his shoulder as if he were afraid something was coming after him. I looked back too, but all I could see was the ramshackle Model T by the kerb, and I had an impression that it was moving slowly after us, but of course it couldn't have been, because there was nobody in the driver's seat.

Phil stepped on the gas and went about twenty miles in fifteen minutes before he relaxed. I was curious, but Phil's expression had been so scared when he came out of that diner that I didn't like to ask questions. He was the first to speak, and then what he said didn't seem to have anything to do with what had scared him.

'Tom,' he asked, 'do you remember your first car?'

'I'll say I do! Why, there's never been another one like –'

Phil raised a protesting hand from the steering wheel. 'Then you know how I felt about mine: I got it around 1925, when I was seventeen, and I blew the proceeds of a summer's work for it. And gosh, how I loved it!'

'I know,' I said sympathetically. 'Now, I got mine –'

'It was a sweet little car, too, for those days,' Phil went on. 'A Model T. I was so proud of it, I used to get up nights and go out to the garage and see if it was still there. You know how a kid can be. Why, I'd pat it like you'd pat a horse. I spent every week-end shining it up and kept it brimful of gas and oil. Every few months I'd have it checked over, just in case.'

By this time I was letting Phil talk himself out, though I couldn't see where he was getting. 'I kept it six years,' he told me. 'A long time. But, you know, I was so fond of it I couldn't bear to give it up. You think I'm screwy?'

'Not at all,' I said. 'I know just how –'

'Why, I felt like it was part of my family! I felt it respond. The wheel practically turned of itself in my hands. I felt that it was fond of me too. I *knew* it was.'

'Don't get so excited, Phil,' I said. 'I get you. But what's this all about?'

Well, he went on to tell me the story. He was working his way up in business, and a good appearance, including a good-looking car, was important in his line of work.

So he finally traded the Model T in, and didn't know what became of it. About that time the company he was working for moved him to Texas. And after he'd been in Texas awhile, he fell in love.

Of course a man in love never knows what has hit him. She was pretty, Phil said, and flirtatious. He was still a young man, and didn't bother to find out what she was really like. But he did notice one thing, that she was pretty much impressed by anything showy. Nice places, good clothes, big cars. So Phil got himself a new car. He didn't mind trading in the one he had at the time, because he'd never really got fond of it, like he'd been of the old Model T.

The new car was a Streamline Special, bright green, with white-walled tyres. Phil called the girl up and said, 'Look, honey, put on your best clothes. I've got a new car that'll knock your eyes out, and we're going riding.' She was thrilled pink. She came into the room all done up in furs and flowers, and said that she just couldn't wait to see the car.

Phil told her to look out the window, and stood back with a big grin waiting to hear her exclaim. But she turned to him and said, very nastily, 'If you think that's a good joke, Philip Barnes, just think again. Trying to be so funny! You just get in that old rattletrap and drive away. If you think I'm going out with you in that, you're crazy.'

Phil went to the window and saw that another car had come up behind the Streamline Special, where it was the first thing the girl would see. He started to laugh and say, 'Why, honey, you're making a mistake.'

Then he looked at her again, and saw that her pretty face didn't look pretty with the angry, sullen expression on it. And it occurred to him that she must be mighty dumb, and mighty snobbish. And he thought about the kind of wife a girl like that would make, and made a few pleasant remarks and picked up his hat and drove away in the Streamline Special. A couple of years later, he met Susan and married her, and every now and then he's taken time off to thank his lucky stars he saw through the girl in Texas before it was too late.

'But,' Phil finished his story, 'before I went away in the Streamline Special, I had a look at the car behind, And, Tom, it was my old Model T! I knew by the way the front fender was bent and the windshield was splintered.'

'That's quite a coincidence,' I told him.

'Yeah,' said Phil. 'Coincidence. Well, next place the company sent me was to Washington, and of course I didn't ever expect to see the old buggy again. But I did.'

'Did you?' I asked. I was beginning to suspect what was up by now, though I couldn't really believe that Phil meant it. Phil took a deep breath.

'The first time I saw it,' he said, 'the time I just told you about, it did me a good turn in my private life. But the second time – well, I'll tell you.' He'd been about to close a big order, Phil said, with a guy named W. G. Foxbaum. Foxbaum was an odd bird. He kept a Flit gun of antiseptic in his office and sprayed everything each hour, on account of germs. He had a fixation on the idea of absolute cleanliness. Anyone who wanted an order from Foxbaum had to show up with his pants pressed and his nails manicured, or he didn't stand a chance.

Phil was all set, and he had an appointment with Foxbaum at three o'clock to wind up the details. Foxbaum was as strong on punctuality as he was on neatness, and Phil was planning to be there on time. He'd had his pants cleaned and pressed. He'd had a shave and a manicure and a haircut. He was going down the street, very spruce, with his briefcase in his hand. He was so anxious not to be even half a minute late, because of the way those things counted with Foxbaum, that he was crossing the street against a red light when a car came up from behind and nuzzled him.

'Nuzzled?' I asked.

'Nuzzled,' Phil affirmed. And he went on to tell how he'd lost his balance and fallen into a mud-puddle. He dropped the briefcase and it opened and his papers got all splashed with mud and water. So did his nice, clean pants. By the time he'd picked himself up, cursing, he just saw the rear end of the car going around the corner. But he was sure that it was his old Model T.

'I didn't know whether to take time off to get cleaned up and arrive late, or to arrive on time in the mess I was in,' Paul finished. 'So I compromised. I got brushed off and straightened out my papers as well as I could, which wasn't very good, and I got to Foxbaum's office only fifteen minutes late and only moderately dirty, and I lost the order. Two weeks later Foxbaum went bankrupt, owing fifty thousand dollars.'

I said, 'Funny coincidence, huh?'

'Yeah,' said Phil. 'Too funny. I wrote to the Motor Vehicle Bureau, and they traced the Model T for me. Seems that a year after I'd sold it, the car was sold again to a junk dealer, and as far as they knew it's been standing in a junkyard ever since.'

'That's impossible,' I said.

'Sure it's impossible,' said Phil. 'But, did you notice, when we saw the car outside the diner, that it didn't have any licence plates? That it was sort of dusty? *That it didn't look as if it belonged to anyone?*'

'Phil,' I said, 'I see what you're getting at, and I think you're nuts. You figure that car has been –'

'Yeah,' said Phil. 'That's what I figure. It was junked, and it got out, and it's been following me all over the country. It's found me twice, and both times the company moved me away right afterwards, so it had to start out again. Now it's found me once more, and it's going to follow me. It's fond of me. Tom!' His voice rose in a shrill crescendo! 'Tom!' he yelled. 'It can't happen! A car can't do that! Can it, Tom?'

'Of course it can't,' I said. 'Obviously not. You'll never see it again.' But there were prickles up and down my spine. Because, though I tried to tell myself it was just Phil's suggestion that made me think so, it didn't seem to me that there *had* been any licence plates on the old Model T parked out in front of the diner.

By the time Phil and I got up to the Catskills, he'd calmed down a bit. After a day of fishing, he was quite himself again. He even essayed a word or two of apology. 'I guess you thought I was nuts, Tom,' he said. 'Maybe I am. Of course, you were right. It was just a series of coincidences, and my imagination.'

'I'm sure of it,' I answered. But I really wasn't sure at all because, as I've said, Phil had no imagination. None at all. And there were points in his story that a man would have needed imagination to make up.

Anyhow, everything was serene when we started back, and even the Sunday traffic on the Storm King Highway didn't bother us. The spring dusk was lovely, and we could hear the fresh noise of waters coming down the slopes. Of course, we didn't pay any more attention than people usually do to the signs which said 'Drive Carefully' and 'Watch Out for Falling Rocks'.

Then everything happened at once.

We were going around an especially narrow, dangerous curve, and another car came up behind us on the outside, forcing us over against the rock wall. Phil cursed under his breath, watching the other car pass horribly close to the steep slope beside us.

'Darn fool!' he said. 'Risking his life like that.' He wrenched the wheel over. And then the car ahead came suddenly to a stop, making Phil jam his brakes on abruptly. There was barely time for me to experience a sickening flash of realisation as to the identity of that other car, when a roaring, gnashing noise sounded above our heads.

And, down upon the road ahead, smashing the other car to a crumpled heap of tin, came a thirty-ton boulder. And then another, and another, streams of boulders of all sizes, enough to crush any car into nothingness and send its occupants to glory.

In a minute, it was all over. The echoes died away, and the mountains again were silent. Phil and I got out and ran to look at the car on the road ahead, the little Model T which had been buried and crushed under the gigantic rocks of the landslide.

Ghost car or not, it would never run again. Phil laid a hand on the battered fender which projected from the wreckage, then straightened up slowly and looked at me. 'If it hadn't forced us to stop,' he said, 'we'd have been in the path of that.'

I nodded. Neither of us wanted to talk about it. We peered under the boulders which lay atop the car, into the front seat, searching for a driver, but both of us knew beforehand that there was no driver in the car, and no licence plates, nor any signs of human life or ownership.

THE GHOST CAR

Ken Batten

The range of Rolls-Royce cars produced in the eighty years since the two founders joined their unique talents has made the vehicles a byword around the world for elegance, power and superlative motoring. Charles Stewart Rolls (1877–1910) was an automobilist and aeronaut who experimented with some of the earliest motor cars in 1895 before later forming a partnership with the engineer Frederick Henry Royce (1863–1933) who had also been experimenting with engines since 1884 and cars from 1904. The two men then built up a business making fine motor vehicles and outstanding engines which has no peer.

The story about a Rolls-Royce which appears here is a particularly curious one because it is claimed to be true! It was first published in October 1928 in the American magazine, Ghost Stories, *a monthly journal which specialised in accounts of supernatural experiences from readers which were then rewritten by staff writers. A close scrutiny of copies of the magazine, however, reveals that not a few of the stories are quite patently fiction – though the case of 'The Ghost Car' is less clear-cut. Ken Batten (1893–1959) produced a number of* Ghost Stories' *most highly acclaimed yarns, and this story is credited with having been told to him by a certain 'Betty B'. Fact or fiction, one would not wish anyone to have to experience the hair-raising events which befall the drivers of this particular Rolls-Royce. Indeed, it gives a new dimension to the name of that best-known of all Rolls-Royces – the 'Silver Ghost' . . .*

Things happen in this life which not only change character but put the soul through an acid test that purifies it and reveals undreamed-of realms of thought and emotion.

Such a thing happened to me when I was only twenty-one, and as light-hearted and frivolous a girl as ever had a doting father to spoil her.

For a birthday present I had asked for a Rolls-Royce automobile. Father remonstrated with me and suggested a less expensive make of car, but spoilt girl that I was, I wanted a 'Rolls' or no car at all. On the morning of my birthday Dad took me to our garage and there, to my surprise and joy, was a beautiful, yellow Rolls-Royce roadster!

Dad, being strictly truthful, explained that it was a second-hand car, but as good as new in every respect. Experts had examined the motor and pronounced it perfect. The car was only two years old, which is young for a Rolls-Royce. Nothing was known of its previous history, except that it had never been driven in this country. And obviously, whoever had owned or driven it in England, had taken great care of it and driven it only a few times.

We decided to christen my car at once, so Dad and I started out for a little spin. I was at the wheel, going about forty miles an hour on a little-travelled country road. I saw a car on the cross-road to the right and I made my calculations to slow down because it had the right-of-way. About a hundred yards from the intersection I put my foot on the brake. To my surprise and horror, my car, instead of slowing down, continued at forty. The other car was approaching the crossing with equal speed.

Again I pushed down on the brake, but without result. Dad never stirred or said a word. Both cars reached the intersection at the same moment. With a violent jerk I swung my steering wheel to the left, just as I heard the grinding of the other car's brakes as its driver swung to the right. There came a crunching of mud-guards, then both cars stopped in their tracks.

I was too stunned for speech, whether from shock or fear I scarcely know. The occupants of the other car were furious, and Dad apologised and explained that we were trying out our car and that the brakes hadn't worked. No serious damage had been done and the other car drove off.

Then Dad got out and examined the brakes. Nothing seemed to be wrong with them. We turned homeward, driving slowly and testing the brakes frequently. They worked perfectly!

We drove in silence, yet I knew that my father was sharing my troubled and confused thoughts. I was conscious of a vague fear and a sense of mystery such as I had never felt before. It was not a natural, healthy fear. What had happened was uncanny – sinister – and we both felt it intensely.

When we put up the car, Dad spoke for the first time, saying that he would have the motor thoroughly overhauled. Then he suggested casually that it might be better not to mention our experience to the family.

Mechanics examined the car and pronounced it in absolutely first-class condition. I decided that I was a young fool. I determined to put that morning's incident out of my mind and to take my car out at once. For days I drove it for long stretches, and all was well.

At breakfast one morning my mother asked me if she might use my car that day, as I was going to town by train. With quick assent on my lips I felt my eyes drawn to Dad's. He was looking at me with a queer expression, and I knew that he didn't want Mother to drive the Rolls.

She caught my hesitation and said, 'My dear, if you'd prefer for me not to drive your new car, just say so frankly.'

Of course I couldn't let it pass that way; so I assured Mother that I didn't, in the least, mind her driving it.

That night she came to my room after I had gone to bed. She looked worried and she spoke very low.

'Betty, don't mention what I'm going to tell you, to your father. I want to ask you, first, if you've had any trouble with your Rolls-Royce?'

I caught my breath but I managed to say casually:

'Nothing in particular – why?'

'Because,' Mother said excitedly, 'something happened this afternoon that was so mysterious and left me so weak with fear that I wanted to tell you about it. It's beyond my understanding.'

Her story was briefly this: on a narrow road she saw a big car approaching at high speed. She slowed down, and when she was within fifty yards of the oncoming car, she turned her steering wheel to the right. To her horror the car stayed in the centre of the road, close in the path of the onrushing car.

Again she wrenched at the steering wheel, and then, at the last moment of desperation, she used the emergency brake. The roadster stopped with a terrific jolt and she heard a screeching and grinding of brakes. The other driver had used his own brakes just in time, and when his car stopped, the bumpers of the two cars were touching.

The other driver had been considerate, seeing that Mother was on the verge of fainting. After hearing her explanation about the steering wheel, he examined it and tested it. It worked perfectly.

When he started away in his car, his expression seemed to say: 'These women drivers!'

Mother had driven home cautiously and safely, but her mind had been confused and her nerves had had a fearful shock.

'I'm not a coward,' she summed up. 'You know that, Betty, and it wasn't ordinary fright I felt. I can't put into words the horrible and uncanny chill of fear that completely mastered me. Why, I wouldn't drive that car of yours, my dear, or even take a ride in it, for anything in the world! And I advise you to get rid of it. I can't explain what I feel, and perhaps you think me silly.'

I managed a natural laugh and told her that she certainly was silly, and that she should look upon her experience as an ordinary motorist's adventure and forget it.

As for me, I dismissed Mother's story from my mind – or tried to – and assured myself that it was merely an unpleasant coincidence, our both having had such queer experiences with my Rolls-Royce. I continued to drive my car, although far back in my mind was always an uneasy expectation of trouble.

One day my brother Dick asked me for a loan of twenty-five dollars. He was in the habit of borrowing money from me, and I usually let him have small sums without question. But on this occasion he looked worried, and I asked him why he needed twenty-five dollars.

'Got a ticket for speeding,' he said curtly.

'Is that all?' I said, laughing at him, for it wasn't his first summons to court.

He frowned angrily and his eyes held a mystified and baffled expression.

'But I *wasn't* speeding this time. That's the damn funny part of it. You see . . .' He hesitated. 'Well, Sis, I took out your roadster for a spin. Didn't think you'd mind as you were in town. At a traffic signal I tried to slow down but that *blankety blank* car shot ahead like a bullet.'

Under other circumstances I would have resented his using my car without permission, but now I said eagerly:

'Oh, Dick, you *must* have ignored that signal, or done something you shouldn't have done!'

'You're as bad as the cops!' he said angrily. 'They thought I was lying, and they jeered at me when I told them the car ran away. But, darn it all, Sis, that's exactly what it did!'

I knew he was speaking the truth. But I would not admit it to him. I argued, saying feebly, 'But I don't see . . .'

'Neither do I,' he interrupted excitedly. 'That Rolls is cuckoo. I simply couldn't stop the darn thing, and believe me, I was scared to death – I admit it frankly. I wasn't afraid of being killed – but something I can't understand or explain made me feel as weak as a baby.'

It seemed that he just missed hitting a huge truck, escaped collision with a wall by a miracle, and then the cops caught him.

'There's something spooky about that car!' he finished.

I laughed and said lightly, 'Nonsense! Who ever heard of an automobile being spooky?'

Inwardly I did not laugh and for a few days I did not use my car. Then one evening Dad took me to one side and said quietly:

'Betty, don't you think we'd better get rid of your Rolls and get another car?'

I could see by his face that he was holding something back. I asked what had happened.

He surprised me with this question: 'Did you notice the weather today?'

I nodded my head.

'Fine and clear, wasn't it? Absolutely dry roads for the last two weeks. Couldn't imagine skidding on such roads, could you?'

'Skidding!' I was amazed, for all the highways were as dry and dusty as the desert.

'Well,' Dad continued, frowning, 'going about thirty an hour, on a bone-dry road, that car skidded clear across. I just missed smashing into a bus. If I had, there'd have been nothing left of me. And it wasn't ordinary, human fear I felt! It was worse than that first day with you. Betty, that car isn't safe! Heaven knows why, but the fact remains. Not for *us* at any rate. I'm going to put it on the market at once.'

I agreed eagerly. I never wanted to ride in that Rolls-Royce again. But Fate decreed that I should. The next day I received a wire calling me to a hospital twenty miles away, cross-country –

where a dear friend was on the verge of death. By train it would have taken half a day. It happened that our two family cars were out. There was nothing to do but drive the Rolls roadster. Heavens! How I hated even to get into the thing, but if I wanted to reach the hospital in time, I had to act quickly.

The roadster ate up the road for about fifteen miles, and behaved beautifully. I confess that I didn't let my thoughts run ahead of me to my sick friend. I concentrated on what I was doing – driving a car that had played every one of us some queer trick, and that demanded every ounce of agility of my mind and body.

I saw a grade crossing just ahead to the right, and a sharp curve in the track. I did as I always do at one of those dangerous crossings – slowed up, strained my eyes and ears, then, hearing and seeing nothing, stepped on the gas, but only to about thirty. It sounds unbelievable, but right in the middle of that crossing, the car came to a halt, with a jerk that almost threw me out.

I was seized with such fright that I could not move a muscle. All I had to do was to jump out and leave the car to be wrecked if a train came along. Instead, I tried to press the self-starter and shift gears but my legs and arms were as if paralysed.

At that moment I heard the whistle of an approaching train!

I remember nothing more until after the train had stopped and people were crowding around my car, excitedly seeking an explanation of my extraordinary conduct. All I could tell them was that my car had stalled and that I had almost fainted from fright. But I knew well enough that some mysterious power beyond my puny control or understanding had stalled that car in the middle of the track, and left me shaking with an unnameable fear.

Then, to the amusement of the crowd and to my own horrible embarrassment, that car started off as quietly as a lamb. I reached the hospital without mishap and found my friend out of danger, which partly soothed my overwrought nerves. But it took all my grit to drive home in that roadster. Nothing happened, but I had reached the point where no mortal power could have induced me to drive that car again.

Dad had advertised the car for sale, but a week passed without a single bid. I did not tell him about getting stalled on the grade crossing. Then, one afternoon, a strange thing happened. I was alone in the house, except for the servants.

Suddenly I felt that I was being controlled as if by some hypnotic influence!

Consciously, but against my own will, I went to the garage, stood staring at the Rolls and struggling to escape back to the house. But the next instant I was in the car, with my foot on the self-starter and my hand on the gear-shift. Outwardly calm but seething inside with the most terrific fear I have ever felt, I started that car down the road.

It was like a nightmare, for I was powerless to escape from the spell that bound me. Faster and faster went the car. Soon I was doing sixty miles an hour along an embankment that I knew well. To the right the ground sloped down about fifty feet into marshy land. Suddenly the car headed for the edge of the embankment. It jolted horribly over the rough ground. The left front wheel hit a telegraph pole and I hung to the steering-wheel as the car leaped into the air, then rolled sideways down the embankment. I was thrown out and knocked senseless.

At that time, as I knew nothing of the occult, I had never heard that just before physical dissolution the soul leaves the body, but is still earth-bound until life is actually extinct.

But while I was lying there almost at the point of death, my soul did leave my body, as surely as I have lived to write of this experience. And the eyes of my soul, as it hovered near its physical shell, witnessed a drama more vivid than anything I had ever seen in actuality.

This is what I saw: a quiet country road with fields on either side and some very old trees standing here and there. It was early dusk and the sky was faintly streaked with reds and yellows. It seemed to be a road in rural England.

By the side of the road stood a car (*my* car, which, in reality, lay shattered and useless at the bottom of the embankment) and so vivid was this picture that I saw the licence number distinctly – and it was *not* an American licence plate!

Two men were sitting in the roadster, deep in conversation. The man at the wheel was dark, with a thick, stocky figure. His face was singularly evil with small, dark eyes and an unhealthy complexion. He seemed to be irritated, for he kept tugging at his moustache with quick, angry gestures.

His companion was younger, a semi-blond with a frank, clean-cut face. He was calm and spoke little, although he watched the older man with a piercing intensity. Then the dark man made a violent statement which he emphasised by bringing his fist down with a bang on the steering wheel. The younger man turned pale – his face looked very white in the fading light – and said something quickly which seemed to infuriate his companion.

For a brief instant the man at the wheel stared at the other, without speaking, but his face twitched and he seemed to hesitate. Then, with a lightning movement, he reached for the side pocket in the door of the car and drew out a revolver. Quick as he was, the younger man, watchful and silent, was ready for him. The next minute they were grappling for possession of the gun.

I could see that the blond man was trying desperately to get hold of the weapon without injury to either of them. He tried with all his strength to unclinch the other man's fingers that gripped the butt of the revolver, so that it would drop to the floor of the car.

Up and down, backwards and forwards the revolver waved, still held in the dark man's hand. He was trying to aim it at his adversary – to turn it towards his stomach. It was a struggle to the death, but I knew, as I watched, that only one of those men *wanted* to kill; the other struggled only to prevent any injury to either one. However, if those murderous fingers gripping the revolver butt could not be loosened, then it must be death to one or the other – to the one who was the weaker of the two!

Then – I saw, with those eyes of my detached soul, that the hand holding the gun was slowly, slowly, turning inwards. Steadily it moved towards the body of its owner, and he was powerless to stop it. There was a sharp flash, and I saw the dark, evil man straighten up for a second, then fall back.

The picture gradually faded and I saw nothing more.

Two days later, lying in a hospital bed, I regained consciousness and could think rationally once more. I recognised my parents standing near the bed, and I saw a nurse and the doctor. In reply to my feeble inquiries they told me quietly that I had been thrown from my car and knocked unconscious. (As if I didn't know that much, and oh, so much more!) I had been picked up by motorists and hurried to the hospital. I had been delirious but was now on the road to recovery.

The scene that my soul had witnessed while my body lay inert by the side of the lonely road, was still so vivid in my mind that I was sure I had talked about it in my delirium. Tremulously eager and weak from emotional strain, I asked if I had talked in delirium of two men fighting in a car.

I saw the glances exchanged between those watching me, and the doctor said, 'Do you mean that you recall what you talked about while you were unconscious?'

I nodded my head and said that I knew I had talked of seeing two men struggling over a revolver until one man shot the other.

'That's very extraordinary,' the doctor remarked, looking puzzled. 'In all my experience I have never known a patient to recall, after regaining consciousness, the ravings of delirium.'

'Did I keep repeating a certain number?' I asked anxiously.

'Yes, you did,' the nurse said quickly, with a swift glance at the doctor.

'It was – "MX 2198",' I said slowly.

For a moment there was dead silence in that hospital room. Then the nurse went to a desk and came back with a slip of paper.

'Here it is,' she said gently. 'You repeated it so many times that I wrote it down. It corresponds exactly.'

I needed no proof of the reality of my vision, but there was something terribly uncanny in this strange corroboration of the licence number on that ghost car. I felt the blood rushing to my head and thought I was going to faint. The doctor whispered to the nurse and she poured something between my lips which calmed me at once. Soon I fell into a profound and dreamless sleep.

As the days passed and I slowly regained my strength, I tried to talk to the nurse about what I had seen when I lay unconscious by the roadside. But she would not let me talk, and when I grew restive she always gave me a sedative. It is a wonder that I recovered as rapidly as I did, for my mind and soul were in turmoil.

The day I returned home from the hospital, Dad and I had a heart-to-heart talk. Not only did he understand all the mental perturbation I had suffered, but he shared my intense desire to investigate the mysterious phenomenon of that fatal Rolls-Royce. Mother, of course, was taken into our confidence when we decided that we must go at once to England.

Money and wire-pulling can accomplish a good deal, even at the eleventh hour, and we sailed on one of the larger steamers two days later.

On reaching London, we went straight to the Automobile Licence Bureau. We discovered that the number 'MX 2198' had been issued in 1924 to a Mr Bernard Stanley, with an address at Surbiton, a town near London. The licence, however, had not been renewed after that year. The next step was to find Mr Stanley of Surbiton, and this we set out to do the next day.

The address proved to be a large and well-kept house. The servant who answered our ring told us that Mr Stanley no longer lived there. We asked for a forwarding address, and the maid, after some hesitation, ushered us into the presence of her mistress, a gracious lady who asked if we were friends of Mr Stanley. Dad told her frankly that we have never met Mr Stanley but that it was highly important for us to find him.

'I am sorry,' the lady said gently, 'but Mr Stanley died two years ago. We are distant relatives of his.'

It may have been her voice or it may have been an expression in her eyes that quickened my intuition. But the conviction that seized me was so impelling that without hesitation I said quickly, looking her squarely in the eyes: 'Did he die a violent death?'

She drew back a little, surprised and startled, but she said quietly, 'Yes, he did, although I cannot understand by what right you are questioning me.'

'Oh, please,' I said eagerly, 'believe me when I say that we are here on a very serious mission. Later we will explain. But you must tell me,' I rushed on – 'was he shot in his own automobile?'

Her face paled and she stared at me and at Father. Evidently she was convinced of our sincerity, for she answered that her cousin had been killed in his own car.

I quivered with excitement – now I *knew* who was the man I had seen shot. But I must find out who the other man was, and what had happened to him. I begged the lady to tell me if she knew of anyone who had been closely connected with the tragedy, with whom I could talk. My desperate earnestness and Dad's impressive personality must have convinced her beyond all doubt that we had very good reasons for our probing questions.

She replied, 'The sister of the man who is serving a twenty-year term for the murder of Bernard Stanley, lives only a few miles from here. Her name is Eileen Bassett.' Then she gave Miss Bassett's address and we departed.

I went alone to call on Eileen Bassett and I found her at home. She was a very charming girl, only a little older than myself. I went straight to the point and told her that I had come to talk with her regarding her brother's conviction for murder.

Her face turned so white that I thought she was going to faint, and her blue eyes grew almost black with emotion. Her lips trembled in her effort to speak, and I put my hand on her arm and asked her to sit down and listen to what I had to tell her.

As briefly as possible, I told her everything. Then I said, gently and sympathetically:

'I don't know if you will be incredulous of my story – as I would have been a short time ago – but from the bottom of my heart I want to help you to prove your brother's innocence, for I *know* what happened in that car that fatal night. I know, as surely as I know that I'm alive, that he shot Bernard Stanley in self-defence.'

At that point the girl broke down and wept, assuring me between her sobs that she believed in psychic phenomena and that she thanked God for sending me to her brother's rescue.

'Never for a minute,' she said earnestly, 'have I doubted my brother's innocence – I mean his declaration that he shot Bernard Stanley in self-defence.'

Then she told me the story. Stanley had met and fallen in love with her some four years back. He was several years her senior and had a sinister type of face, but he had fascinated her from the beginning. Even while her instinct warned her against him, another side of her nature was thrilled by his love and responded to it. Finally she had promised to marry him on a certain date – the very month that was his last on earth.

Her brother Tom had disliked Stanley and distrusted him. He did everything in his power to dissuade his sister from marrying the man, and had put many obstacles in the way of her seeing him. She had to use subterfuge to meet him, and it made her angry with her brother, whom she had always loved dearly. When she told him of her intention to marry Stanley, Tom Bassett went white to the lips and said that if she did, it would be over his dead body. (They were orphans and he was the elder.)

She regarded Tom's attitude as personal antagonism to Stanley, and she defied him to prevent her marriage. One day, when her fiancé left the Bassett home, Tom said he would ride back with him, as he wished to have a talk with him. That was the last time Eileen Bassett saw Stanley alive.

Her brother had come straight home after the shooting, told her his version of what had happened, and then had given himself up to the police. He was tried and convicted, and received a twenty-year sentence, which, to Tom Bassett, had seemed worse than hanging.

'The awful part of it for me,' Eileen Bassett said, with her face drawn in pain, 'is that I was the cause of the tragedy. If I had heeded my brother, he would not be serving a sentence for murder. And the strange thing is, that from the hour when he confessed to killing Stanley, I believed him absolutely. And although I would have brought Bernard back to life if I could have done so, my love for him died with him. I despised him – for Tom, wanting me to know the truth, told me why Bernard turned on him with the gun. It was because Tom had threatened, as a last resort, to tell me things he had found out about Bernard's life – things that he knew would turn me completely against the man I had promised to marry. The rest of his story – which the jury refused to believe – was just what you have described seeing that night a few weeks ago.'

I was deeply stirred, and filled with eagerness to free this girl's brother from an unhappy fate.

I outlined my plans, then she said: 'Before going to Scotland Yard, you must give your story to the Psychical Research Society, for they will stand back of you and help you with the police. You see,' she said wistfully, 'we English do not scoff, as most Americans do, at spiritual manifestations. Even if, as individuals, we cannot understand or experience these things, we know that others do. We are all interested and unprejudiced, when it comes to psychic phenomena. The Society will not scoff at your testimony.'

'They will not dare!' I cried excitedly. 'My inmost soul told me the first time that I drove the Rolls-Royce roadster, that something uncanny had come into my prosaic life – and the feeling grew and grew until the final catastrophe. I don't understand why the evil spirit of Bernard Stanley tried so hard to destroy me, but I do know that he failed, and that I have it in my power to right a great wrong.'

Dad and I got a letter of introduction to a certain peer prominent in the Psychical Research Society, and his interest in my story and his full acceptance of it were very inspiring. Perhaps his chief interest lay in the fact that I had contributed another bit of evidence for the Society, but he was only too glad to help us prove Tom Bassett's innocence.

This man – his name is well known throughout the world – accompanied us to Scotland Yard and into the rather plain office of the Chief.

For the third time in as many days, I related the story of the Rolls-Royce roadster, of my vision and of my purpose in coming to England – and of my added purpose in proving that Tom Bassett had shot Bernard Stanley in self-defence.

I knew as I talked, that the Chief – a kindly, humane man – was politely incredulous, although believing in my sincerity.

When I had finished, he asked quietly, 'Had you ever seen either Bassett or Stanley before the night when you say you saw them fighting over a gun in the roadster?'

'Never,' I told him quickly. 'But their faces were indelibly stamped on my memory that night. I could never forget either of them.'

The Chief gave an order over the telephone in a low voice; then he looked from me to Dad, and said slowly:

'I remember that case. As far as we knew, Bassett was a fine young chap. But when a man testifies that he killed another man to prevent that man killing him, and when there isn't a single witness, it's not so easy to convince a jury that the accused individual is telling the truth. But the case puzzled me, and I felt very sorry for young Bassett.'

At that point a man entered and laid some papers on the Chief's desk. The latter turned to me, saying that he was going to show me twenty-five photographs of different men, and that one of them was the picture of one of the men I had seen in my vision.

'See if you can pick him out, Miss,' he said, handing me a package of photographs.

I examined them, first rapidly, with a fast-beating heart, then more slowly, fingering each one with reluctant conviction that something was wrong.

Handing them back to the Chief, I said, 'There is no photograph there of either Tom Bassett of Bernard Stanley.'

I stared into the Chief's grey eyes with a puzzled and questioning glance. I wondered what he was up to. Then he handed me, without a word, another packet of photographs. I seized them eagerly – and on looking at the third picture in the stack, I cried out excitedly:

'That's Bernard Stanley – the man who was shot to death in his own car!'

I saw surprise on the Chief's face, and the representative of the Psychical Research Society patted my shoulder encouragingly. Then the Chief told me that I must forgive him for playing a little trick on me, but that he had wanted to put my identification to the test.

'You can test me as much as you like,' I said, laughing for sheer relief. 'If you had shown me a hundred pictures, I would have picked out that man's face if it had been among them. I could never forget it, nor Tom Bassett's, either.'

'Well, Miss,' the Chief said kindly, 'may I ask you two or three questions? You never met Miss Bassett before yesterday?'

'Never,' I told him promptly.

'Did she show you any picture of her brother or did you see one in her house?'

'No, to both questions.' I spoke quietly, looking into the Chief's shrewd eyes, and I knew that he believed me.

Then he said, 'I'll take you to the jail where Tom Bassett is serving his term and see if you can identify him among the other prisoners.'

The next day we four (Dad, myself, the Chief and the psychic investigator) visited the prison. The details of the trip are unimportant. All that matters is that presently I found myself in a room where many prisoners were standing in rows of ten. Then I was directed to identify Tom Bassett.

Like a field-marshal inspecting troops, I walked the length of the first row. Tom Bassett was not in it. The same with the second row. I wondered if they were playing a trick on me.

Then, in the row next to the last, fifth from the far end, I came face to face with him! In that flashing second before I spoke his name aloud, impressions and thoughts tore like lightning through my brain.

There was no possible doubt that the face I stared into was that of the blond young man I had seen so plainly in my vision, but he was terribly changed. There was strength and nobility in his face, but all the youthful radiance was gone. His expression was flat, defeated, dead – and the pain of it made me catch my breath.

I turned to the others and said, 'This is Tom Bassett!'

I heard excited murmurs and exclamations, but I was more intensely conscious of the look of puzzled wonder on Tom Bassett's pale face. When the situation was explained to him, his expression of utter amazement changed quickly and the tears came to his tired eyes. Then we left him, because we had work before us, out beyond the walls of that prison.

The Chief gave us advice, if not hope.

'Your identifications, Miss, would convince most people that Tom Bassett's testimony in court was gospel truth. But it takes more than a haunted car to get a man pardoned, once he's been convicted of murder. I advise you to go and see the Home Secretary. It's in his power to help you. But I'll have to warn you that there isn't much chance of his seeing the matter the way you do, Miss.'

With as little delay as possible, we called on the Home Secretary, by appointment. After I had narrated my experiences in the realm of the psychic, we told of my identification of the two men.

The Home Secretary – a dark-eyed, rather stern-visaged man of about fifty – looked thoughtfully at us and said slowly:

'There is one point – an important point – in this story of the Rolls-Royce, that rather mystifies me. I cannot see exactly *why* the evil spirit of the dead man should have attempted to destroy this young lady.'

'That's what I wondered about,' I burst out eagerly. 'I cannot understand why he wanted to get me out of the way.'

As my glance turned to the member of the psychic society who had accompanied us on our important mission, I saw his face light up with enthusiasm.

He said eagerly: 'If every psychic phenomenon were as easy to explain as the point you have raised, all the world would accept our beliefs.' He glanced from the Home Secretary to me. 'This young lady is what is called a "sensitive." I realised the moment I saw her, that she was psychic. The evil spirit of Bernard Stanley knew that sooner or later she would discover the truth about the car in her possession. He determined to kill her. In the final catastrophe he nearly succeeded in his evil purpose, for her soul did leave her body and it was in that moment that everything was revealed to her.'

I stared at him, amazed at the simplicity and clarity of his explanation. Then an astounding thing occurred. The Home Secretary told us that he had always been profoundly interested in psychical research and had followed the activities of the Society in London. He was absolutely convinced, he said of the innocence of Tom Bassett.

'Such a belief,' he ended quietly, 'and such a statement as you have made, are obviously outside the scope of English law. But feeling and believing as I do, I shall urgently advise His Majesty to pardon the young man.'

And so it came about that full pardon was granted by the King to Tom Bassett. He was once more a free man, although he would have to bear the cross of a tragic memory to the end. But as the years have passed, the cross has grown less heavy. Thank Heaven I have done my small part in bringing happiness into his life, for – Tom and I were married about a year after his release from prison – after his new lease on life, which he insists he owes to me.

NEW CORNER

L. T. C. Rolt

The racing of motor cars developed as a sport early in the history of the automobile, and though some of the speeds achieved by drivers at those pioneer meetings back in the first few decades of this century may seem ludicrously slow by today's standards, the demands of skill and bravery placed upon the drivers were none the less exacting. Old-time enthusiasts of the sport will eagerly regale any listener with stories of long-dead drivers who, they claim, have no equal among today's speed merchants. They will also talk of the defunct machines those stars raced and of the circuits they made famous. For who has not heard of Brooklands, Silverstone, Le Mans or Watson's Glen? Of such are motor racing memories made . . .

Lionel Thomas Caswell Rolt (1910–1974), the author of this next story, was a well-known authority on all forms of transport. He acquired a garage in 1934 and for nearly forty years specialised in veteran, vintage and racing cars. His fascination with the car inspired him to write Horseless Carriage *(1938), the first popular history of the motor car in England. He was also a founder member of the Vintage Sports Car Club and was responsible for organising the famous Anglo-American Vintage Car Rally in 1954. L. T. C. Rolt liked a good mystery story, too, and in 1948 wrote 'New Corner', which not only reveals his special knowledge of the motor-racing world but also a very real talent at mixing ancient traditions with modern technology.*

The Blighs were late as usual, and practice day was nearly over when their familiar old Vauxhall with its loaded trailer rumbled into the paddock.

It was the first meeting of the 1938 season at the famous Highbury Hill, and promised to be the best of a long series, for the enthusiastic organisers, the Mercia Motor Club, had been preparing for the event as never before. Not only had they managed to secure an international date for the first time, but they had improved the hill out of all recognition, widening, resurfacing and constructing one entirely new section of road. These efforts had been justly rewarded by what was probably the finest entry list that a speed hill climb in this country had ever produced.

Germany had sent over one of her Grand Prix Rheinwagens – a 3-litre, 16-cylinder, rear-engined job – to be handled by no less a person than Von Eberstraum himself. France had entered her most successful driver, Camille, with Monsieur Rene Lefevre's latest masterpiece, a double-cam straight-eight of conventional design – somewhat untried, but a joy to the eye, like all Rene's cars. Most noteworthy of all, Italy was to be represented by her veteran 'Maestro', Emilio Volanti, driving a marque which had not been associated with his name for some time, a 3-litre Maturati, the first Italian car seriously to challenge German speed supremacy.

The British reply to this formidable Continental opposition was provided by the works team of B.R.C.s, and a host of sprint 'specials'. The former were smaller than their Continental rivals, but the course suited them and, with the exception of the new section, their drivers had the advantage of knowing the hill intimately.

The 'specials' were, as always, an unknown quantity. Some, in their day, were quite capable of matching the performance of the Grand Prix cars over such a short course, while others might merely provide comic relief by emitting remarkably irregular noises and bestrewing the course with intimate parts of their machinery.

There was no doubt about it, the stage was set for a record meeting. No wonder Mr Nelson, the genial little secretary and moving spirit of the MMC, had felt excited and pleased with himself that morning when he had watched lorries bearing names famous on all the circuits of Europe come rolling into his paddock.

Brothers Peter and John lost no time in unloading the Bligh Special from its trailer.

'If you go and rout out the scrutineer,' said Peter, as they man-handled the Special into its bay, 'I'll go and talk nicely to Nelson and see if I can't wangle one run before dark.'

John had barely finished unloading from the tonneau of the Vauxhall the cans of dope, the tools and all the other paraphernalia that accompanies the sprint car, when Peter came back at the double.

'It's okay,' he called. 'But we shall have to hurry; Nelson's sending over the scrutineer. Meantime, we've got to go for a walk, blast it! All drivers have got to go over the new section on foot and report to the timing-box that they've done so before they're allowed a run.' He paused, peering roung the paddock. 'I wonder where those silly asses can have got to? I told them to keep a look-out for us,' he complained.

'Maybe they've got fed up with waiting and gone off to the Crown,' John hazarded.

'I'll half break their silly necks if they have,' Peter swore. 'No, there they are snooping around the Maturati. Oi!' he bellowed. 'Mike! George!'

Two tall, untidy figures detached themselves from the curious group about the Italian car and came towards them at a jog-trot.

'Where the hell have you been?' shouted one as soon as he came within earshot. 'We'd just given you up – thought you must have thrown the trailer away again on the way, so we were just going to make for the local tap-house.'

'Never mind about that now,' Peter silenced him. 'Your thirst will improve with keeping. The great thing at the moment is to get a practice run before dark. John and I have got to walk over the new bit of the course, so if you'd like to make yourself really useful for a change, you can get her ready and warmed up while we're away. That's the dope-can, the one with the white top. It's all ready mixed. The soft plugs are in, but you'd better have a look at them before you try a start. When she's just about sizzling, put in the R2s, they're in that yellow box. Oh, and another thing,' he added, 'the scrutineer is on his way, so none of your rudery or he may take a poor view of John's idea of independent suspension.'

'As you say, Chief,' Mike replied with mock humility, and pulled his forelock. Yet he took his coat off and set to work with a will, ably assisted by the quiet George, while the others set off up the course.

Whereas the old road wound its way up through the wood in a series of zigzag curves, thus gaining height on an easy gradient, the new section left the old at the first of these corners, and cut straight and steeply up the hillside for a distance of 300 yards to a single left-handed turn. This was followed by another straight on a slightly easier gradient, which ran parallel with the flank of the hill until it rejoined the old course, at what had previously been the very slow Creek Hairpin.

Peter and John stood on the apex of the new corner, surveying it with critical and practised eyes.

'There's no doubt about it, this is a great improvement,' John decided. 'It'll make the course much faster and more interesting, too. This "swerve" reminds me of the first bend of the "esse" at Shelsley; same gradient up to it, I should think, same curvature and camber, and the same bank on the outside, too, for the unwary to clout.

'Of course, it's difficult to judge just how steep that approach is, so that one can't tell exactly where the cut-off point will be, but I should say it will be just about opposite those stones there.'

He pointed to two great boulders that stood like monoliths, one on each side of the road. Peter nodded.

'I think you're right,' he agreed. 'It looks straightforward enough and yet – oh, I don't know – there's something I don't like about it, but exactly what it is I couldn't tell you. Phew!' he exclaimed and laughed shortly, 'what a stink! Old socks and rotten eggs aren't in it. Something must have died here a long time ago, I should think.'

'That's funny,' said John, sniffing. 'I don't notice it. Anyway, we'd better get down, it seems to be getting dark all of a sudden under these trees, so unless we hurry we shan't have enough light for a run.'

When they got back to the paddock practically everyone had packed up for the night, but the faithful Mike and his shadow George had the Special ready and only awaiting a push to the line. Peter wriggled his way into the narrow bucket-seat in front of the two potent 'Vee' twin engines and the others pushed.

Letting in the clutch, he was greeted with the deafening staccato bark of four open exhausts belching blue flame and a reek of dope and castor-oil. For a few moments the air about the timing-box was filled with an intensity of urgent sound that literally stung the ear-drums to painful protest, while Peter tightened his body-belt, pulled down his goggles and exchanged a last shouted word or two with John.

Then at a nodded signal Mike released the plungers of the two oil-pumps and stepped back, the note of the engines rose even more fiercely, and the next instant the car was snaking out of sight in a series of power slides, leaving in its wake two long, black streaks of pungent burnt rubber from the tyres.

'A bit too much loud pedal there,' Mike commented.

Although invisible to him, John could follow Peter's progress by the noise that now resounded through the wood and echoed about the surrounding hills. Now he had cut-out and changed down for the first corner into the wood – a sharp one that – now he was round and accelerating away for all he was worth up the steep straight to the new corner; he was through to second, now into third – that was a surprise, he had not expected that Peter would get into third. Now he had cut-out for the new corner.

John waited expectantly for a renewed burst of sound, but no sound came. He must have crashed. Then, after what seemed an age of suspense, but must in reality have been but a second or two, he heard the sound of one engine come to life and continue over the top of the hill. John heaved a sigh of relief and walked round to meet the car at the foot of the return road; anyway, Peter and the Special were still in one piece.

Peter came coasting back in a fine fury, consigning with great fluency the MMC, the hill, the local inhabitants, and the new corner to a particularly lurid hell. John gave him a few moments in which to simmer down before he dared to inquire what had happened.

'What happened?' Peter exploded with renewed fury. 'Well, I was going a treat, as you probably heard. Pulling third on the straight, too, when just as I came into the new corner some suicidal idiot came flapping out at me waving his arms plumb in the middle of the road. It meant that I had to brake and alter course right in the middle of the corner, and it was no fault of his that I didn't pile up the whole outfit. As it was, I just touched the bank on the outside, shot across the road, went up on the grass on the inside and eventually managed to get back on to the road again. By that time one engine had cut out; still, I think the car's all right. We shall have to get up bright and early and get in a couple of runs tomorrow morning, that's all, there's not enough light in the wood for another run now.'

When the Blighs eventually arrived at the Crown in Winchford where they had arranged to stay, they found Mr Nelson leaning on the bar, chatting to Camille and Butt, the number one BRC driver. He looked up and smiled as they came in.

'Well, how did you get on, Bligh?' he inquired.

Peter grinned ruefully.

'Oh, all right, thanks, as far as it went, which wasn't very far, I'm afraid.'

'You're not going to tell me you had trouble on the new corner, are you?' Mr Nelson implored. 'Everyone seems to have been in difficulties there. I've heard nothing but complaints about it all day. The surface, the camber, the light – nothing seems to be right about it. It's pretty disheartening for me after so much work. Even Volanti said he had a nasty moment there, although he put up an excellent time. Three people have hit the bank, fortunately without serious damage, and several others had their engines die quite unaccountably when they came to open up after the corner.' Mr Nelson looked quite downcast.

'Oh, no,' Peter hastened to assure him. 'I've got no complaint to make against the corner itself, but just as I came into it some fool popped out from nowhere right into the middle of the road, waving his arms like a lunatic. Result was, I had a very busy time indeed, and while I was motoring about on the grass and dodging trees I lost one engine.'

Poor conscientious Mr Nelson looked more harassed than ever and swore under his breath.

'I'm most frightfully sorry to hear about this, Bligh,' he apologised. 'I can't think who can have done such a crazy thing. When you went up, the marshals had just come down and reported to me that there were no spectators left on the hill, and only Arthur Day was still up there, hanging on in the top timing-box until you had made your run. Tell me, what did this idiot look like?'

Peter thought for a moment before replying.

'Well,' he explained, 'the light was pretty poor under the trees there by the time I went up, and anyway you can't notice much detail when you're "dicing", but he seemed a tall, thin bloke wearing something white. It looked like an overall coat, or it may have been a very light-coloured mackintosh.

'The odd thing that struck me, now I come to think of it, was that he didn't seem to have the coat on properly – his arms through the sleeves I mean – but slung round his shoulders, so that it looked like – well – more like a surplice than anything else.'

He laughed.

'I'm not trying to suggest, though, that it may have been the local padre in his war-paint or anything like that. Just as I got the car back on to the road,' he went on, 'I had a quick look round, but he must have made a lightning getaway, for I couldn't see a sign of him. Anyway,' Peter concluded, 'I'm not worrying, it was my own fault for turning up so late. What'll you have to drink?' he asked.

The conversation became general and the usual topics that are raised on the eve of a speed event were discusseed at length. Talk was of blowers and blower pressures, of gear ratios, suspension and braking systems and of twin rear wheels versus single.

Mr Nelson played his part nobly in this discussion, for he was secretly a prey to a vague feeling of uneasiness, a dim sense of foreboding, which began to get the upper hand later, when he found himself alone in his room for the night. That confounded new corner seemed to be at the bottom of everying, he reflected; what an unlucky job it had been from start to finish! A constant worry. At one time he had seriously doubted whether the road would ever be ready in time, they had had such a long chapter of accidents and irritating annoyances.

In the first place, the local wiseacres had been even more pig-headed and obstinate than usual, and had not only refused to help the work of the club in any way, but had actually seemed bent on putting obstacles in their path. None of the local contractors could be persuaded to take on the job, and he had been compelled to employ a London firm at much greater expense. All this because of some archaic superstition about a ring of old stones through which the road would pass.

To begin with, some foolish practical joker, presumably one of the villagers, kept moving the surveyor's pegs and sights overnight, and once they had even been collected together and burnt. Next, a large oak-tree they were felling, thanks to an unexpected and violent gust of wind on an otherwise calm day, fell unexpectedly in the wrong direction. It trapped the foreman, seriously injuring him, while several of the men had narrow escapes.

The mechanical navvy broke down repeatedly, until finally a subsidence occurred beneath it, and it required days of digging and the erection of shear-legs before it could be extricated. Just when the excavations were nearly at an end, and they were preparing to lay the foundations of the road, a spring had been struck, which made the whole hillside a hopeless quagmire of mud.

Then the trouble began among the workmen. Several of them fell victims to a peculiar and singularly unpleasant complaint, from which two had subsequently died, and the remainder had become restless and uneasy, saying there was no luck on the job. No doubt local talk was responsible.

Seeing the work was so behind time, he had tried to persuade the contractor to put on a night shift, offering to provide them with flares, but the men had resolutely refused to work after sundown. It was only by the dogged persistence of Mr Nelson himself that the road had been completed in time for the event, and it was with a sense of personal triumph that he had opened the course to competitors.

When beset by all these difficulties, he had actually begun to wonder at times whether there might not, after all, be some truth in local superstitions, but when the new road was at last finished and he toured up it at the wheel of his blue saloon Le Fevre, this disturbing thought had been forgotten. Now, the unfortunate mishaps in practice and particularly Bligh's story had recalled his past uneasiness.

He recollected how he had dismissed impatiently the workmen's talk of something or someone flitting about among the trees; never seen in broad daylight, but only after sundown, often glimpsed in the corner of the eye, but never directly seen. Strange, too, that both workmen and drivers had complained of the unpleasant stench that occasionally seemed to hang about the corner.

In an attempt to put a stop to these disquieting and unprofitable thoughts, Mr Nelson decided to indulge in his favourite relaxation of reading in bed. After a while the book slipped from his hand on to the coverlet and he fell into an uneasy sleep, which brought with it a very vivid and disturbing dream.

He was sitting in his favourite position in the lower timing-box at Longbury. It was evidently late in the day, for the light seemed subdued. Through the window he could see the Rheinwagen on the starting-line with Von Eberstraum at the wheel.

For no apparent reason this perfectly normal spectacle seemed to inspire him with dreadful uneasiness. He felt as though he was the unwilling witness of some sinister sequence of events which he was quite powerless to interrupt.

He saw the starter place the contact shoe before the front wheel of the car, and as he did so a voice said quite clearly and distinctly:

'He's out for blood.'

Then the Rheinwagen made its anticipated meteoric get-away. Mr Nelson realised that he had the head-phones on, and he listened anxiously for the reassuring voice of Arthur Day to announce the time. It did not come.

Instead his head became filled with a distant but penetrating reverberation of sound. It was like nothing he had ever heard before, but it most closely resembled the far-off booming of a great gong. Then a thin, high voice began to intone in a tongue that was unintelligible, and yet somehow indescribably menacing. Finally, and seemingly much nearer at hand, someone screamed.

At this point Mr Nelson awoke with the scream still ringing in his ears, to find himself bathed in perspiration, despite the fact that he had kicked most of the bedclothes on to the floor. Disinclined to court further sleep that night, and feeling wretchedly ill at ease, he propped himself upright with his pillows and resigned himself to read his novel, with as much concentration as he could muster, for the rest of the night.

A brilliant spring morning without a cloud in the sky did much to dispel Mr Nelson's gloomy fears and to make amends for his wretched night. He felt inclined to attribute his nightmare to over-indulgence in the Crown's excellent Stilton at dinner the previous evening.

When he opened the course at noon, accompanied by the President of the Club and a minor Royalty, he felt in excellent humour once more. A record crowd of spectators thronged the banks and enclosures on the hill and the fields below were black with cars.

In the interval between the first and second runs Mr Nelson felt justified in laughing at his forebodings, for the unfortunate incidents of practice day had not recurred, and the programme had been run off like clockwork. It was obvious that the honour of fastest time of the day lay between Von Eberstraum and Volanti with the Maturati. Von Eberstraum, it appeared, had a slightly faster car, but he held an advantage of a mere fifth of a second over Volanti, who was handling his car with that almost fabulous skill for which he was justly famous.

A brilliantly judged climb by Butt in No. 1 B.R.C. won him first place in the 1½-litre class, and third in the general classification, while the Bligh Special had made an ear-splitting run to record the fastest time by a sprint 'special'. The performance of the new Lefevre was a little disappointing, and Camille could only manage fifth place. Mr Nelson could see him in the paddock now, explaining volubly and with a wealth of gesture typically Gallic, to a group of equally vociferous mechanics, why the car was quite useless and unfit for him, the great Camille, to drive.

It was just as the first car was being brought to the line for its second run that an unfortunate and most unusual mishap occurred to delay the proceedings. Without any warning a section of the bank above the new corner gave way and slid down into the road, carrying several spectators with it. Fortunately no one was injured, and amidst much laughter and jesting a gang of amateur navvies was hastily recruited, and set to work with a will to clear the earth on to the inside of the corner. Even so, the delay caused was such that Mr Nelson realised that unless the rest of the programme was run off extremely promptly, the light would fail the last cars.

However, once the obstruction had been cleared and the spectators moved back as a precautionary measure, the second runs were made amidst much excitement, but again without untoward incident. Von Eberstraum and Volanti both made faster, but this time identical, times, and sent a message to the timing-box requesting that they be allowed an additional run each to decide the tie. This was granted, though the two drivers were urged to come to the line as soon as possible on account of failing light. The announcement that the tie was about to be run off provoked a murmur of excited anticipation and speculation from the dense crowds on the hill.

Volanti appeared first, as the Rheinwagen mechanics were changing rear wheels. As he was pushed to the line and the engine of the Maturati was started the sun was just sinking beyond the horizon of the vale, and already the outlines of the woods and of the farther hills were becoming indistinct in a blue evening haze.

The 'Maestro' went off like a bullet, his hatchet face set in the determined way that meant business. His time came through surprisingly quickly, Arthur Day's usually quiet voice raised with excitement. It was two-fifths of a second better than his previous run.

Now Von Eberstraum! The silver Rheinwagen was pushed up to the line by the impassive German mechanics. The driver climbed into the cockpit. One mechanic fixed the detachable steering-wheel in place, while another inserted the starting-handle in the tail. At a signal from the driver he gave one sharp flick of the wrist and the engine broke into its characteristic deep-throated roar, little puffs of black smoke spurting vertically upward from sixteen short pipes as the throttle was 'blipped'. Von Eberstraum looked grimly determined as he drew on his gloves and adjusted his goggles. A marshal bent towards Mr Nelson in the timing-box.

'He's out for blood,' he shouted above the roar.

Mr Nelson's heart sank within him, for in a moment he realised that his nightmare of the previous night was being re-enacted before his eyes. Every detail was horribly familiar; the particular quality of the light which seemed to have suddenly become dim; a little unimportant gesture which the starter made as he acknowledged the nod from the timing-box and placed the contact shoe before the wheel.

Once more a sense of inevitably impending tragedy made him feel powerless, but mastering it, he got to his feet and hammered on the glass of the window to the consternation of his colleagues.

'Stop!' he called despairingly. 'Stop him!'

Too late; the words were scarcely out of his mouth when the Rheinwagen left the line with smoking tyres and rocketed away in one terrific, sustained burst of acceleration.

Mr Nelson knew then that what he was about to hear through the head-phones would not be the familiar voice of Arthur Day. He was right.

People started to run and the ambulance dashed up the course. Mercifully, perhaps Mr Nelson did not see them; he had fainted.

The tragic duel between Volanti and Von Eberstraum was almost the sole topic of discussion in motor-racing circles for months afterwards. As usual, theories as to the cause of the disaster were legion. On only one point were the theorists unanimous. The new corner was in some obscure way highly dangerous.

First Volanti had approached the corner at a fantastic speed, crammed on his brakes, and got into a terrifying and inexplicable slide as though the road had suddenly become a sheet of ice. To the horrified spectators it looked as though a crash was inevitable, and only Volanti's uncanny skill and presence of mind can have saved him. The little man's elbows worked like flails as he fought for control. Instead of the head-on impact which seemed so inevitable, the Maturati caught the bank a glancing blow as the tail swung wide, then rocketed across to the inside as though it must surely plunge over the bank to disaster, but was corrected and held on the very brink, all in a moment of time. Finally, and before the astounded spectators had time to draw breath, the car was on the road again, the howl of the blower burst forth once more like a triumphant cry, and Volanti was gone in a flurry of turf, dust and smoke to set up his incredible record.

A marshal walked up and examined the road surface, suspecting oil, but there was none visible. Many spectators were then driven away from the corner by an appalling stench which suddenly arose. Others, oddly enough, failed to notice it.

Then came Von Eberstraum. The Rheinwagen appeared to be travelling equally rapidly, but seemed quite steady under the terrific braking, and was taking the corner very fast, but apparently under perfect control, when once more the inexplicable happened. In the middle of the corner Von Eberstraum braked suddenly and appeared to alter course, with the result that the car went completely out of control, spun round, and disappeared backwards over the bank on the inside. There was a sickening crashing and splintering as the car bounded over and over through the undergrowth until it eventually came to rest, a mangled wreck, against a great upright block of stone.

The most popular theory of the accident was that the brakes seized, the arm-chair theorists talking glibly of the fluid boiling in the brake pipes as a result of the heavy braking immediately before the corner. They ignored the fact that the braking system fitted to the car had undergone many far more gruelling tests in Grand Prix races.

There were other witnesses of the disaster who had their own shadowy inkling of the possible cause, but preferred to keep it to themselves, because they doubted the evidence of their eyes, having seen what many had apparently failed to see. As Von

Eberstraum came into the corner they had fancied that something darted out from the shadow of the bank below them into the path of the car. It was only a fleeting glimpse seen out of the corners of eyes intently focused on the car alone. After the car had gone the road was deserted.

Peter Bligh was amongst those who had vague but disturbing ideas about the accident, which he decided to keep to himself.

Mr Nelson was the only person who was not in the slightest doubt as to the cause, although he, too, preferred to keep his own counsel. His first action after his recovery from a severe nervous breakdown was to order a high and unclimbable fence to be erected all round the new corner.

Some of you may have wondered, like I did, why such a promising and costly improvement of Longbury Hill should be allowed to fall into disuse so soon. I have at last managed to get the real facts from Mr Nelson and Peter Bligh. So now you know, and may draw your own conclusions. Personally, I agree with Mr Nelson. I think there is something on the inside of that fence that is best left alone.

'JUST LIKE WILD BOB'

William F. Nolan

One of the most famous of racing drivers was the American Barney Oldfield whose exploits on the track have made him a legend and also the subject of a biography by my next contributor, William Francis Nolan (1928–). Motor racing is, in fact, a subject in which Nolan is well versed, for he raced cars himself in his younger days and has since published eight books and over a hundred shorter pieces on the topic. Of all these, however, 'Just Like Wild Bob', written in 1964 and not previously published in a book, remains his personal favourite.

'It is a story very close to my heart,' he told me, 'since it is really about my late father, based on all the stories he used to tell me about the great Barney Oldfield. In fact, I finally wrote Oldfield's biography inspired by my Dad's tales of those "golden days of motor cars".'

I have to be honest here and say that this is not a strange, bizarre or even horrific story, but it is one about the 'transformation' of a boy's feelings for his father from near-hate to pride and love. I found it quite irresistible on reading, and it also provides what I think is a most necessary bit of light relief after some of the horrors we have so far encountered! I should just add for the benefit of fantasy-fiction lovers, that Bill Nolan is the same Nolan who has been writing fine tales of fantasy for some thirty years, including that superb story 'Logan's Run' which was filmed in 1976 with Michael York and Jenny Agutter, and then became a television series the following year.

It was hot, desperately hot, in the car, and McAllister felt the heat under his clothes, felt the perspiration gathering beneath his armpits and along his trousered thighs. Damn the California sun, he thought, and damn having to drive through it in an old Ford with 80,000 tired miles on the odometer.

He looked over at his father who sat bolt upright in the heat, as straight as a soldier. And Paul McAllister thought; nothing bothers him; he just sits there in this blast-furnace air and nothing bothers him at all. My God, I hope things like heat and cold and long rides bother me when I'm eighty; I hope to God they do. He isn't even human. He's some kind of insensitive machine that keeps on operating no matter what happens to it. People look at him and say: isn't he wonderful, isn't it *grand* to be that way? And I feel like yelling at them, McAllister thought. I feel like yelling: if you think he's so damn wonderful and grand why don't you take him to live with you? Why don't *you* put up with his senility and his deafness and his dirt? You'd soon find out how grand he is.

Highway 99 ribboned ahead of them, flat and grey-white, rippling slightly in the heat-haze. Paul held the Ford at 65. Not fast on a weekday like this with no cops out, but plenty fast for the old Ford. It rolled and heaved drunkenly around curves and on a straight like this it took both hands to keep it steady at anything over 50.

The thing is, I should have gone to San Berdoo without him, McAllister told himself; I should have said: hell no you can't go with me! This is business and I have to see this guy about something you wouldn't understand . . . But his father had begged to be taken along, whined like a puppy, and McAllister had given in. Hours up and hours back in the August heat with the sun strong enough to suck the water from a camel's hump – but the old man had not complained once. He knew better. If he said a word McAllister would cut him to pieces with his tongue. He'd done it often enough before.

I'm 31 and he's 80 and he's got no business messing up my life, McAllister's inner monologue continued. I ought to be married, have a wife and family of my own – and maybe I would if it weren't for him. Oh, well, I guess I wouldn't, but hell, who knows, really, whether I would or not? He's always there, around the house all day like some kind of vulture, crouched over the TV, maybe an inch from the screen because of his eyes, always giving me terrible suggestions about how to sell real estate, about what to say to people.

If Mother were alive things might be different. They *would* be, no doubt of it. She'd let him talk to her while she ironed or cooked and the words would go on past her because she never really listened to him, never really heard the same tired, dreadful stories over and over. The words would disappear in her mind like invisible ink on white paper.

But with her gone, he's just got me. Only me. And I can't ignore him the way Mother could. When I'm home he's talking all the time and I keep wanting to tell him to shut up, to shut his damn old mouth up, that I've heard all he's got to say a million times and just can't stand the words any longer. And sometimes, McAllister told himself with a bitter satisfaction, sometimes I *do* just that. I yell like fury at him and he shuts up for maybe an afternoon – or even an entire day – and pouts like a slapped kid.

The old man coughed violently next to McAllister. He pulled a grey handkerchief from his pants pocket and began to dab at his watering eyes with it.

'My God, *look* at that thing!' snapped McAllister. 'I told you to make sure you had a clean one before you left.'

'Sorry,' the old man said, and smiled toothlessly. 'Sorry, son, but I forgot to get another one from the drawer. I did.'

'All right,' Paul sighed. 'But just put it away. You'll fill the car with germs.'

McAllister's father nodded in the heat, his long yellow-white hair pasted thinly to his lined forehead. He looked over at his son and attempted another smile, but to Paul it was a grimace, a toothless grimace – and, perversely, did not smile back.

'You didn't *have* to go along, you know,' he told his father, eyes coldly fastened on the road ahead. 'I warned you about the heat.'

The old man seemed puzzled. 'I didn't say nothing about the heat did I?' he asked. 'I didn't say nothing.'

McAllister sighed again and kept his eyes on the wide, flat highway running up into the hills. Sweat had gathered like a cluster of tiny seed-pearls on his upper lip and he ran the edge of his left sleeve over the skin, immediately angry with himself for not using his clean handkerchief and showing his father what it meant to carry fresh, laundered things.

Hell, he'd live like a pig if I ever left him, McAllister assured himself. He never washes really well, just kind of *pats* some water over him when he's in the tub. His bathtowel shows it. Why is it that old people are so dirty? Not all of them, though. My grandfather on my mother's side was as neat as a pin right up to the day he died. And he was 83. Yet most old people would live like pigs if they could.

A half-mile ahead of them, near the right side of the highway, McAllister made out a small figure, waving. As they drew nearer he braked to 45 and squinted for a clearer look. A boy of maybe 18 in blue denims with sandy, crewcut hair was waving and shouting something. Just a few feet behind the boy, completely off the highway on the grass verge, McAllister saw a light-green panel truck. Gas, that's it, thought Paul; the kid's out of gas.

'There's a guy stuck up ahead,' McAllister told his father. 'I'm going to stop and give him a lift.'

'Fine with me,' the old man replied. 'That's all right.'

Paul had never believed in picking up hitch-hikers. Never can tell about them. Maybe only one in a thousand's a sour apple, but he might be the one you pick up. Might be he's got a gun and he needs your car for some kind of getaway. But not this kid, McAllister was certain, not this kid here in the middle of the open highway in broad daylight with his own panel truck. Not a chance in a million. I'd be a heel if I passed him by.

McAllister brought the Ford to a halt by the truck and motioned to the boy in the denims. 'Need a ride?' he asked.

'Sure do, mister,' answered the boy, trotting over to the car. 'Ran plain out of gas about a mile back and just coasted this far hoping I'd make a station. But don't seem like there's one around for miles.'

'That's right,' said Paul. 'Nearest station is a good bit up the highway. Hop in, I'll take you. It's on the way.'

'Thanks a lot,' the boy said and was about to open the front door when Paul said: 'Get in back. More room there.'

'Okay.' The boy slid into the rear of the Ford, slamming the door. McAllister accelerated away, leaving the green panel truck parked and silent behind them in the heat.

'My name is Springer,' the boy said from the back seat. 'Anson Springer.'

'Mine's Paul McAllister,' said Paul mechanically, watching the road. 'This is my father.'

'Hi,' said the boy.

'Glad to make your acquaintance,' smiled the old man,

twisting in the seat and extending one withered yellow hand. The boy shook it briskly. 'Same here.'

'You work around these parts?' the old man asked – and Paul thought: hell, he's got someone to listen to him now and he's going to start talking up a storm. Maybe picking up this kid was a lousy idea after all. Dad knows when I'm sore and he stays quiet, but give him an extra pair of ears to bend and off he goes.

'I'm a mechanic in LA,' replied the boy. 'I help my brother in his garage.'

'Then . . . you know cars, eh boy?' The old man twisted even farther around in the seat.

'Yeah, a little I guess.' He hesitated. 'I can take an engine apart if that's what you mean.'

'Ever hear about a car called the Stevens-Duryea?' The old man's voice held a trace of urgency, of tenseness, and McAllister drew in a sharp breath and swore silently. God, he's going to start the business about the early days; he's going to go into the whole long, involved, exhausting bit.

'I doubt if he's ever heard of the car, Dad,' said Paul, forcing a degree of pleasantness into his voice. He flicked his glance to the rearview mirror, hoping the boy would back up his statement. If so the talk could be slanted, pushed away from the familiar subject at hand.

'As a matter of plain fact,' the boy grinned, 'I sure have. I mean, I've seen pictures of it. My brother's an old-car bug. Knows all about Barney Oldfield and like that.'

From the corner of his eye McAllister could see his father straighten in triumph and nod quickly like a bird, the wrinkles on his veined neck folding deeply one upon another. It was too late now. When the boy mentioned Barney Oldfield McAllister realised it was too late.

'I knew him,' piped the old man, still nodding. 'Yes sir, I knew Barney. I raced against him when he drove a White Steamer in Missouri. Big White Steamer down in Missouri. Cross-country it was, maybe 200 miles, through mud so deep you could swim in it. I was in a Chalmers-Bluebird then and I let Barney break ground for me. I mean following his big Steamer, staying right in his tracks while all the other cars bogged down. Near the end of the race old Barney he ran out of water and had to stop and leave his car on the road while he went into a farmhouse and asked for some. For the Steamer, you know. Had to have water for the Steamer.'

Paul made one more desperate attempt. 'Maybe he doesn't want to hear about all that stuff, Dad,' McAllister said, his voice now edged and crisp. 'It's a pretty damn hot day and maybe –'

'Oh no, I'm glad to listen,' the boy cut in. 'Golly! . . . Al – that's my brother, Al – he'll be mighty surprised when I tell him I met somebody that actually raced Barney Oldfield. Did you finally beat him, Mr McAllister?'

Paul sighed and kept his eyes fixed on the road. It was no use, none at all, and now all he could hope for was a gas station. He pressed his foot down on the pedal and the speedometer needled up to 68, then 70. The Ford began to shudder and Paul eased off. No use wrecking the car just to keep from hearing it all again, he thought. Won't be much longer. We'll get there soon. I know there's a new station opened up about five miles or so down the highway.

'Well, I never *did* beat ole Barney,' his father was saying. 'I passed him when he went for water that time, but my car threw a rod and I never finished that race at all. Ole Barney, he won fair an' square.'

I doubt if Oldfield ever drove a White Steamer, McAllister thought bitterly. Sure, you probably raced a couple of times, but I bet you never came any closer to Oldfield than a sparrow comes to a hawk.

'I knew Bobby Burman too,' the old man went on, warming to his subject. His eyes began to water under the wrinkled lids and he blinked rapidly. 'We called him Wild Bob because he was a regular hellion behind the wheel. This was 1909 you know, and he used to come out to Missouri and race at the Elm Ridge track.' The old man took out his grey handkerchief and scrubbed at his watering eyes.

Filthy, thought McAllister; that's just plain filthy. You can't tell an old man anything. Tell him to keep that thing out of sight and he'll be blowing his nose with it in front of the Queen of England five minutes later! Like a 3-year-old. You can't tell them anything they remember.

'Wild Bob was in a Stoddard-Dayton out at Elm Ridge one Sunday,' the old man continued, 'and it was beginning to rain cats and dogs. Well, Bobby was cuttin' up the track, you know, with that big car of his and so I went out to flag him down. I was chairman of the racing committee then and we didn't want the track all cut up in the rain. We'd have a real bad time packing it all down again if he cut it up and so I tried to flag him and get him off there.'

Who cares, thought McAllister, Dear Lord who the hell cares what happened 49 lousy years ago on some lousy dirt track in Missouri? He's failed at everything he ever tried in his life, lost all my mother's money, made her sell our house to invest in one of his crazy schemes and lived just as he wanted to live, not caring for what other people wanted, what my mother wanted, or me, or anyone. He's a failure and I hope to God I'm never like him. But to hear him talk you'd think he was a big, raging success at everything. From auto racing to raising chickens . . . I'll bet he never won a race in his life, Paul thought, never in his life.

'So he hits me,' the old man was saying, his voice droning on in the heat, behind McAllister's thoughts. 'He skidded, comes sideways across the wet track and hits me.' The old man threw up a leathery hand. 'Knocked me ten feet in the air and broke every bone in my body. Even today I got a plate in my left leg that aches when it rains.' He tapped the spot. 'Silver plate just like on a dinner table. Right here in my leg.'

'Golly . . . that's something,' said the boy from the rear seat. McAllister found it impossible to tell whether he was simply bored and being polite or whether he really wanted to hear more of this.

'They put me in the morgue. Left me for dead!' The old man nodded again, chuckling with a sound like wind in high grass. A rustling, repulsive kind of chuckle, thought McAllister.

'But I woke up and threw off that sheet and crawled across that cold floor to the feller in charge and scared him half to death. They took me to the hospital and I was out and walking in two weeks!'

Yes, and tell him about your fistula and your ulcers and the cancer you got over like it was a cold in the head, McAllister silently prodded. Tell him how you're stronger even than God in his heaven! Roosevelt dies and Stalin and Ronald Colman but you go right on. Not human, that's all; you're just not human.

'I drove the Pathfinder car for the Star Cup Tour back in 1910,' the old man said. 'That was in the Stevens-Duryea I mentioned. We called 'er the Big Six and she was 60 horsepower. Steering her was like grabbing a wagon wheel and it took a mile to get her rolling good. But then she's do 80. Roads were gumbo in those days. We couldn't get her movin' very fast on those roads. I had the agency for Stevens-Duryea in Kansas City then and I was selected over forty other dealers to blaze the way for the Star Cup runners. I mean, I drove the whole two thousand miles and we laid out the route for the auto tour that came later that year. We were the first car over the Glorietta mountains in New Mexico, first car to ever travel the Old Sante Fe trail.' Paul's father was caught up afresh in the emotion of the Golden Era, and McAllister wondered where in hell that new gas station was, how many more miles they had to go before the kid could be dumped and the conversation terminated.

'Oh, we had ourselves a *time*,' the old man chuckled. He needed a shave and the sun picked up the spiny edge of beard along his lower jaw. 'Dust, gumbo, rocks so big it took the four of us to move 'em, rain and cold and roads like goat trails. Had ten rain storms the first two and a half days out of Kansas City. But we made it, the whole way and back, and when we rolled into Kansas they tied wheat to the sides of the Big Six and we came on into Missouri, into Kansas City, and the crowds were out in the streets shouting at us and cheering and yelling our names . . .' The old man's voice dimmed away into memory.

'Didn't you have any breakdowns?' asked the boy.

'None major. We never missed an explosion in all the two thousand miles. I mean, the engine didn't. Ran like a clock. I tell you if they ran like they used to they wouldn't need mechanics like you these days. Young buck like you could get out and hustle for work 'cus there just wouldn't be none if the cars were all like my Big Six. Oh, we broke a wheel in the Gloriettas, but we got her changed quick enough. Had to use a mule team to haul us outa one big mudhole in Colorado but she never missed an explosion. No sir, she never missed.'

Ahead of them, near a broad intersection, McAllister spotted the gas station. Thank God, he thought, for the sign of the Flying Red Horse! Never looked so good to me before. And just in time, too, or else he would have gone into the business of his entering the Star Cup tour and leading most of the way and then breaking down near the end and the whole long bit. I couldn't take that, thought McAllister, as he approached the intersection, I just couldn't take that. A cream-coloured Oldsmobile was moving rapidly out of the station and Paul had to twist the wheel and hard-brake to avoid him.

'Well, here we are,' he said to the boy. 'You can get a can of gas and hitch a ride back to your truck with no trouble.'

'Thanks, thanks a lot, mister,' said the boy, jumping out and slamming the car door behind him. 'And . . .' He hesitated, looking into the seamed face of the old man. 'I sure do want to thank you for telling me about Barney Oldfield and all. I'll tell Al when I get back to LA and he'll have a fit he wasn't along. He'll just have himself a plain fit he didn't meet you.'

They shook hands, Paul's father and the teenaged boy in blue denims – and just before the boy was about to turn away the old man raised an ivoried hand and gripped Paul's shoulder. 'You see the way my boy handles this Ford? You see him whip it in here and miss that other feller? Handles this Ford like it was a kiddy car. Well, now, he drives, don't he? I watch him and I think of the way Wild Bob used to drive and I'm proud. Cuz he's just like him. My son here drives just like Wild Bob.'

'I'll see ya,' the boy said, and he waved as Paul rolled the car back onto the long flat highway.

'Nice youngster,' the old man said, and he folded his bony arms across his chest. He coughed once and lapsed into silence.

In the midday heat, driving the tired Ford towards Los Angeles, Paul McAllister tried not to think about his father, or 1910, or a car named the Stevens-Duryea, or a man they called Wild Bob. And, most particularly, he tried not to think of the compliment his father had paid him, of the words and the pride behind the words. The old man had no business saying a thing like that and making him feel the way he suddenly felt. It threw everything out of perspective; it didn't fit the pattern.

I didn't ask him for it, McAllister thought angrily, I didn't *want* him to say it.

But the words of pride had been spoken and although McAllister gripped the wheel tighter and pressed harder on the gas pedal the rush of highway and the heat and his own inner voice telling him to forget, to ignore the words, failed. They failed to dull the sudden ache within his chest, the pain that stabbed at him from a place he could never hope to reach.

Beside him, sitting as straight as a soldier, his father produced the grey handkerchief and scrubbed at his watering eyes.

AUTO SUGGESTION

Charles Beaumont

Real car enthusiasts are quick to tell you that every vehicle has its own characteristics – some are good-tempered and reliable, others unpredictable and even downright stubborn. Not for nothing, they will add, are motor cars referred to as female! This observation is not made with any intention of annoying any ladies who may have picked up this book, but merely as a means of introducing this next story in which the character of the car in question affects both its owner and the outcome of the events into which he is plunged. I will hint no more for fear of spoiling your surprise . . .

The author, Chicago-born Charles Beaumont (1929–1967) was a lover of fine automobiles as a glance at several of his stories will indicate. He was also an excellent writer of fantasy fiction who, after years of struggle trying to get his work published, finally achieved great acclaim in the pages of Playboy *magazine. This led to several collections of his stories being published, as well as employment as a Hollywood script-writer. Tragically, at the height of his success, a terrible disease struck him and when he died aged just 38 he had disintegrated into a gnarled old man. Fortunately, we have stories like 'Auto Suggestion' (which, curiously, has not previously been collected) to remind us of his inventive mind and storytelling skill. This story is all the more memorable because it was written in 1965 and pre-dates by almost two decades horror-story writer Stephen King's novel about another car with a sinister character of its own, 'Christine', which has recently been filmed.*

'Why?' Mr Llewellyn demanded, listening to the symphony of hate behind him. 'Why!' he moaned.

He twisted his head around and shuddered: a great shining sea of cars, all the cars in the world it seemed, honking in outrage, honking in anger, honking, honking.

Mr Llewellyn closed his eyes. Well, at least Miss Minifee wasn't along. That would have made it so much worse. He tried to think: be calm, be calm. For the tenth time he put his foot onto the starter, swallowed drily. *Please*, he thought, *please car, Non Omnis my old friend, please . . .*

He listened to the grinding noise and felt droplets of cold perspiration soak into his shirt.

Urrr-urrr-urrr. Urrr-rrr.

Terrified, he removed his foot. The percussion sounds were rising in back, louder, louder, unspeakably furious. HONK! *You're a fool, Abner Llewellyn!* HONK! *You're a bungling* HONK! *incompetent silly* BEEP! *ineffectual* RRROOOGA! *pathetic little* MOVE IT FOR CHRISSAKES MAC! –

Mr Llewellyn wrenched open the door, got out and went around to the front of his car and lifted the hood.

Something with the sparkplugs, he thought. Those little white things. He touched them. Then he touched other things, wires, the dipstick, the generator, ran his fingers over the rubber and metal. Oh God. It could be anything, anything!

Suddenly he wished that he were dead; dead in some graveyard where no cars honked and no wives shrieked and no bosses bellowed, where it was quiet and rest –

'The ignition,' someone said softly.

Mr Llewellyn jerked at the sound, hitting his head smartly on the upraised hood, crushing his hat. Things started to go purple. 'What?'

'The ignition – you forgot to turn it back on.'

Mr Llewellyn turned to face the scornful smile, the patronising snickering unbelieving –

But no one was there. Just the freeway and the illimitable vista of stalled automobiles; and the people in the automobiles, angry, redfaced.

'Hurry!'

The voice was firmer this time, not so soft. And – Mr Llewellyn felt faint – it appeared to be issuing from beneath his own vehicle.

'Hurry, hurry! The ignition!'

A truck's air horn began some car lengths away. A frightening sound, a terrible sound, like the scream of a wounded elephant, and it led the other smaller cars to renew their anger, shrill now beneath the dump-truck's mighty bellow, shrill and chittering, like arboreal creatures gone mad.

Mr Llewellyn slammed down the hood.

'Gently!' someone said in his car.

He ran to the door and scrambled quickly into the driver's position. In the rear-view mirror: people piling out onto the pavement: men, women, walking towards him.

'The ignition, you idiot! Wake up!'

Mr Llewellyn looked at the keys. It was true. He reached down and turned the key. His right foot came down upon the starter. An everlasting second of waiting, while things abraded loudly, waiting for the inscrutable but familiar feelings and signs, and then the sound of life, the rising pulse and roar of the motor breathing: power.

He took a quick swipe at his forehead and depressed the clutch. People were standing outside now, looking in.

He took his foot from the accelerator pedal and attempted to wrest the gearshift into place. It wouldn't go. More people outside. Laughing? Was that laughing he heard?

Low. Get into low. Get in there! He pulled the shift down with all his strength, listening to the awful grinding: at last – it was done. Now. He let out the clutch. Too fast. The car jerked, bounced, bobbed, threatened to stall. Mr. Llewellyn fought it, hard: control, control. Just get away is the thing now, away from the faces and their expressions of awe and stupefaction, away from the mockers.

He didn't wait for complete mastery over his vehicle. He stabbed at the clutch another time, mindless of the picture he was presenting, mindless that the car was bucking like a Brahma bull, and shoved the gearshift into second. And down again to high.

He was on his way.

'Knobheads!' someone said.

Mr Llewellyn twitched at the voice, forgot about the road, examined the interior of the car and swung back in time to miss a concrete lamp post, narrowly.

'What's that? Who's talking?'

There was a short silence. Then: 'Me.'

Mr Llewellyn revolved a finger in his ears. He shook his head several times. Someone was talking to him. But no one was there. A bad business.

'Perfectly normal cats,' the voice said, 'but let 'em get inside us and right away what are they? Schnooks! Inconsiderate, ill-mannered and sadistic. Check?'

'What?' Mr Llewellyn said. 'What?' He reached for the radio, remembered that he'd never had one installed. No radio.

Cars were passing in faster lanes. People scowling, grinning, shrugging. Honking.

'Loud-mouthed bastards! Give me a pain in the piston. I'm sick of it. Aren't you?'

Mr Llewellyn said nothing; he stared straight ahead.

'Well, *aren't* you?' the voice demanded.

'W-what?'

'Sick of these loud-mouths?'

'I – that is –'

'Man, enough is too much. Honk me.'

'I beg pardon?'

'Honk me! Toot me!'

'Good heavens!' Dazedly, Mr Llewellyn permitted a finger to touch the round black horn button, lightly. It reminded him that in his entire life he had never honked the horn of a car. Never. Well – this was an old car. Wouldn't make more than a courteous beep, wouldn't even be heard, probably. No harm in it.

He pressed the button.

The noise burst out instantly, from a shrill whine to an eardrum-fracturing cacophony. Paralysed with astonishment, Mr Llewellyn forgot to remove his finger from the horn, and he could see other automobiles ahead lurching, veering, skittering at the blast. And above the caterwaul, loud as new, overpoweringly loud – he now recalled the salesman years ago mentioning something about special triple horns – there was a wild chuckling. Then his hand slipped off and the noise stopped.

'That'll teach 'em!' the chuckling voice said.

'See here,' Mr Llewellyn cried, beside himself, 'who are you? Who's talking to me?'

'*I* am.' The voice seemed to come from the dashboard, or from behind the dashboard.

'Cars,' Mr Llewellyn said after a long while, 'cannot talk.'

He drove silently, thinking. About numerous things. *Non Omnis*, particularly: *Non Omnis Moriar*, the name he had given to the car on a whim . . . He had whims in those days, the days before Charlotte and the job and – the rest of it.

He became lost in thought and so was not entirely conscious of the low-throated snarl until it had pulled alongside him. He glanced over and saw the other car, a sleek convertible with its top down. The driver was smiling, not good-naturedly. One last smile and then the rumble and spit of dual exhausts and the canary-coloured racer was off, leaving the fumes of ignominy in Mr Llewellyn's nostrils.

'We gonna take that?' someone asked.

'Oh,' Mr Llewellyn said.

'Come on – he's fast, but we're clever. We'll out-think him.'

Mr Llewellyn kept the speedometer needle at a steady thirty-five, as set forth in the Vehicle Code, Section –

'Come *on!* We can still take him. Look at the schlemiel: all he knows is speed. Abner, you gonna let a dumb jerk make a fool of you – again? Aren't you fed up with being low man?'

Mr Llewellyn felt his foot sink down on the accelerator pedal. The speedometer rose slowly from thirty-five to forty, to fifty, to fifty-five –

'That's it! That's it! Now cut right – there's a hole!'

Mr Llewellyn breathed deep, fought to keep himself from throwing a glance over his shoulder. But he seemed to have lost all control over himself. He slid into the temporary opening between cars.

'Great! Now! Into the other lane!'

Fifty-five – sixty – sixty-five – Mr Llewellyn had never driven so fast before in his life. He didn't even know the car would do over fifty. He saw himself creeping up behind the yellow convertible.

'Okay. Fine. Easy now, be careful – wait for that Olds. Good: he's blocked off. Now swing back to the other lane. Come on, come on!'

Mr Llewellyn pulled out and listened to the scream of tyres against cement as he plugged another small hole in traffic. The horns were going wild.

'Okay,' the voice cried. 'Wrap it up!'

Mr Llewellyn's foot planked down hard against the floor, straining. *Non Omnis* shot forward orgiastically and the convertible was passed in a blur of yellow.

'Atta boy! Atta boy!'

Mr Llewellyn slowed down in time for the turn-off to his street. He crossed both lanes of traffic, just missing a pickup truck and a startled little Austin.

But Mr Llewellyn was no less startled. At his reflection in the mirror, for example: he was grinning. He listened for the voice, but there was no voice now: only the tinkle of pistons, the many motor sounds of an old car.

He shuddered slightly at the memory of the past hour and remembered that he was late, very late, and that Charlotte would be angry, very angry.

He parked in the garage, listened a moment. *'Non Omnis?'* he said softly. *'Non Omnis?'*

Then he switched off the engine, picked up his newspaper and went inside the house.

A bank teller is a bank teller, Mr Llewellyn thought. Is a husband is a poor provider is a misser-out is a dweller in the world which is a world immutable irrevocable irremediable and rotten. That is all, that is the end, you die.

Therefore: It's possible that you were overwrought, nervous, susceptible. Therefore: It's impossible that your car actually talked to you.

A bird may crawl on the ground, but a snake may never fly. And –

'Abner.'

Mr Llewellyn descended abruptly from the high plateau of abstract thought and faced Miss Minifee, little Miss Minifee, smiling and pink-dressed.

'Going to work overtime, Abner?'

'No. Just tidying up.'

'Can I catch a ride with you?'

Mr Llewellyn became excited. She had stopped riding with him when Charley Doolittle arrived on the scene. He had thought it was all over, all those pleasant painful minutes.

'Of course. You surely may.'

Miss Minifee blushed slightly. 'Charley usually goes right by my place. He's working late, though.'

And then they were in the car and the day was behind them.

And Mr Llewellyn thought about Miss Minifee. In her pink dress. He saw her skin, the smoothness of milk, the colour of copper. Oh, she had liked him, once. She really had.

He eased aside the picture of Charlotte, porcine of construction, skin like a worn gladstone bag, shrill-voiced, old. He dizzied from the perfume smell of Miss Minifee, from the forever invitation of her smile.

'Why not?'

Mr Llewellyn's heart constricted. That voice again.

'No, no,' he whispered.

'How's that?' Miss Minifee said.

It must not happen. Not again. 'Nothing – I didn't say anything.'

She turned away, after a long look.

There was a chuckling.

'Yes, Abner?'

Mr Llewellyn was about to explain that it hadn't been he, but thought the better of it. He smiled blankly.

Miss Minifee swung around in her seat to face him, mouth slightly parted to reveal very white teeth and behind them a tongue which was small and moist.

You had your chance, that mouth almost said, you had it and you fluffed it because you're weak and that's why I ride home with Charley now.

The disembodied voice boomed with cordiality. 'Hey,' it said, 'I want to ask you a question.'

Mr Llewellyn stiffened. The voice sounded now exactly like his own.

'Uh huh?' Miss Minifee said.

'Just wondering if you had anything on tonight.'

'Just what you see, honey,' Miss Minifee said, sliding closer to him at a curve of insufficient excuse.

'How about dinner?'

'You mean – us, Abner?'

'That I do.'

'Well – I mean, what about the Mrs?'

'Charlotte and I are through. Finished. Washed up. She'll go her way, I'll go mine.'

'You wouldn't kid a girl, would you?'

'Miss Minifee, do I strike you as the "kidding" sort?'

'Nooo –' Miss Minifee studied him. Then she smiled. 'Okay,' she said. 'You know where I live. About seven?'

'Seven it is.'

'And – you're sure it's all right?'

'All *right?* Baby, it's the greatest!'

Mr Llewellyn wiped his forehead and applied the brake. Miss Minifee touched his arm and squeezed. 'I got a dress,' she said, 'that's going to knock you out.'

The voice like Mr Llewellyn's said, 'You'd be a knockout in anything, baby!'

Miss Minifee looked puzzled, then she laughed, squeezed his arm again and got out. Mr Llewellyn roared off immediately, beating out a Cadillac to the freeway entrance.

A block from home, he could see his wife standing at the kerb, staring at him. He tried to slow down, as he had been trying, but it was no use. The car thundered along the residential street at a steady fifty-five and screeched to within three feet of the large woman, who yelped and jumped backwards.

'Abner! Have you gone crazy? Get out of that car this instant and come inside. I've got some talking to do with you.'

'Now what?' Mr Llewellyn sank down in the seat, looking about him for escape frantically. The voice was loud and arrogant.

Mr Llewellyn's wife opened her mouth. *'Well!'* she said at last, 'if you don't care what the neighbours think, then I'm sure I don't. It so happens that Mrs Purdy saw you with that awful girl from work.'

'Now, now, my dear –' Mr Llewellyn began, but his voice was submerged by the voice from the dashboard – or was it from the dashboard? 'You can tell Mrs Purdy to go take a flying leap –'

*'Ab*ner!'

Mr Llewellyn strained, tried to force his hand to the door, but he couldn't move. *Non Omnis* idled noisily.

'Abner, come into the house. Supper is ready.'

'Tough luck, Fatso. I got other plans.'

'I – I –'

'Maybe I'll get home tonight, maybe not – don't hold your breath.' The voice began to sing: 'Man, I'm all knocked out, I've got a fit, for a chick with a body that just won't quit!'

Mrs Llewellyn clutched at her heart. She reeled.

Mr Llewellyn could no longer move. His eyes bulged grotesquely. 'Stop it,' he hissed. 'Shut up. Keep quiet. Be still.'

'You come inside this very minute, do you hear, Abner?'

'Got *news* for you, baby: You've had it.'

'What are you talking about?'

'What am I talking about? Sugar, I mean I just don't dig your jazz no mo'.'

'Wh – What are you going to do?' the fat woman stammered, chins quivering.

'Have a ball, man,' the voice hollered. 'A B-A-double-L ball!

'Bye now.' With which Mr Llewellyn was off, leaving a cloud of rich black smoke.

The chuckling was insane.

Out of sight of the house, Mr Llewellyn fell back against the seat limply.

'I don't understand,' he said. 'I don't understand. *Non Omnis* – why are you doing this? Why haven't you ever talked before?'

'Never felt like it,' the voice answered.

'But – it's impossible. Good grief, can *all* cars talk?'

'Isn't that just a little ridiculous?'

Mr Llewellyn nodded. He glanced at his watch. It was six-fifteen.

A custom job, chopped and channelled, blown and stroked, passed by in a wild splutter of exhaust.

Mr Llewellyn stopped fighting it. He felt his foot come down hard on the accelerator.

Outside it was dark, still and dark, desolate. The beach wind was icicle-cold. The girl with the cinnamon skin sighed luxuriously as they came to a stop high in the hills. 'Mmmm' she sighed, stretching.

'Baby,' said the voice like Mr Llewellyn's, 'where have you been all of my life?'

'Around,' Miss Minifee said. Her off-the-shoulder angora sweater came down off the other shoulder. Mr Llewellyn studied the thin prominences of collar-bone and neck muscle.

'Have kicks tonight?'

'Plenty, I'll say,' she murmured.

'Then explain to me what you're doing all the way over there.'

'Mmm.' Miss Minifee had lost her puzzled look. She slid across the seat until her body touched Mr Llewellyn's own. He jumped.

'That's more like it.'

'Abner – you're so different,' she said. 'Where have *you* been all your life?'

Whereupon, for a reason he did not pause to analyse, Mr Llewellyn turned, put his arms about Miss Minifee and kissed her upon the lips. This caused a peculiar reaction from Miss Minifee, who was now saying 'Mmm' regularly.

Time passed.

At length they were on the road again.

Mr Llewellyn, too assailed by emotion to speak, barely heard the voice say: 'Gloria, you are the greatest!'

But he heard Miss Minifee's answer. 'Abner, I've always gone for you.'

'But what about Charley Doolittle?' Mr Llewellyn asked.

'Doolitle, schmoolittle, that square! I mean, it didn't look like I was getting no place with you, and a girl has got to have somebody . . . even second best . . .'

'Well, you're getting someplace with me now.'

'A lot of good! Here you're married and all – it's hopeless, I guess.'

'Nuts!' said the voice, loudly. 'Gloria – let's run away together!'

'Okay. Where to?'

'Zapotec, Azerzaijan – what's it matter? Get away from it all – live, sweetheart, live!'

'Gee,' Miss Minifee said, 'but that'll take dough, won't it?'

Mr Llewellyn felt his hand curl around the girl's shoulder and listened to his answer.

'Don't worry. I'll get the dough.'

The speedometer rose to seventy and the surf became a roar merged with the motor's roar, and Mr Llewellyn shivered.

'But,' he whispered hoarsely, 'that would be illegal!'

'So what? Listen, dad, it's almost morning now – check?'

Mr Llewellyn nodded. Almost morning: the latest he had ever stayed up. Why wouldn't *Non Omnis Moriar* even let him get out? They'd gone to a drive-in, he'd honked for Gloria from the kerb – he hadn't been out of the car for almost fifteen hours!

'So what could be simpler? You got a key. What's-his-name the guard you know. You walk in, say you forgot something, let him have it, open the vault, grab the dough – and, man! You're gone with the wind! Think of it: Gloria, money, a new life: no more banks, no more Charlottes – think about it.'

Mr Llewellyn thought about it. He shook his head. 'Absolutely not,' he said.

The car kept talking, wheedling, cajoling, yelling – then, the voice changed to a low Machiavellian tone. 'If,' it said, 'you don't – I'll drive us both off a cliff. How'd you like that?'

'All right. All right!'

They discussed it lengthily. Then, Mr Llewellyn found himself in front of the Corn Husker's Security Building.

'It's all up to you now, Jack. All up to you. Charlotte or Gloria. The life you've led or the one you *could* lead if you've got the guts. Make your choice.'

Mr Llewellyn trembled. He looked up and down the streets: no one afoot, at this hour. For the first time he summoned the power to open the door.

'Make it snappy,' the voice said. 'I'll leave my motor running.'

Run away, Mr Llewellyn thought. But something held him. His life passed in a grey parade across his mind. He went to the door, turned the key, closed the door again.

'Yes, sir?' the guard said.

'Correction in the tapes, Frank,' Mr Llewellyn said; he knew he would be believed, as the only combination teller entrusted with a key.

The guard smiled and started for the lights. Mr Llewellyn opened his jacket and removed the lug wrench.

The guard moaned softly and crumpled to the floor.

Mr Llewellyn moved to the inert body, found some keys, went to the vault. Two doors opened. A big steel one did not open. It had a combination lock. Mr Llewellyn remembered the numbers, tried them.

The door snapped open, and Mr Llewellyn proceeded to select from the safe numerous bundles of currency, for the most part crisp. A moment later, he closed and locked the steel door and hurried outside.

'Did you get it?' the car croaked.

'Shut up!' Mr Llewellyn barked. 'Just get going!'

He peeled rubber for several feet and then began to zigzag across town.

'Man,' the voice screamed, 'we're in! We're in!'

Mr Llewellyn pulled to a noisy stop in front of a small white-plaster house. He kicked the gear into neutral, dashed into the house and emerged some ten seconds afterwards with Miss Minifee in his arms.

'But –' Miss Minifee said. 'But –'

At sight of the money, however, a smile came to her face. She put her arms around Mr Llewellyn and kissed him, saying 'Oh! Oh!'

Mr Llewellyn dumped the nightgowned girl into *Non Omnis*, slammed the door and jumped into the driver's seat.

'Where'll it be?' he yelled above the engine's frenzy. 'Yucatan? Madrid? Palm Beach?'

Miss Minifee had just begun to clap her hands, when, quite suddenly, the air was torn by the treble whine of sirens. Tiny cycloped eyes winked redly in the rear-view mirror.

Grimly, Mr Llewellyn poured on the gas and cackled as he took a corner on no more than two wheels.

'Abner,' Miss Minifee wailed, 'have you done something wrong?'

'No,' he answered, cornering sharp and going into a flat-out slide.

Early morning houses whipped by like a film run too fast. But manoeuvre as he might, Mr Llewellyn could not be rid of the frenetic red eyes, nor could he expunge the nightmare sound of sirens, more sirens now.

'Hang on, baby!' he called and pointed them up the slender ribbon of road which led through the hills to the valley on the other side.

Miss Minifee hung on.

'Don't worry, Abner,' someone other than Miss Minifee chortled, 'we'll shake 'em!'

The hairpin turns were accomplished by dint of a skill edging on genius. As he climbed, happy now the night behind was only dawn-darkness, Mr Llewellyn invariably headed for the cliff-sides, for the emptiness of space and the dizzying drops, only to brake, slide and whip around at the last possible instant.

Finally they hit a straightaway. Miss Minifee had fainted: her Italian-boy-haircutted head lolled on its shoulders with a dreamy motion. Her chestnut skin seemed to have blanched.

Mr Llewellyn patted the girl's behind in a gesture of profound understanding and camaraderie. Soon the red eyes were back again and gaining, always gaining.

At the second entrance to the cliffs, the first shot was fired. He could not hear it, but he saw the white puff.

'YAHH, missed!' Mr Llewellyn screeched, attempting to push the accelerator pedal clear through the floorboard.

More shots. 'Close!' someone whispered.

And more. They were buzzing like hornets and from time to time, Mr Llewellyn could feel the leaden plosh of a hit.

He smiled fiercely, even when the tyre exploded, didn't stop smiling for a moment as *Non Omnis* went into a spin.

Just before they went over the side, he managed to get the door opened. A mighty lunge threw Miss Minifee to safety on the green and gentle sward.

The tyres clung an infinite second: as they were suspended there on the brink, Mr Llewellyn smiled, if anything, more brightly than before.

Then they went over. Over and over. Around and around. And *Non Omnis* cried with pain every time a new boulder was struck.

Many hundreds of feet below, Mr Llewellyn tried to move and found he could not. Metal enveloped him like the bandages of a mummy. He was able to get one hand free.

With this hand he stroked the twisted remains of a wooden steering wheel – tenderly, gently, softly.

'Non Omnis – Non Omnis –'

'Moriar,' the car said; and, with a last metallic rattle, died.

Mr Llewellyn saw the little specks of light descending the abyss. Then there were more specks until his mind was a microscope under which coruscated a million disks of light. Getting dimmer, getting dimmer . . .

He rubbed the pitted plaster wall. White. All so white. And clean and sterile –

And he kept thinking – he had not stopped saying it to himself –: *I am insane. Buggy, mad as a March Hare* . . .

Schizophrenia was the word they used.

'Of course your car talked you into it, Mr Llewellyn, of course it did. Nothing unusual in that. Now everything's all right. We've put your car in another room and as soon as it's able to get around, why, we'll have it visit you. And won't that be nice?'

Normal matter, they said. Actually harmless case. Repressed personality builds ideal other self: ideal other self is embodiment of all repressed personality's frustrations transfigured into complete antithesis . . .

And I'm a looney.

Mr Llewellyn sat on the bed. Then he arose, for this always made him think of the girl with the inviting smile who would have gone far away with him, who would go yet, even now, he was sure, sure of it.

He stared out the window gloomily at the grotesquely pleasant rolls of lawn and beyond, the high white wall.

If only there were some way to get out – some way – He would be more careful. He wouldn't let them catch him.

Then he looked at the solemn gates of the wall. 'Bars!' he

murmured. 'Always, bars. And I'll never get out. Never.'

There was suddenly the sound of splintering pottery. A vase had fallen to the floor and crashed into hundreds of pieces, sharp pieces, sharp enough to cut flesh.

'Want to take bets?' the vase said, softly.

DUEL

Richard Matheson

Although Stephen King's novel 'Christine' may be the most recent book about a car to be turned into a movie, for my money it is neither the best nor the most famous. That honour belongs to the film based on this next story, which was filmed in 1970 and was directed by a young man now accepted as the most successful film maker of the century, Stephen Spielberg. Quite simply, 'Duel' is the most terrifying and engrossing picture ever made about motor vehicles as well as being one of the finest of all macabre films.

Richard Matheson (1926–   ) is one of Hollywood's leading scriptwriters of horror pictures, and apart from adapting a number of Edgar Allan Poe stories for the screen, has also re-worked several of his own books for the cinema including two classics, I Am Legend *(1954) about a world full of vampires, and* The Incredible Shrinking Man *(1956). Mr Matheson has explained how he came to create 'Duel': 'I was playing golf with another fantasy writer Jerry Sohl on the day that President Kennedy was assassinated. We broke off our game and headed for home. As we were driving, muttering and moaning about the assassination, a truck started tailgating us on the narrow pass we were driving through. This went on for miles and miles with us screaming infuriatedly, until we finally pulled over to the side of the road and let the son of a bitch pass us. While we were stopped, I wrote the idea for "Duel" down on the back of an envelope that Jerry had in his car.' Later, the story was published in* Playboy *magazine, and from there picked up by Universal Pictures who cast Dennis Weaver as the hounded driver and gave the directing job to the young Spielberg. The rest is history. Curiously, though, despite the fame of the film, this marks the first publication of the story in an anthology – a fact which delights me and will, I am sure, now chill you to the very marrow . . .*

At 11.32 a.m., Mann passed the truck.

He was heading west, en route to San Francisco. It was Thursday and unseasonably hot for April. He had his suit coat off, his tie removed and shirt collar opened, his sleeve cuffs folded back. There was sunlight on his left arm and on part of his lap. He could feel the heat of it through his dark trousers as he drove along the two-lane highway. For the past 20 minutes, he had not seen another vehicle going in either direction.

Then he saw the truck ahead, moving up a curving grade between two high green hills. He heard the grinding strain of its motor and saw a double shadow on the road. The truck was pulling a trailer.

He paid no attention to the details of the truck. As he drew behind it on the grade, he edged his car towards the opposite lane. The road ahead had blind curves and he didn't try to pass until the truck had crossed the ridge. He waited until it started around a left curve on the downgrade, then, seeing that the way was clear, pressed down on the accelerator pedal and steered his car into the eastbound lane. He waited until he could see the truck front in his rearview mirror before he turned back into the proper lane.

Mann looked across the countryside ahead. There were ranges of mountains as far as he could see and, all around him, rolling green hills. He whistled softly as the car sped down the winding grade, its tyres making crisp sounds on the pavement.

At the bottom of the hill, he crossed a concrete bridge and, glancing to the right, saw a dry stream bed strewn with rocks and gravel. As the car moved off the bridge, he saw a trailer park set back from the highway to his right. How can anyone live out here? he thought. His shifting gaze caught sight of a pet cemetery ahead and he smiled. Maybe those people in the trailers wanted to be close to the graves of their dogs and cats.

The highway ahead was straight now. Mann drifted into a reverie, the sunlight on his arm and lap. He wondered what Ruth was doing. The kids, of course, were in school and would be for hours yet. Maybe Ruth was shopping; Thursday was the day she usually went. Mann visualised her in the supermarket, putting various items into the basket cart. He wished he were with her instead of starting on another sales trip. Hours of driving yet before he'd reach San Francisco. Three days of hotel sleeping and restaurant eating, hoped-for contacts and likely disappointments. He sighed; then, reaching out impulsively, he switched on the radio. He revolved the tuning knob until he found a station playing soft, innocuous music. He hummed along with it, eyes almost out of focus on the road ahead.

He started as the truck roared past him on the left, causing his car to shudder slightly. He watched the truck and trailer cut in abruptly for the westbound lane and frowned as he had to brake to maintain a safe distance behind it. What's with you? he thought. He eyed the truck with cursory disapproval. It was a huge gasoline tanker pulling a tank trailer, each of them having six pairs of wheels. He could see that it was not a new rig but was dented and in need of renovation, its tanks painted a cheap-looking silvery colour. Mann wondered if the driver had done the painting himself. His gaze shifted from the word FLAMMABLE printed across the back of the trailer tank, red letters on a white background, to the parallel reflector lines painted in red across the bottom of the tank to the massive rubber flaps swaying behind the rear tyres, then back up again. The reflector lines looked as though they'd been clumsily applied with a stencil. The driver must be an independent trucker, he decided, and not too affluent a one, from the looks of his outfit. He glanced at the trailer's licence plate. It was a California issue.

Mann checked his speedometer. He was holding steady at 55 miles an hour, as he invariably did when he drove without thinking on the open highway. The truck driver must have done a good 70 to pass him so quickly. That seemed a little odd. Weren't truck drivers supposed to be a cautious lot?

He grimaced at the smell of the truck's exhaust and looked at the vertical pipe to the left of the cab. It was spewing smoke, which clouded darkly back across the trailer. Christ, he thought. With all the furor about air pollution, why do they keep allowing that sort of thing on the highways?

He scowled at the constant fumes. They'd make him nauseated in a little while, he knew. He couldn't lag back here like this. Either he slowed down or he passed the truck again. He didn't have the time to slow down. He'd gotten a late start. Keeping it at 55 all the way, he'd just about make his afternoon appointment. No, he'd have to pass.

Depressing the gas pedal, he eased his car towards the opposite lane. No sign of anything ahead. Traffic on this route seemed almost nonexistent today. He pushed down harder on the accelerator and steered all the way into the eastbound lane.

As he passed the truck, he glanced at it. The cab was too high for him to see into. All he caught sight of was the back of the truck driver's left hand on the steering wheel. It was darkly tanned and square-looking, with large veins knotted on its surface.

When Mann could see the truck reflected in the rearview mirror, he pulled back over to the proper lane and looked ahead again.

He glanced at the rearview mirror in surprise as the truck driver gave him an extended horn blast. What was that? he wondered; a greeting or a curse? He grunted with amusement, glancing at the mirror as he drove. The front fenders of the truck were a dingy purple colour, the paint faded and chipped; another amateurish job. All he could see was the lower portion of the truck; the rest was cut off by the top of his rear window.

To Mann's right, now, was a slope of shalelike earth with patches of scrub grass growing on it. His gaze jumped to the clapboard house on top of the slope. The television aerial on its roof was sagging at an angle of less than 40 degrees. Must give great reception, he thought.

He looked to the front again, glancing aside abruptly at a sign printed in jagged block letters on a piece of plywood: NIGHT CRAWLERS – BAIT. What the hell is a night crawler? he wondered. It sounded like some monster in a low-grade Hollywood thriller.

The unexpected roar of the truck motor made his gaze jump to the rearview mirror. Instantly, his startled look jumped to the side mirror. By God, the guy was passing him *again*. Mann turned his head to scowl at the leviathan form as it drifted by. He tried to see into the cab but couldn't because of its height. What's with him, anyway? he wondered. What the hell are we having here, a contest? See which vehicle can stay ahead the longer?

He thought of speeding up to stay ahead but changed his mind. When the truck and trailer started back into the westbound lane, he let up on the pedal, voicing a newly incredulous sound as he saw that if he hadn't slowed down, he would have been prematurely cut off again. Jesus Christ, he thought. What's *with* this guy?

His scowl deepened as the odour of the truck's exhaust reached his nostrils again. Irritably, he cranked up the window on his left. Damn it, was he going to have to breathe that crap all the way to San Francisco? He couldn't afford to slow down. He had to meet Forbes at a quarter after three and that was that.

He looked ahead. At least there was no traffic complicating matters. Mann pressed down on the accelerator pedal, drawing close behind the truck. When the highway curved enough to the left to give him a completely open view of the route ahead, he jarred down on the pedal, steering out into the opposite lane.

The truck edged over, blocking his way.

For several moments, all Mann could do was stare at it in blank confusion. Then, with a startled noise, he braked, returning to the proper lane. The truck moved back in front of him.

Mann could not allow himself to accept what apparently had taken place. It had to be a coincidence. The truck driver couldn't have blocked his way on purpose. He waited for more than a minute, then flicked down the turn-indicator lever to make his intentions perfectly clear and, depressing the accelerator pedal, steered again into the eastbound lane.

Immediately, the truck shifted, barring his way.

'Jesus Christ!' Mann was astounded. This was unbelievable. He'd never seen such a thing in 26 years of driving. He returned to the westbound lane, shaking his head as the truck swung back in front of him.

He eased up on the gas pedal, falling back to avoid the truck's exhaust. Now what? he wondered. He still had to make San Francisco on schedule. Why in God's name hadn't he gone a little out of his way in the beginning, so he could have travelled by freeway? This damned highway was two lane all the way.

Impulsively, he sped into the eastbound lane again. To his surprise, the truck driver did not pull over. Instead, the driver stuck his left arm out and waved him on. Mann started pushing down on the accelerator. Suddenly, he let up on the pedal with a gasp and jerked the steering wheel around, raking back behind the truck so quickly that his car began to fishtail. He was fighting to control its zigzag whipping when a blue convertible shot by him in the opposite lane. Mann caught a momentary vision of the man inside it glaring at him.

The car came under his control again. Mann was sucking breath in through his mouth. His heart was pounding almost painfully. My God! he thought. *He wanted me to hit that car head on*. The realisation stunned him. True, he should have seen to it himself that the road ahead was clear; that was his failure. But to wave him on . . . Mann felt appalled and sickened. Boy, oh, boy, oh, boy, he thought. This was really one for the books. That son of a bitch had meant for not only him to be killed but a totally uninvolved passer-by as well. The idea seemed beyond his comprehension. On a California highway on a Thursday morning? *Why?*

Mann tried to calm himself and rationalise the incident. Maybe it's the heat, he thought. Maybe the truck driver had a tension headache or an upset stomach; maybe both. Maybe he'd had a fight with his wife. Maybe she'd failed to put out last night. Mann tried in vain to smile. There could be any number of reasons. Reaching out, he twisted off the radio. The cheerful music irritated him.

He drove behind the truck for several minutes, his face a mask of animosity. As the exhaust fumes started putting his stomach on edge, he suddenly forced down the heel of his right hand on the horn bar and held it there. Seeing that the route ahead was clear, he pushed in the accelerator pedal all the way and steered into the opposite lane.

The movement of his car was paralleled immediately by the truck. Mann stayed in place, right hand jammed down on the horn bar. Get out of the way, you son of a bitch! he thought. He felt the muscles of his jaw hardening until they ached. There was a twisting in his stomach.

'*Damn!*' He pulled back quickly to the proper lane, shuddering with fury. 'You miserable son of a bitch,' he muttered, glaring at the truck as it was shifted back in front of him. What the hell is wrong with you? I pass your goddamn rig a couple of times and you go flying off the deep end? Are you nuts or something? Mann nodded tensely. Yes, he thought; he *is*. No other explanation.

He wondered what Ruth would think of all this, how she'd react. Probably, she'd start to honk the horn and would keep on honking it, assuming that, eventually, it would attract the attention of a policeman. He looked around with a scowl. Just where in hell *were* the policemen out here, anyway? He made a scoffing noise. What policemen? Here in the boondocks? They probably had a sheriff on horseback, for Christ's sake.

He wondered suddenly if he could fool the truck driver by passing on the right. Edging his car towards the shoulder, he peered ahead. No chance. There wasn't room enough. The truck driver could shove him through that wire fence if he wanted to. Mann shivered. And he'd want to, sure as hell, he thought.

Driving where he was, he grew conscious of the debris lying beside the highway: beer cans, candy wrappers, icecream containers, newspaper sections browned and rotted by the weather, a FOR SALE sign torn in half. Keep America beautiful, he thought sardonically. He passed a boulder with the name WILL JASPER painted on it in white. Who the hell is Will Jasper? he wondered. What would he think of this situation?

Unexpectedly, the car began to bounce. For several anxious moments, Mann thought that one of his tyres had gone flat. Then he noticed that the paving along this section of highway consisted of pitted slabs with gaps between them. He saw the truck and trailer jolting up and down and thought: I hope it shakes your brains loose. As the truck veered into a sharp left curve, he caught a fleeting glimpse of the driver's face in the cab's side mirror. There was not enough time to establish his appearance.

'Ah,' he said. A long, steep hill was looming up ahead. The truck would have to climb it slowly. There would doubtless be an opportunity to pass somewhere on the grade. Mann pressed down on the accelerator pedal, drawing as close behind the truck as safety would allow.

Halfway up the slope, Mann saw a turnout for the eastbound lane with no oncoming traffic anywhere in sight. Flooring the accelerator pedal, he shot into the opposite lane. The slow-moving truck began to angle out in front of him. Face stiffening, Mann steered his speeding car across the highway edge and curved it sharply on the turnout. Clouds of dust went billowing up behind his car, making him lose sight of the truck. His tyres buzzed and crackled on the dirt, then, suddenly, were humming on the pavement once again.

He glanced at the rearview mirror and a barking laugh erupted from his throat. He'd only meant to pass. The dust had been an unexpected bonus. Let the bastard get a sniff of something rotten smelling in *his* nose for a change! he thought. He honked the horn elatedly, a mocking rhythm of bleats. Screw you, Jack!

He swept across the summit of the hill. A striking vista lay ahead: sunlit hills and flatland, a corridor of dark trees, quadrangles of cleared-off acreage and bright-green vegetable patches; far off, in the distance, a mammoth water tower. Mann felt stirred by the panoramic sight. Lovely, he thought. Reaching out, he turned the radio back on and started humming cheerfully with the music.

Seven minutes later, he passed a billboard advertising CHUCK'S CAFÉ. No thanks, Chuck, he thought. He glanced at a grey house nestled in a hollow. Was that a cemetery in its front yard or a group of plaster statuary for sale?

Hearing the noise behind him, Mann looked at the rearview mirror and felt himself go cold with fear. The truck was hurtling down the hill, pursuing him.

His mouth fell open and he threw a glance at the speedometer. He was doing more than 60! On a curving downgrade, that was not at all a safe speed to be driving. Yet the truck must be exceeding that by a considerable margin, it was closing the distance between them so rapidly. Mann swallowed, leaning to the right as he steered his car around a sharp curve. Is the man *insane*? he thought.

His gaze jumped forward searchingly. He saw a turnoff half a mile ahead and decided that he'd use it. In the rearview mirror, the huge square radiator grille was all he could see now. He stamped down on the gas pedal and his tyres screeched unnervingly as he wheeled around another curve, thinking that, surely, the truck would have to slow down here.

He groaned as it rounded the curve with ease, only the sway of its tanks revealing the outward pressure of the turn. Mann bit trembling lips together as he whipped his car around another curve. A straight descent now. He depressed the pedal farther, glanced at the speedometer. Almost 70 miles an hour! He wasn't used to driving this fast!

In agony, he saw the turnoff shoot by on his right. He couldn't have left the highway at this speed, anyway; he'd have overturned. Goddamn it, what was wrong with that son of a bitch? Mann honked his horn in frightened rage. Cranking down the window suddenly, he shoved his left arm out to wave the truck back. '*Back!*' he yelled. He honked the horn again. 'Get back, you crazy bastard!'

The truck was almost on him now. He's going to kill me! Mann thought, horrified. He honked the horn repeatedly, then had to use both hands to grip the steering wheel as he swept around another curve. He flashed a look at the rearview mirror. He could see only the bottom portion of the truck's radiator grille. He was going to lose control! He felt the rear wheels start to drift and let up on the pedal quickly. The tyre treads bit in, the car leaped on, regaining its momentum.

Mann saw the bottom of the grade ahead, and in the distance there was a building with a sign that read CHUCK'S CAFÉ. The truck was gaining ground again. This is insane! he thought, enraged and terrified at once. The highway straightened out. He floored the pedal: 74 now – 75. Mann braced himself, trying to ease the car as far to the right as possible.

Abruptly, he began to brake, then swerved to the right, raking his car into the open area in front of the café. He cried out as the car began to fishtail, then careered into a skid. *Steer with it!* screamed a voice in his mind. The rear of the car was lashing from side to side, tyres spewing dirt and raising clouds of dust. Mann pressed harder on the brake pedal, turning further into the skid. The car began to straighten out and he braked harder yet, conscious on the sides of his vision, of the truck and trailer roaring by on the highway. He nearly sideswiped one of the cars parked in front of the café, bounced and skidded by it, going almost straight now. He jammed in the brake pedal as hard as he could. The rear end broke to the right and the car spun half around, sheering sideways to a neck-wrenching halt 30 yards beyond the café.

Mann sat in pulsing silence, eyes closed. His heartbeats felt like club blows in his chest. He couldn't seem to catch his breath. If he were ever going to have a heart attack, it would be now. After a while, he opened his eyes and pressed his right palm against his chest. His heart was still throbbing labouredly. No wonder, he thought. It isn't every day I'm almost murdered by a truck.

He raised the handle and pushed out the door, then started forward, grunting in surprise as the safety belt held him in place. Reaching down with shaking fingers, he depressed the release button and pulled the ends of the belt apart. He glanced at the café. What had its patrons thought of his breakneck appearance? he wondered.

He stumbled as he walked to the front door of the café. TRUCKERS WELCOME, read a sign in the window. It gave Mann a queasy feeling to see it. Shivering, he pulled open the door and went inside, avoiding the sight of its customers. He felt certain they were watching him, but he didn't have the strength to face their looks. Keeping his gaze fixed straight ahead, he moved to the rear of the café and opened the door marked GENTS.

Moving to the sink, he twisted the right-hand faucet and leaned over to cup cold water in his palms and splash it on his face. There was a fluttering of his stomach muscles he could not control.

Straightening up, he tugged down several towels from their dispenser and patted them against his face, grimacing at the smell of the paper. Dropping the soggy towels into a wastebasket beside the sink, he regarded himself in the wall mirror. Still with us, Mann, he thought. He nodded, swallowing. Drawing out his metal comb, he neatened his hair. You never know, he thought. You just never know. You drift along, year after year, presuming certain values to be fixed; like being able to drive on a public thoroughfare without somebody trying to murder you. You come to depend on that sort of thing. Then something occurs and all bets are off. One shocking incident and all the years of logic and acceptance are displaced and, suddenly, the jungle is in front of you again. *Man, part animal, part angel*. Where had he come across that phrase? He shivered.

It was entirely an animal in that truck out there.

His breath was almost back to normal now. Mann forced a smile at his reflection. All right, boy, he told himself. It's over now. It was a goddamned nightmare, but it's over. You are on your way to San Francisco. You'll get yourself a nice hotel room, order a bottle of expensive Scotch, soak your body in a hot bath and forget. Damn right, he thought. He turned and walked out of the washroom.

He jolted to a halt, his breath cut off. Standing rooted, heartbeat hammering at his chest, he gaped through the front window of the café.

The truck and trailer were parked outside.

Mann stared at them in unbelieving shock. It wasn't possible. He'd seen them roaring by at top speed. The driver had won; he'd *won*! He'd had the whole damn highway to himself! *Why had he turned back?*

Mann looked around with sudden dread. There were five men eating, three along the counter, two in booths. He cursed himself for having failed to look at faces when he'd entered. Now there was no way of knowing who it was. Mann felt his legs begin to shake.

Abruptly, he walked to the nearest booth and slid in clumsily behind the table. Now wait, he told himself; just wait. Surely, he could tell which one it was. Masking his face with the menu, he glanced across its top. Was it that one in the khaki work shirt? Mann tried to see the man's hands but couldn't. His gaze flicked nervously across the room. Not that one in the suit, of course. Three remaining. That one in the front booth, square-faced, black-haired? If only he could see the man's hands, it might help. One of the two others at the counter? Mann studied them uneasily. Why hadn't he looked at faces when he'd come in?

Now *wait*, he thought. Goddamn it, *wait*! All right, the truck driver was in here. That didn't automatically signify that he meant to continue the insane duel. Chuck's Café might be the only place to eat for miles around. It *was* lunchtime, wasn't it? The truck driver had probably intended to eat here all the time. He'd just been moving too fast to pull into the parking lot before. So he'd slowed down, turned around and driven back, that was all. Mann forced himself to read the menu. Right, he thought. No point in getting so rattled. Perhaps a beer would help relax him.

The woman behind the counter came over and Mann ordered a ham sandwich on rye toast and a bottle of Coors. As the woman turned away, he wondered, with a sudden twinge of self-reproach, why he hadn't simply left the café, jumped into his car and sped away. He would have known immediately, then, if the truck driver was still out to get him. As it was, he'd have to suffer through an entire meal to find out. He almost groaned at his stupidity.

Still, what if the truck driver *had* followed him out and started after him again? He'd have been right back where he'd started. Even if he'd managed to get a good lead, the truck driver would have overtaken him eventually. It just wasn't in him to drive at 80 and 90 miles an hour in order to stay ahead. True, he might have been intercepted by a California Highway Patrol car. What if he weren't, though?

Mann repressed the plaguing thoughts. He tried to calm himself. He looked deliberately at the four men. Either of two seemed a likely possibility as the driver of the truck: the square-faced one in the front booth and the chunky one in the jump suit sitting at the counter. Mann had an impulse to walk over to them and ask which one it was, tell the man he was sorry he'd irritated him, tell him anything to calm him, since, obviously, he wasn't rational, was a manic-depressive, probably. Maybe buy the man a beer and sit with him awhile to try to settle things.

He couldn't move. What if the truck driver were letting the whole thing drop? Mightn't his approach rile the man all over again? Mann felt drained by indecision. He nodded weakly as the waitress set the sandwich and the bottle in front of him. He took a swallow of the beer, which made him cough. Was the truck driver amused by the sound? Mann felt a stirring of resentment deep inside himself. What right did that bastard have to impose this torment on another human being? It was a free country, wasn't it? Damn it, he had every right to pass the son of a bitch on a highway if he wanted to!

'Oh, hell,' he mumbled. He tried to feel amused. He was making entirely too much of this. Wasn't he? He glanced at the pay telephone on the front wall. What was to prevent him from calling the local police and telling them the situation? But, then, he'd have to stay here, lose time, make Forbes angry, probably lose the sale. And what if the truck driver stayed to face them? Naturally, he'd deny the whole thing. What if the police believed him and didn't do anything about it? After they'd gone, the truck driver would undoubtedly take it out on him again, only worse, *God!* Mann thought in agony.

The sandwich tasted flat, the beer unpleasantly sour. Mann stared at the table as he ate. For God's sake, why was he just *sitting* here like this? He was a grown man, wasn't he? Why didn't he settle this damn thing once and for all?

His left hand twitched so unexpectedly, he spilled beer on his trousers. The man in the jump suit had risen from the counter and was strolling towards the front of the café. Mann felt his heartbeat thumping as the man gave money to the waitress, took his change and a toothpick from the dispenser and went outside. Mann watched in anxious silence.

The man did not get into the cab of the tanker truck.

It had to be the one in the front booth, then. His face took form in Mann's remembrance: square, with dark eyes, dark hair; the man who'd tried to kill him.

Mann stood abruptly, letting impulse conquer fear. Eyes fixed ahead, he started towards the entrace. Anything was preferable to sitting in that booth. He stopped by the cash register, conscious of the hitching of his chest as he gulped in air. Was the man observing him? he wondered. He swallowed, pulling out the clip of dollar bills in his right-hand trouser pocket. He glanced towards the waitress. Come *on*, he thought. He looked at his check and, seeing the amount, reached shakily into his trouser pocket for change. He heard a coin fall onto the floor and roll away. Ignoring it, he dropped a dollar and a quarter onto the counter and thrust the clip of bills into his trouser pocket.

As he did, he heard the man in the front booth get up. An icy shudder spasmed up his neck. Turning quickly to the door, he shoved it open, seeing, on the edges of his vision, the square-faced man approach the cash register. Lurching from the café, he started towards his car with long strides. His mouth was dry again. The pounding of his heart was painful in his chest.

Suddenly, he started running. He heard the café door bang shut and fought away the urge to look across his shoulder. Was that a sound of other running footsteps now? Reaching his car, Mann yanked open the door and jarred in awkwardly behind the steering wheel. He reached into his trouser pocket for the keys and snatched them out, almost dropping them. His hand was shaking so badly he couldn't get the ignition key into its slot. He whined with mounting dread. Come on! he thought.

The key slid in, he twisted it convulsively. The motor started and he raced it momentarily before jerking the transmission shift to drive. Depressing the accelerator pedal quickly, he raked the car around and steered it towards the highway. From the corners of his eyes, he saw the truck and trailer being backed away from the café.

Reaction burst inside him. 'No!' he raged and slammed his foot down on the brake pedal. This was idiotic! Why the hell should he run away? His car slid sideways to a rocking halt and, shouldering out the door, he lurched to his feet and started towards the truck with angry strides. *All right, Jack*, he thought. He glared at the man inside the truck. You want to punch my nose, OK, but no more goddamn tournament on the highway.

The truck began to pick up speed. Mann raised his right arm. 'Hey!' he yelled. He knew the driver saw him. '*Hey!*' He started running as the truck kept moving, engine grinding loudly. It was on the highway now. He sprinted towards it with a sense of martyred outrage. The driver shifted gears, the truck moved faster. 'Stop!' Mann shouted. 'Damn it, *stop*!'

He thudded to a panting halt, staring at the truck as it receded down the highway, moved around a hill and disappeared. 'You son of a bitch,' he muttered. 'You goddamn, miserable son of a bitch.'

He trudged back slowly to his car, trying to believe that the truck driver had fled the hazard of a fistfight. It was possible, of course, but, somehow, he could not believe it.

He got into his car and was about to drive onto the highway when he changed his mind and switched the motor off. That crazy bastard might just be tooling along at 15 miles an hour, waiting for him to catch up. Nuts to that, he thought. So he blew his schedule; screw it. Forbes would have to wait, that was all. And if Forbes didn't care to wait, that was all right, too. He'd sit here for a while and let the nut get out of range, let him think he'd won the day. He grinned. You're the bloody Red Baron, Jack; you've shot me down. Now go to hell with my sincerest compliments. He shook his head. Beyond belief, he thought.

He really should have done this earlier, pulled over, waited. Then the truck driver would have had to let it pass. *Or picked on someone else*, the startling thought occurred to him. Jesus, maybe that was how the crazy bastard whiled away his work hours! Jesus Christ Almighty! was it possible?

He looked at the dashboard clock. It was just past 12.30. Wow, he thought. All that in less than an hour. He shifted on the seat and stretched his legs out. Leaning back against the door, he closed his eyes and mentally perused the things he had to do tomorrow and the following day. Today was shot to hell, as far as he could see.

When he opened his eyes, afraid of drifting into sleep and losing too much time, almost 11 minutes had passed. The nut must be an ample distance off by now, he thought: at least 11 miles and likely more, the way he drove. Good enough. He wasn't going to try to make San Francisco on schedule now, anyway. He'd take it real easy.

Mann adjusted his safety belt, switched on the motor, tapped the transmission pointer into drive position and pulled onto the highway, glancing back across his shoulder. Not a car in sight. Great day for driving. Everybody was staying at home. That nut must have a reputation around here. When Crazy Jack is on the highway, lock your car in the garage. Mann chuckled at the notion as his car began to turn the curve ahead.

Mindless reflex drove his right foot down against the brake pedal. Suddenly, his car had skidded to a halt and he was staring down the highway. The truck and trailer were parked on the shoulder less than 90 yards away.

Mann couldn't seem to function. He knew his car was blocking the westbound lane, knew that he should either make a U-turn or pull off the highway, but all he could do was gape at the truck.

He cried out, legs retracting, as a horn blast sounded behind him. Snapping up his head, he looked at the rearview mirror, gasping as he saw a yellow station wagon bearing down on him at high speed. Suddenly, it veered off towards the eastbound lane, disappearing from the mirror. Mann jerked around and saw it hurtling past his car, its rear end snapping back and forth, its back tyres screeching. He saw the twisted features of the man inside, saw his lips move rapidly with cursing.

Then the station wagon had swerved back into the westbound lane and was speeding off. It gave Mann an odd sensation to see it pass the truck. The man in that station wagon could drive on, unthreatened. Only he had been singled out. What happened was demented. Yet it was happening.

He drove his car onto the highway shoulder and braked. Putting the transmission into neutral, he leaned back, staring at the truck. His head was aching again. There was a pulsing at his temples like the ticking of a muffled clock.

What was he to do? He knew very well that if he left his car to walk to the truck, the driver would pull away and repark farther down the highway. He may as well face the fact that he was dealing with a madman. He felt the tremor in his stomach muscles starting up again. His heartbeat thudded slowly, striking at his chest wall. Now what?

With a sudden, angry impulse, Mann snapped the transmission into gear and stepped down hard on the accelerator pedal. The tyres of the car spun sizzlingly before they gripped; the car shot out onto the highway. Instantly, the truck began to move. He even had the motor on! Mann thought in raging fear. He floored the pedal, then, abruptly, realised he couldn't make it, that the truck would block his way and he'd collide with its trailer. A vision flashed across his mind, a fiery explosion and a sheet of flame incinerating him. He started braking fast, trying to decelerate evenly, so he wouldn't lose control.

When he'd slowed down enough to feel that it was safe, he steered the car onto the shoulder and stopped it again, throwing the transmission into neutral.

Approximately 80 yards ahead, the truck pulled off the highway and stopped.

Mann tapped his fingers on the steering wheel. *Now* what? he thought. Turn around and head east until he reached a cutoff that would take him to San Francisco by another route? How did he know the truck driver wouldn't follow him even then? His cheeks twitched as he bit his lips together angrily. No! He wasn't going to turn around!

His expression hardened suddenly. Well, he wasn't going to *sit* here all day, that was certain. Reaching out, he tapped the gearshift into drive and steered his car onto the highway once again. He saw the massive truck and trailer start to move but made no effort to speed up. He tapped at the brakes, taking a position about 30 yards behind the trailer. He glanced at his speedometer. Forty miles an hour. The truck driver had his left arm out the cab window and was waving him on. What did that mean? Had he changed his mind? Decided, finally, that this thing had gone too far? Mann couldn't let himself believe it.

He looked ahead. Despite the mountain ranges all around, the highway was flat as far as he could see. He tapped a fingernail against the horn bar, trying to make up his mind. Presumably, he could continue all the way to San Francisco at this speed, hanging back just far enough to avoid the worst of the exhaust fumes. It didn't seem likely that the truck driver would stop directly on the highway to block his way. And if the truck driver pulled onto the shoulder to let him pass, he could pull off the highway, too, It would be a draining afternoon but a safe one.

On the other hand, outracing the truck might be worth just one more try. This was obviously what that son of a bitch wanted. Yet, surely, a vehicle of such size couldn't be driven with the same daring as, potentially, his own. The laws of mechanics were against it, if nothing else. Whatever advantage the truck had in mass, it had to lose in stability, particularly that of its trailer. If Mann were to drive at, say, 80 miles an hour and there were a few steep grades – as he felt sure there were – the truck would have to fall behind.

The question was, of course, whether he had the nerve to maintain such a speed over a long distance. He'd never done it before. Still, the more he thought about it, the more it appealed to him; far more than the alternative did.

Abruptly, he decided. *Right,* he thought. He checked ahead, then pressed down hard on the accelerator pedal and pulled into the eastbound lane. As he neared the truck, he tensed, anticipating that the driver might block his way. But the truck did not shift from the westbound lane. Mann's car moved along its mammoth side. He glanced at the cab and saw the name KELLER printed on its door. For a shocking instant, he thought it read KILLER and started to slow down. Then, glancing at the name again, he saw what it really was and depressed the pedal sharply. When he saw the truck reflected in the rearview mirror, he steered his car into the westbound lane.

He shuddered, dread and satisfaction mixed together, as he saw that the truck driver was speeding up. It was strangely comforting to know the man's intentions definitely again. That plus the knowledge of his face and name seemed, somehow, to reduce his stature. Before, he had been faceless, nameless, an embodiment of unknown terror. Now, at least, he was an individual. All right, Keller, said his mind, let's see you beat me with that purple-silver relic now. He pressed down harder on the pedal. *Here we go,* he thought.

He looked at the speedometer, scowling as he saw that he was doing only 74 miles an hour. Deliberately, he pressed down on the pedal, alternating his gaze between the highway ahead and the speedometer until the needle turned past 80. He felt a flickering of satisfaction with himself. All right, Keller, you son of a bitch, top that, he thought.

After several moments, he glanced into the rearview mirror again. Was the truck getting closer? Stunned, he checked the speedometer. Damn it! He was down to 76! He forced in the accelerator pedal angrily. *He mustn't go less than 80!* Mann's chest shuddered with convulsive breath.

He glanced aside as he hurtled past a beige sedan parked on the shoulder underneath a tree. A young couple sat inside it, talking. Already they were far behind, their world removed from his. Had they even glanced aside when he'd passed? He doubted it.

He started as the shadow of an overhead bridge whipped across the hood and windshield. Inhaling raggedly, he glanced at the speedometer again. He was holding at 81. He checked the rearview mirror. Was it his imagination that the truck was gaining ground? He looked forward with anxious eyes. There had to be some kind of town ahead. To hell with time; he'd stop at the police station and tell them what had happened. They'd have to believe him. Why would he stop to tell them such a story if it weren't true? For all he knew, Keller had a police record in these parts. *Oh, sure, we're on to him,* he heard a faceless officer remark. *That crazy bastard's asked for it before and now he's going to get it.*

Mann shook himself and looked at the mirror. The truck *was* getting closer. Wincing, he glanced at the speedometer. God-damn it, pay attention! raged his mind. He was down to 74 again! Whining with frustration, he depressed the pedal. Eighty! – 80! he demanded of himself. There was a murderer behind him!

His car began to pass a field of flowers; lilacs, Mann saw, white and purple, stretching out in endless rows. There was a small shack near the highway, the words FIELD FRESH FLOWERS painted on it. A brown-cardboard square was propped against the shack, the word FUNERALS printed crudely on it. Mann saw himself, abruptly, lying in a casket, painted like some grotesque mannequin. The overpowering smell of flowers seemed to fill his nostrils. Ruth and the children sitting in the first row, heads bowed. All his relatives ——

Suddenly, the pavement roughened and the car began to bounce and shudder, driving bolts of pain into his head. He felt the steering wheel resisting him and clamped his hands around it tightly, harsh vibrations running up his arms. He didn't dare look at the mirror now. He had to force himself to keep the speed unchanged. Keller wasn't going to slow down; he was sure of that. *What if he got a flat tyre, though?* All control would vanish in an instant. He visualised the somersaulting of his car, its grinding, shrieking tumble, the explosion of its gas tank, his body crushed and burned and ——

The broken span of pavement ended and his gaze jumped quickly to the rearview mirror. The truck was no closer, but it hadn't lost ground, either. Mann's eyes shifted. Up ahead were hills and mountains. He tried to reassure himself that upgrades were on his side, that he could climb them at the same speed he was going now. Yet all he could imagine were the downgrades, the immense truck close behind him, slamming violently into his car and knocking it across some cliff edge. He had a horrifying vision of dozens of broken, rusted cars lying unseen in the canyons ahead, corpses in every one of them, all flung to shattering deaths by Keller.

Mann's car went rocketing into a corridor of trees. On each side of the highway was a eucalyptus windbreak, each trunk three feet from the next. It was like speeding through a high-walled canyon. Mann gasped, twitching, as a large twig bearing dusty leaves dropped down across the windshield, then slid out of sight. Dear God! he thought. He was getting near the edge himself. If he should lose his nerve at this speed; it was over. Jesus! That would be ideal for Keller! he realised suddenly. He visualised the square-faced driver laughing as he passed the burning wreckage, knowing that he'd killed his prey without so much as touching him.

Mann started as his car shot out into the open. The route ahead was not straight now but winding up into the foothills. Mann willed himself to press down on the pedal even more. Eighty-three now, almost 84.

To his left was a broad terrain of green hills blending into mountains. He saw a black car on a dirt road, moving towards the highway. *Was its side painted white?* Mann's heartbeat lurched. Impulsively, he jammed the heel of his right hand down against the horn bar and held it there. The blast of the horn was shrill and racking to his ears. His heart began to pound. Was it a police car? *Was* it?

He let the horn bar up abruptly. *No,* it *wasn't*. Damn! his mind raged. Keller must have been amused by his pathetic efforts. Doubtless, he was chuckling to himself right now. He heard the truck driver's voice in his mind, coarse and sly. *You think you gonna get a cop to save you, boy? Shee-it. You gonna die*. Mann's heart contorted with savage hatred. *You son of a bitch!* he thought. Jerking his right hand into a fist, he drove it down against the seat. Goddamn you, Keller! I'm going to kill you, if it's the last thing I do!

The hills were closer now. There would be slopes directly, long steep grades. Mann felt a burst of hope within himself. He was sure to gain a lot of distance on the truck. No matter how he tried, that bastard Keller couldn't manage 80 miles an hour on a hill. But *I* can! cried his mind with fierce elation. He worked up saliva in his mouth and swallowed it. The back of his shirt was drenched. He could feel sweat trickling down his sides. A bath and a drink, first order of the day on reaching San Francisco. A long, hot bath, a long, cold drink. Cutty Sark. He'd splurge, by Christ. He rated it.

The car swept up a shallow rise. Not steep enough, goddamn it! The truck's momentum would prevent its losing speed. Mann felt mindless hatred for the landscape. Already, he had topped the rise and tilted over to a shallow downgrade. He looked at the rearview mirror. *Square*, he thought, everything about the truck was square: the radiator grille, the fender shapes, the bumper ends, the outline of the cab, even the shape of Keller's hands and face. He visualised the truck as some great entity pursuing him, insentient, brutish, chasing him with instinct only.

Mann cried out, horror-stricken, as he saw the ROAD REPAIRS sign up ahead. His frantic gaze leaped down the highway. Both lanes blocked, a huge black arrow pointing towards the alternative route! He groaned in anguish, seeing it was dirt. His foot jumped automatically to the brake pedal and started pumping it. He threw a dazed look at the rearview mirror. The truck was moving as fast as ever! It *couldn't*, though! Mann's expression froze in terror as he started turning to the right.

He stiffened as the front wheels hit the dirt road. For an instant, he was certain that the back part of the car was going to spin; he felt it breaking to the left. 'No, don't!' he cried. Abruptly, he was jarring down the dirt road, elbows braced against his sides, trying to keep from losing control. His tyres battered at the ruts, almost tearing the wheel from his grip. The windows rattled noisily. His neck snapped back and forth with painful jerks. His jolting body surged against the binding of the safety belt and slammed down violently on the seat. He felt the bouncing of the car drive up his spine. His clenching teeth slipped and he cried out hoarsely as his upper teeth gouged deep into his lip.

He gasped as the rear end of the car began surging to the right. He started to jerk the steering wheel to the left, then, hissing, wrenched it in the opposite direction, crying out as the right rear fender cracked into a fence pole, knocking it down. He started pumping at the brakes, struggling to regain control. The car rear yawed sharply to the left, tyres shooting out a spray of dirt. Mann felt a scream tear upward in his throat. He twisted wildly at the steering wheel. The car began careering to the right. He hitched the wheel around until the car was on course again. His head was pounding like his heart now, with gigantic, throbbing spasms. He started coughing as he gagged on dripping blood.

The dirt road ended suddenly, the car regained momentum on the pavement and he dared to look at the rearview mirror. The truck was slowed down but was still behind him, rocking like a freighter on a storm-tossed sea, its huge tyres scouring up a pall of dust. Mann shoved in the accelerator pedal and his car surged forward. A good, steep grade lay just ahead; he'd gain that distance now. He swallowed blood, grimacing at the taste, then fumbled in his trouser pocket and tugged out his handkerchief. He pressed it to his bleeding lip, eyes fixed on the slope ahead. Another 50 yards or so. He writhed his back. His undershirt was soaking wet, adhering to his skin. He glanced at the rearview mirror. The truck had just regained the highway. *Tough!* he thought with venom. Didn't get me, did you, Keller?

His car was on the first yards of the upgrade when steam began to issue from beneath its hood. Mann stiffened suddenly, eyes widening with shock. The steam increased, became a smoking mist. Mann's gaze jumped down. The red light hadn't flashed on yet but had to in a moment. How could this be happening? Just as he was set to get away! The slope ahead was long and gradual, with many curves. He knew he couldn't stop. Could he U-turn unexpectedly and go back down? the sudden thought occurred. He looked ahead. The highway was too narrow, bound by hills on both sides. There wasn't room enough to make an uninterrupted turn and there wasn't time enough to ease around. If he tried that, Keller would shift direction and hit him head on. 'Oh, my God!' Mann murmured suddenly.

He was going to die.

He stared ahead with stricken eyes, his view increasingly obscured by steam. Abruptly, he recalled the afternoon he'd had the engine steam cleaned at the local car wash. The man who'd done it had suggested he replace the water hoses, because steam-cleaning had a tendency to make them crack. He'd nodded, thinking that he'd do it when he had more time. *More time!* The phrase was like a dagger in his mind. He'd failed to change the hoses and, for that failure he was now about to die.

He sobbed in terror as the dashboard light flashed on. He glanced at it involuntarily and read the word HOT, black on red. With a breathless gasp, he jerked the transmission into low. Why hadn't he done that right away! He looked ahead. The slope seemed endless. Already, he could hear a boiling throb inside the radiator. How much coolant was there left? Steam was clouding faster, hazing up the windshield. Reaching out, he twisted at a dashboard knob. The wipers started flicking back and forth in fan-shaped sweeps. There had to be enough coolant in the radiator to get him to the top. *Then* what? cried his mind. He couldn't drive without coolant, even downhill. He glanced at the rearview mirror. The truck was falling behind. Mann snarled with maddened fury. *If it weren't for that goddamned hose, he'd be escaping now!*

The sudden lurching of the car snatched him back to terror. If he braked now, he could jump out, run and scrabble up that slope. Later, he might not have the time. He couldn't make himself stop the car, though. As long as it kept on running, he felt bound to it, less vulnerable. God knows what would happen if he left it.

Mann stared up the slope with haunted eyes, trying not to see the red light on the edges of his vision. Yard by yard, his car was slowing down. Make it, make it, pleaded his mind, even though he thought that it was futile. The car was running more and more unevenly. The thumping percolation of its radiator filled his ears. Any moment now, the motor would be choked off and the car would shudder to a stop, leaving him a sitting target. *No,* he thought. He tried to blank his mind.

He was almost to the top, but in the mirror he could see the truck drawing up on him. He jammed down on the pedal and the motor made a grinding noise. He groaned. It had to make the top! Please, God, help me! screamed his mind. The ridge was just ahead. Closer. Closer. Make it. 'Make it.' The car was shuddering and clanking, slowing down – oil, smoke and steam gushing from beneath the hood. The windshield wipers swept from side to side. Mann's head throbbed. Both his hands felt numb. His heartbeat pounded as he stared ahead. Make it, please, God, make it. Make it. *Make* it!

Over! Mann's lips opened in a cry of triumph as the car began descending. Hand shaking uncontrollably, he shoved the transmission into neutral and let the car go into a glide. The triumph strangled in his throat as he saw that there was nothing in sight but hills and more hills. Never mind! He was on a downgrade now, a long one. He passed a sign that read TRUCKS USE LOW GEARS NEXT 12 MILES. Twelve miles! Something would come up. It had to.

The car began to pick up speed. Mann glanced at the speedometer. Forty-seven miles an hour. The red light still burned. He'd save the motor for a long time, too, though; let it cool for 12 miles, if the truck was far enough behind.

His speed increased. Fifty . . . 51. Mann watched the needle turning slowly towards the right. He glanced at the rearview mirror. The truck had not appeared yet. With a little luck, he might still get a good lead. Not as good as he might have if the motor hadn't overheated but enough to work with. There had to be someplace along the way to stop. The needle edged past 55 and started towards the 60 mark.

Again, he looked at the rearview mirror, jolting as he saw that the truck had topped the ridge and was on its way down. He felt his lips begin to shake and crimped them together. His gaze jumped fitfully between the steam-obscured highway and the mirror. The truck was accelerating rapidly. Keller doubtless had the gas pedal floored. it wouldn't be long before the truck caught up to him. Mann's right hand twitched unconsciously towards the gearshift. Noticing, he jerked it back, grimacing, glanced at the speedometer. The car's velocity had just passed 60. Not enough! He had to use the motor now! He reached out desperately.

His right hand froze in mid-air as the motor stalled; then, shooting out the hand, he twisted the ignition key. The motor made a grinding noise but wouldn't start. Mann glanced up, saw that he was almost on the shoulder, jerked the steering wheel around. Again, he turned the key, but there was no response. He looked up at the rearview mirror. The truck was gaining on him swiftly. He glanced at the speedometer. The car's speed was fixed at 62. Mann felt himself crushed in a vice of panic. He stared ahead with haunted eyes.

Then he saw it, several hundred yards ahead: an escape route for trucks with burned-out brakes. There was no alternative now. Either he took the turnout or his car would be rammed from behind. The truck was frighteningly close. He heard the high-pitched wailing of its motor. Unconsciously, he started easing to the right, then jerked the wheel back suddenly. He mustn't give the move away! He had to wait until the last possible moment. Otherwise, Keller would follow him in.

Just before he reached the escape route, Mann wrenched the steering wheel around. The car rear started breaking to the left, tyres shrieking on the pavement. Mann steered with the skid, braking just enough to keep from losing all control. The rear tyres grabbed and, at 60 miles an hour, the car shot up the dirt trail, tyres slinging up a cloud of dust. Mann began to hit the brakes. The rear wheels sideslipped and the car slammed hard against the dirt bank to the right. Mann gasped as the car bounced off and started to fishtail with violent whipping motions, angling towards the trail edge. He drove his foot down on the brake pedal with all his might. The car rear skidded to the right and slammed against the bank again. Mann heard a grinding rend of metal and felt himself heaved downward suddenly, his neck snapped, as the car ploughed to a violent halt.

As in a dream, Mann turned to see the truck and trailer swerving off the highway. Paralysed, he watched the massive vehicle hurtle towards him, staring at it with a blank detachment, knowing he was going to die but so stupefied by the sight of the looming truck that he couldn't react. The gargantuan shape roared closer, blotting out the sky. Mann felt a strange sensation in his throat, unaware that he was screaming.

Suddenly, the truck began to tilt. Mann stared at it in choked-off silence as it started tipping over like some ponderous beast toppling in slow motion. Before it reached his car, it vanished from his rear window.

Hands palsied, Mann undid the safety belt and opened the door. Struggling from the car, he stumbled to the trail edge, staring downward. He was just in time to see the truck capsize like a foundering ship. The tanker followed, huge wheels spinning as it overturned.

The storage tank on the truck exploded first, the violence of its detonation causing Mann to stagger back and sit down clumsily on the dirt. A second explosion roared below, its shock wave buffeting across him hotly, making his ears hurt. His glazed eyes saw a fiery column shoot up towards the sky in front of him, then another.

Mann crawled slowly to the trail edge and peered down at the canyon. Enormous gouts of flame were towering upward, topped by thick, black, oily smoke. He couldn't see the truck or trailer, only flames. He gaped at them in shock, all feeling drained from him.

Then, unexpectedly, emotion came. Not dread, at first, and not regret; not the nausea that followed soon. It was a primeval tumult in his mind: the cry of some ancestral beast above the body of its vanquished foe.

SECOND CHANCE

Jack Finney

Here is another remarkable story which the perceptive reader will see has a similar theme to one of Stephen Spielberg's most recent box office successes, 'Back to the Future'. It is a fact, though, that Jack Finney's story of 'time travel' was written back in 1957, and is just one of several such tales he has created about people escaping from the ugly present day into a more tranquil past. Interestingly, too, 'Second Chance' was adapted for the American television series, 'Dead of Night' by my previous contributor, Richard Matheson, who is a great admirer of Jack Finney's work.

Finney (1911–) has, indeed, become greatly admired in the field of fantasy fiction by fans and critics alike for his remarkable short stories found in collections like The Clock of Time *(1957) and, of course, for his very famous novel,* Invasion of the Body Snatchers *which has twice been successfully filmed. Like that eerie story of an attempted take-over of Earth by aliens, 'Second Chance' is also set in Jack Finney's native North California. Similarly, it demonstrates his knowledge and affection for old cars in what is an eerie and fascinating tale . . .*

I can't tell you, I know, how I got to a time and place no one else in the world even remembers. But maybe I can tell you how I felt the morning I stood in an old barn off the county road, staring down at what was to take me there.

I paid out seventy-five dollars I'd worked hard for after classes last semester – I'm a senior at Poynt College in Hylesburg, Illinois, my home town – and the middle-aged farmer took it silently, watching me shrewdly, knowing I must be out of my mind. Then I stood looking down at the smashed, rusty, rat-gnawed, dust-covered, old wreck of an automobile lying on the wood floor where it had been hauled and dumped thirty-three years before – and that now belonged to me. And if you can remember the moment, whenever it was, when you finally got something you wanted so badly you dreamed about it – then maybe I've told you how I felt staring at the dusty mass of junk that was a genuine Jordan Playboy.

You've never heard of a Jordan Playboy, if you're younger than forty, unless you're like I am; one of those people who'd rather own a 1926 Mercer convertible sedan, or a 1931 Packard touring car, or a '24 Wills Sainte Claire, or a '31 air-cooled Franklin convertible – or a Jordan Playboy – than the newest two-toned, '57 model made; I was actually half sick with excitement.

And the excitement lasted; it took me four months to restore that car, and that's fast. I went to classes till school ended for the summer, then I worked, clerking at J. C. Penney's; and I had dates, saw an occasional movie, ate and slept. But all I really did – all that counted – was work on that car; from six to eight every morning, for half an hour at lunchtime, and from the moment I got home, most nights, till I stumbled to bed, worn out.

My folks live in the big old house my dad was born in; there's a barn off at the back of the lot, and I've got a chain hoist in there, a workbench, and a full set of mechanic's tools. I built hot rods there for three years, one after another; those charcoal-black mongrels with the rear ends up in the air. But I'm through with hot rods; I'll leave those to the high-school set. I'm twenty years old now, and I've been living for the day when I could soak loose the body bolts with liniment, hoist the body aside, and start restoring my own classic. That's what they're called; those certain models of certain cars of certain years which have something that's lasted, something today's cars don't have for us, and something worth bringing back.

But you don't restore a classic by throwing in a new motor, hammering out the dents, replacing missing parts with anything handy, and painting it chartreuse. 'Restore' means what it says, or ought to. My Jordan had been struck by a train, the man who sold it to me said – just grazed, but that was enough to flip it over, tumbling it across a field, and the thing was a wreck; the people in it were killed. So the right rear wheel and the spare were hopeless wads of wire spokes and twisted rims, and the body was caved in, with the metal actually split in places. The motor was a mess, though the block was sound. The upholstery was rat-gnawed, and almost gone. All the nickel plating was rusted and flaking off. And exterior parts were gone; nothing but screw holes to show they'd been there. But three of the wheels were intact, or almost, and none of the body was missing.

What you do is write letters, advertise in the magazines people like me read, ask around, prowl garages, junk heaps and barns, and you trade, and you bargain, and one way or another get together the parts you need. I traded a Winton name plate and hub caps, plus a Saxon hood, to a man in Wichita, Kansas, for two Playboy wheels, and they arrived crated in a wooden box – rusty, and some of the spokes bent and loose, but I could fix that. I bought my Jordan running-board mats and spare-wheel mount from a man in New Jersey. I bought two valve pushrods, and had the rest precision-made precisely like the others. And – well, I restored that car, that's all.

The body shell, every dent and bump gone, every tear welded and burnished down, I painted a deep green, precisely matching what was left of the old paint before I sanded it off. Door handles, windshield rim, and every other nickel-plated part, were restored, re-nickeled, and replaced. I wrote eleven letters to leather supply houses all over the country, enclosing sample swatches of the cracked old upholstery, before I found a place that could match it. Then I paid a hundred and twelve dollars to have my Playboy reupholstered, supplying old photographs to show just how it should be done. And at eight ten one Saturday evening in July, I finally finished; my last missing part, a Jordan radiator cap, for which I'd traded a Duesenberg floor mat, had come from the nickel plater's that afternoon. Just for the fun of it, I put the old plates back on then; Illinois licence 11,206, for 1923. And even the original ignition key, in its old leather case – oiled and worked supple again –

was back where I'd found it, and now I switched it on, advanced the throttle and spark, got out with the crank, and started it up. And thirty-three years after it had bounced, rolled and crashed off a grade crossing, that Jordan Playboy was alive again.

I had a date, and knew I ought to get dressed; I was wearing stained dungarees and my dad's navy blue, high-necked old sweater. I didn't have any money with me; you lose it out of your pockets, working on a car. I was even out of cigarettes. But I couldn't wait, I had to drive that car, and I just washed up at the old sink in the barn, then started down the cinder driveway in that beautiful car, feeling wonderful. It wouldn't matter how I was dressed anyway, driving around in the Playboy tonight.

My mother waved at me tolerantly from a living-room window, and called out to be careful, and I nodded; then I was out in the street, cruising along, and I wish you could have seen me – seen *it*, I mean. I don't care whether you've even given a thought to the wonderful old cars or not, you'd have seen why it was worth all I'd done. Draw yourself a mental picture of a simple, straight-lined, two-seater, open automobile with four big wire wheels fully exposed, and its spare on the back in plain sight; don't put in a line that doesn't belong there, and have a purpose. Make the two doors absolutely square; what other shape should a door be? Make the hood perfectly rounded, louvered at the sides because the motor needs that ventilation. But don't add a single unnecessary curve, jiggle, squiggle, or porthole to that car – and picture the radiator, nothing concealing it and pretending it doesn't exist. And now see that Playboy as I did cruising along, the late sun slanting down through the big old trees along the street, glancing off the bright nickel so that it hurt your eyes, the green of the body glowing like a jewel. It was beautiful, I tell you it was beautiful, and you'd think everyone would see that.

But they didn't. On Main Street, I stopped at a light, and a guy slid up beside me in a great big, shining, new '57 car half as long as a football field. He sat there, the top of the door up to his shoulders, his eyes almost level with the bottom of his windshield, looking as much in proportion to his car as a two-year-old in his father's overcoat; he sat there in a car with a pattern of chrome copied directly from an Oriental rug, and with a trunk sticking out past his back wheels you could have landed a helicopter on; he sat there for a moment, then turned, looked out, and smiled at *my* car!

And when I turned to look at him, eyes cold, he had the nerve to smile at *me*, as though I were supposed to nod and grin and agree that any car not made day before yesterday was an automatic side-splitting riot. I just looked away, and when the light changed, he thought he'd show me just how sick his big four-thousand-dollar job could make my pitiful old antique look. The light clicked, and his foot was on the gas, his automatic transmission taking hold, and he'd already started to grin. But I started when he did, feeding the gas in firm and gentle, and we held even till I shot into second faster than any automatic transmission yet invented can do it, and I drew right past him, and when I looked back it was me who was grinning. But still, at the next light, every pedestrian crossing in front of my car treated me to a tolerant understanding smile, and when the light changed, I swung off Main.

That was one thing that happened; the second was that my date wouldn't go out with me. I guess I shouldn't blame her. First she saw how I was dressed, which didn't help me with her. Then I showed her the Jordan at the kerb, and she nodded, not even slightly interested, and said it was very nice; which didn't help her with me. And then – well, she's a good-looking girl, Naomi Weygand, and while she didn't exactly put it in these words, she let me know she meant to be seen tonight, preferably on a dance floor, and not waste her youth and beauty riding around in some old antique. And when I told her I was going out in the Jordan tonight, and if she wanted to come along, fine, and if she didn't – well, she didn't. And eight seconds later she was opening her front door again, while I scorched rubber pulling away from the kerb.

I felt the way you would have by then, and I wanted to get out of town and alone somewhere, and I shoved it into second, gunning the car, heading for the old Cressville road. It used to be the only road to Cressville, a two-lane paved highway just barely wide enough for cars to pass. But there's been a new highway for fifteen years; four lanes, and straight as a ruler except for two long curves you can do ninety on, and you can make the seven miles to Cressville in five minutes or less.

But it's a dozen winding miles on the old road, and half a mile of it, near Cressville, was flooded out once, and the concrete is broken and full of gaps; you have to drive it in low. So nobody uses the old road nowadays, except for four or five farm families who live along it.

When I swung onto the old road – there are a lot of big old trees all along it – I began to feel better. And I just ambled along, no faster than thirty, maybe, clear up to the broken stretch before I turned back towards Hylesburg, and it was wonderful. I'm not a sports-car man myself, but they've got something when they talk about getting close to the road and into the outdoors again – the way driving used to be before people shut themselves behind great sheets of glass and metal, and began rushing along super-highways, their eyes on the white line. I had the windshield folded down flat against the hood, and the summer air streamed over my face and through my hair, and I could see the road just beside and under me flowing past so close I could have touched it. The air was alive with the heavy fragrances of summer darkness, and the rich nostalgic sounds of summer insects, and I wasn't even thinking, but just living and enjoying it.

One of the old Playboy advertisements, famous in their day, calls the Jordan 'this brawny, graceful thing,' and says, 'It revels along with the wandering wind and roars like a Caproni biplane. It's a car for a man's man – that's certain. Or for a girl who loves the out of doors.' Rich prose for these days, I guess; we're afraid of rich prose now, and laugh in defence. But I'll take it over a stern sales talk on safety belts.

Anyway, I liked just drifting along the old road, a part of the summer outdoors and evening, and the living country around me; and I was no more thinking than a collie dog with his nose thrust out of a car, his eyes half closed against the air stream, enjoying the feeling human beings so often forget, of simply being a living creature. '"I left my love in Avalon,"' I was bawling out at the top of my lungs, hardly knowing when I'd started, '"and saaailed awaaay!"' Then I was singing 'Alice Blue Gown,' very softly and gently. I sang, 'Just a Japanese Saaandman!,' and 'Whispering,' and 'Barney Google,' the fields and trees and cattle, and sometimes an occasional car, flowing past in the darkness, and I was having a wonderful time.

The name 'Dempsey' drifted into my head, I don't know why – just a vagrant thought floating lazily up into my consciousness. Now, I saw Jack Dempsey once; six years ago when I was fourteen, my dad, my mother, and I took a vacation trip to New York. We saw the Empire State Building, Rockefeller Center, took a ride on the subway, and all the rest of it. And we had dinner at Jack Dempsey's restaurant on Broadway, and he was there, and spoke to us, and my dad talked to him for a minute about his fights. So I saw him; a nice-looking middle-aged man, very big and broad. But the picture that drifted up into my mind now, driving along the old Cressville road, wasn't that Jack Dempsey. It was the face of a young man not a lot older than I was, black-haired, black-bearded, fierce and scowling. Dempsey, I thought, that snarling young face rising up clear and vivid in my mind, and the thought completed itself: He beat Tom Gibbons last night.

Last night; Dempsey beat Gibbons *last night* – and it was true. I mean it *felt* true somehow, as though the thought were in the very air around me, like the old songs I'd found myself singing, and suddenly several things I'd been half aware of clicked together in my mind. I'd been dreamily and unthinkingly realising that there were more cars on the road than I'd have expected, flowing past me in the darkness. Maybe some of the farm families along here were having some sort of Saturday-night get-together, I thought. But then I knew it wasn't true.

Picture a car's headlights coming towards you; they're two sharp beams slicing ahead into the darkness, an intense blue-white in colour, their edges as defined as a ruler's. But these headlights – two more sets of them were approaching me now – were different. They were entirely orange in colour, the red-orange of the hot filaments that produced them; and they were hardly even beams, but just twin circles of wide, diffused orange light, and they wavered in intensity, illuminating the road only dimly.

The nearer lights were almost upon me, and I half rose from my seat, leaning forward over the hood of the Jordan, staring at the car as it passed me. It was a Moon; a cream-coloured nineteen-twenty-two Moon roadster.

The next car, those two orange circles of wavering light swelling, approached, then passed, as I stared and turned to look after it. It looked something like mine; wire wheels, but with the spare on a side mount, and with step plates instead of running boards. I knew what it was; a Haynes Speedster, and the man at the wheel wore a cloth cap, and the girl beside him wore a large pink hat, coming well down over her head, and with a wide brim all around it.

I sat moving along, a hand on the wheel, in a kind of stunned ecstatic trance. For now, the Saturday-night traffic at its peak, there they all came one after another, all the glorious old cars; a Saxon Six black-bodied touring car with wood-spoke wheels, and the women in that car wore chin-length veils from the edges of their flowered hats; there passed a grey-bodied black-topped Wills Sainte Claire with orange disc wheels, and the six kids in it were singing 'Who's Sorry Now?'; then I saw another Moon, a light blue open four-seater, its cut-out open, and the kid at the wheel had black hair slicked back in a varnished pompadour, and just glancing at him, you could see he was on his way to a date; now there came an Elcar, two Model T Fords just behind it; then a hundred yards back, a red Buick roadster with natural-wood spoke wheels; I saw a Velie, and a roadster that was either a Noma or a Kissel, I couldn't be sure; and there was a high-topped blue Dodge sedan with cut flowers in little glass vases by the rear doors; there was a car I didn't know at all; then a brand-new Stanley Steamer, and just behind it, a wonderful low-slung 1921 Pierce-Arrow, and I knew what had happened, and where I was.

I've read some of the stuff about Time with a capital T, and I don't say I understand it too well. But I know Einstein or sombody compares Time to a winding river, and says we exist as though in a boat, drifting along between high banks. All we can see is the present, immediately around us. We can't see the future just beyond the next curve, or the past in the many bends behind us. But it's all there just the same. There – countless bends back, in infinite distance – lies the past, as real as the moment around us.

Well, I'll join Einstein and the others with a notion of my own; just a feeling, actually, hardly even a thought. I wonder if we aren't barred from the past by a thousand invisible chains. You can't drive into the past in a 1957 Buick because there are no 1957 Buicks in 1923; so how could you be there in one? You can't drive into 1923 in a Jordan Playboy, along a four-lane superhighway; there are no superhighways in 1923. You couldn't even, I'm certain, drive with a pack of modern filter-tip cigarettes in your pocket – into a night when no such thing existed. Or with so much as a coin bearing a modern date, or wearing a charcoal-grey and pink shirt on your back. All those things, small and large, are chains keeping you out of a time when they could not exist.

But my car and I – the way I felt about it, anyway – were

almost *rejected* that night, by the time I lived in. And so there in my Jordan, just as it was the year it was new, with nothing about me from another time, the old '23 tags on my car, and moving along a highway whose very oil spots belonged to that year – well, I think that for a few moments, all the chains hanging slack, we were free on the surface of Time. And that, moving along that old highway through the summer evening, we simply *drifted* – into the time my Jordan belonged in.

That's the best I can do, anyway; it's all that occurs to me. And – well, I wish I could offer you proof. I wish I could tell you that when I drove into Hylesburg again, onto Main Street, that I saw a newspaper headline saying, PRESIDENT HARDING STRICKEN, or something like that. Or that I heard people discussing Babe Ruth's new home-run record, or saw a bunch of cops raiding a speak-easy.

But I saw or heard nothing of the sort, nothing much different from the way it always has been. The street was quiet and nearly empty, as it is once the stores shut down for the weekend. I saw only two people at first; just a couple walking along far down the street. As for the buildings, they've been there, most of them, since the Civil War, or before – Hylesburg's an old town – and in the semidarkness left by the street lamps, they looked the same as always, and the street was paved with brick as it has been since World War I.

No, all I saw driving along Main Street were – just little things. I saw a shoe store, its awning still over the walk, and that awning was striped; broad red and white stripes, and the edges were scalloped. You just don't see awnings like that, outside of old photographs, but there it was, and I pulled over to the kerb, staring across the walk at the window. But all I can tell you is that there were no open-toed shoes among the women's, and the heels looked a little high to me, and a little different in design, somehow. The men's shoes – well, the toes seemed a little more pointed than you usually see now, and there were no suede shoes at all. But the kids' shoes looked the same as always.

I drove on, and passed a little candy and stationery shop, and on the door was a sign that said, *Drink Coca-Cola*, and in some way I can't describe the letters looked different. Not much, but – you've seen old familiar trademarks that have gradually changed, kept up to date through the years, in a gradual evolution. All I can say is that this old familiar sign looked a little different, a little old-fashioned, but I can't really say how.

There were a couple of all-night restaurants open, as I drove along, one of them The New China, the other Gill's, but they've both been in Hylesburg for years. There were a couple of people in each of them, but I never even thought of going in. It seemed to me I was here on sufferance, or by accident; that I'd just drifted into this time, and had no right to actually intrude on it. Both restaurant signs were lighted, the letters formed by electric-light bulbs, unfrosted so that you could see the filaments glowing, and the bulbs ended in sharp glass spikes. There wasn't a neon sign, lighted or unlighted, the entire length of the street.

On West Main I came to the Orpheum, and though the box office and marquee were dark, there were a few lights still on, and a dozen or so cars parked for half a block on each side of it. I parked mine directly across the street beside a wood telephone pole. Brick pavement is bumpy, and when I shut off the motor, and reached for the hand brake – I don't know whether this is important or not, but I'd better tell it – the Jordan rolled ahead half a foot as its right front wheel settled into a shallow depression in the pavement. For just a second or so, it rocked a little in a tiny series of rapidly decreasing arcs, then stopped, its wheel settled snugly into the depression as though it had found exactly the spot it had been looking for – like a dog turning several times before it lies down in precisely the right place.

Crossing over to the Orph, I saw the big posters in the shallow glass showcases on each side of the entrance. *Fri., Sat. and Sun.*, one said, and it showed a man with a long thin face, wearing a monocle, and his eyes were narrowed, staring at a woman with long hair who looked sort of frightened. GEORGE ARLISS, said the poster, in 'The Green Goddess.'

Coming Attraction, said the other poster, *Mon., Tues. and Wed.* 'Ashes of Vengeance,' starring NORMA TALMADGE and CONWAY TEARLE, with WALLACE BEERY. I've never heard of any of them, except Wallace Beery. In the little open lobby, I looked at the still pictures in wall cases at each side of the box office; small, glossy, black and white scenes from the two movies, and finally recognised Wallace Beery, a thin, handsome, young man. I've never seen that kind of display before, and didn't know it was done.

But that's about all I can tell you; nothing big or dramatic, and nothing significant, like hearing someone say, 'Mark my words, that boy Lindbergh will fly the Atlantic yet.' All I saw was a little, shut-down, eleven-o'clock Main Street.

The parked cars, though, were a Dort; a high, straight-lined Buick sedan with wood wheels; three Model T's; a blue Hupmobile touring car with blue and yellow disc wheels; a Winton; a four-cylinder Chevrolet roadster; a Stutz; a spoke-wheeled Cadillac sedan. Not a single car had been made later than the year 1923. And this is the strange thing; they looked *right* to me. They looked as though that were the way automobiles were supposed to look, nothing odd, funny, or old-fashioned about them. From somewhere in my mind, I know I could have brought up a mental picture of a glossy, two-toned, chromium-striped car with power steering. But it would have taken a real effort, and – I can't really explain this, I know – it was as though modern cars didn't really exist; not yet. *These* were today's cars, parked all around me, and I knew it.

I walked on, just strolling down Main Street, glancing at an occasional store window, enjoying the incredible wonder of being where I was. Then, half a block or so behind me, I heard a sudden little babble of voices, and I looked back and the movie was letting out. A little crowd of people was flowing slowly out onto the walk to stand, some of them, talking for a moment; while others crossed the street, or walked on. Motors began starting, the parked cars pulling out from the kerb, and I heard a girl laugh.

I walked on three or four steps maybe, and then I heard a sound, utterly familiar and unmistakeable, and stopped dead in my tracks. My Jordan's motor had caught, roaring up as someone advanced the spark and throttle, and dying to its chunky, revving-and-ticking-over idle. Swinging around on the walk, I saw a figure, a young man's, vague and shadowy down the street, hop into the front seat, and then – the cut-out open – my Jordan shot ahead, tyres squealing, down the stret towards me.

I was frozen; I just stood there stupidly, staring at my car shooting towards me, my brain not working; then I came to life. It's funny; I was more worried about my car, about the way it was treated, than about the fact that it was being stolen. And I ran out into the street, directly into its path, my arms waving, and I yelled, 'Hey! Take it easy!' The brakes slammed on, the Jordan skidding on the bricks, the rear end sliding sideways a little, and it slowed almost to a stop, then swerved around me, picking up speed again, and as I turned, following it with my eyes, I caught a glimpse of a girl's face staring at me, and a man my age at the wheel beside her, laughing, his teeth flashing white, and then they were past, and he yelled back, 'You betcha! Take it easy; I always do!' For a moment I just stood staring after them, watching the single red tail-light shrinking into the distance; then I turned, and walked back towards the kerb. A little part of the movie crowd was passing, and I heard a woman's voice murmur some question; then a man's voice, gruff and half angry, replied, 'Yeah, of *course* it was Vince; driving like a fool as usual.'

There was nothing I could do. I couldn't report a car theft to the police, trying to explain who I was, and where they could reach me. I hung around for a while, the street deserted once more, hoping they'd bring back my car. But they didn't, and finally I left, and just walked the streets for the rest of the night.

I kept well away from Prairie Avenue. If I was where I knew I was, my grandmother, still alive, was asleep in the big front bedroom of our house, and the thirteen-year-old in my room was the boy who would become my father. I didn't belong there now, and I kept away, up in the north end of town. It looked about as always; Hylesburg, as I've said, is old, and most of the new construction has been on the outskirts. Once in a while I passed a vacant lot where I knew there no longer was one; and when I passed the Dorsets' house where I played as a kid with Ray Dorset, it was only half built now, the wood of the framework looking fresh and new in the dark.

Once I passed a party, the windows all lighted, and they were having a time, noisy and happy, and with a lot of laughing and shrieks from the women. I stopped for a minute, across the street, watching; and I saw figures passing the lighted windows, and one of them was a girl with her hair slicked close to her head, and curving down onto her cheeks in sort of J-shaped hooks. There was a phonograph going, and the music – it was 'China Boy' – sounded sort of distant, the orchestration tinny, and . . . different, I can't explain how. Once it slowed down, the tones deepening, and someone yelled, and then I heard the pitch rising higher again as it picked up speed, and knew someone was winding the phonograph. Then I walked on.

At daylight, the sky whitening in the east, the leaves of the big old trees around me beginning to stir, I was on Cherry Street. I heard a door open across the street, and saw a man in overalls walk down his steps, cut silently across the lawn, and open the garage doors beside his house. He walked in, I heard the motor start, and a cream and green '56 Oldsmobile backed out – and I turned around then, and walked on towards Prairie Avenue and home, and was in bed a couple hours before my folks woke up Sunday morning.

I didn't tell anyone my Jordan was gone; there was no way to explain it. Ed Smiley, and a couple other guys, asked me about it, and I said I was working on it in my garage. My folks didn't ask; they were long since used to my working on a car for weeks, then discovering I'd sold or traded it for something else to work on.

But I wanted – I simply had to have – another Playboy, and it took a long time to find one. I heard of one in Davenport, and borrowed Jim Clark's Hudson, and drove over, but it wasn't a Playboy, just a Jordan, and in miserable shape anyway.

It was a girl who found me a Playboy; after school started up in September. She was in my Economics IV class, a sophomore I learned, though I didn't remember seeing her around before. She wasn't actually a girl you'd turn and look at again, and remember, I suppose; she wasn't actually pretty, I guess you'd have to say. But after I'd talked to her a few times, and had a Coke date once, when I ran into her downtown – then she was pretty. And I got to liking her; quite a lot. It's like this; I'm a guy who's going to want to get married pretty early. I've been dating girls since I was sixteen, and it's fun, and exciting, and I like it fine. But I've just about had my share of that, and I'd been looking at girls in a different way lately; a lot more interested in what they were like than in just how good-looking they were. And I knew pretty soon that this was a girl I could fall in love with, and marry, and be happy with. I won't be fooling around with old cars all my life; it's just a hobby, and I know it, and I wouldn't expect a girl to get all interested in exactly how the motor of an old Marmon works. But I would expect her to take some interest in how I feel about old cars. And she did – Helen McCauley, her name is. She really did; she understood what I was talking about, and it wasn't faked either, I could tell.

So one night – we were going to the dance at the Roof Garden, and I'd called for her a little early, and we were sitting out on her lawn in deck chairs killing time – I told her how I wanted one certain kind of old car, and why it had to be just that car. And when I mentioned its name, she sat up, and said, 'Why, good heavens, I've heard about the Playboy from Dad all my life; we've got one out in the barn; it's a beat-up old mess, though. Dad!' she called, turning to look up at the porch where her folks were sitting. 'Here's a man you've been looking for!'

Well, I'll cut it short. Her dad came down, and when he heard what it was all about, Helen and I never did get to the dance. We were out in that barn, the old tarpaulin pulled off his Jordan, and we were looking at it, touching it, sitting in it, talking about it, and quoting Playboy ads to each other for the next three hours.

It wasn't in bad shape at all. The upholstery was gone; only wads of horsehair and strips of brittle old leather left. The body was dented, but not torn. A few parts, including one headlight and part of the windshield mounting, were gone, and the motor was a long way from running, but nothing serious. And all the wheels were there, and in good shape, though they needed renickeling.

Mr McCauley gave me the car; wouldn't take a nickel for it. He'd owned that Jordan when he was young, had had it ever since, and loved it; he'd always meant, he said, to get it in running order again sometime, but knew he never would now. And once he understood what I meant about restoring a classic, he said that to see it and drive it again as it once was, was all the payment he wanted.

I don't know just when I guessed, or why; but the feeling had been growing on me. Partly, I suppose, it was the colour; the faded-out remains of the deep green this old car had once been. And partly it was something else, I don't know just what. But suddenly – standing in that old barn with Helen, and her mother and dad – suddenly I knew, and I glanced around the barn, and found them; the old plates nailed up on a wall, 1923 through 1931. And when I walked over to look at them, I found what I knew I would find; 1923 Illinois tag 11,206.

'Your old Jordan plates?' I said, and when he nodded, I said as casually as I could, 'What's your first name, Mr McCauley?'

I suppose he thought I was crazy, but he said, 'Vincent. Why?'

'Just wondered. I was picturing you driving around when the Jordan was new; it's a fast car, and it must have been a temptation to open it up.'

'Oh, yeah.' He laughed. 'I did that, all right; those were wild times.'

'Racing trains; all that sort of thing, I suppose?'

'That's right,' he said, and Helen's mother glanced at me curiously. 'That was one of the things to do in those days. We almost got it one night, too; scared me to death. Remember?' he said to his wife.

'I certainly do.'

'What happened?' I said.

'Oh' – he shrugged – 'I was racing a train, out west of town one night; where the road parallels the Q tracks. I passed it, heading for the crossroad – you know where it is – that cuts over the tracks. We got there, my arms started to move, to swing the wheel and shoot over the tracks in front of that engine – when I knew I couldn't make it.' He shook his head. 'Two three seconds more; if we'd gotten there just two seconds earlier, I'd have risked it, I'm certain, and we'd have been killed, I know. But we were just those couple seconds too late, and I swung that wheel straight again, and shot on down the road beside that train, and when I took my foot off the gas, and the engine rushed past us, the fireman was leaning out of the cab shaking his fist, and shouting something, I couldn't hear what, but it wasn't complimentary.' He grinned.

'Did anything delay you that night,' I said softly, 'just long enough to keep you from getting killed?' I was actually holding my breath, waiting for his answer.

But he only shook his head. 'I don't know,' he said without interest. 'I can't remember.' And his wife said, 'I don't even remember where we'd been.'

I don't believe – I really don't – that my Jordan Playboy is anything more than metal, glass, rubber and paint formed into a machine. It isn't alive; it can't think or feel; it's only a car. But I think it's an especial tragedy when a young couple's lives are cut off for no other reason than the sheer exuberance nature put into them. And I can't stop myself from feeling, true or not true, that when that old Jordan was restored – returned to precisely the way it had been just before young Vince McCauley and his girl had raced a train in it back in 1923 – when it had been given a second chance, it went back to the time and place, back to the same evening in 1923, that would give them a second chance, too. And so again, there on that warm July evening, actually there in the year 1923, they got into that Jordan, standing just where they'd parked it, to drive on and race that train. But trivial events can affect important ones following them – how often we've all said: If only this or that had happened, everything would have turned out so differently. And this time it did, for now something was changed. This time on that 1923 July evening, someone dashed in front of their car, delaying them only two or three seconds. But Vince McCauley, then, driving on to race along beside those tracks, changed his mind about trying to cross them; and lived to marry the girl beside him. And to have a daughter.

I haven't asked Helen to marry me, but she knows I will; after I've graduated, and got a job, I expect. And she knows that I know she'll say yes. We'll be married, and have children, and I'm sure we'll be driving a modern hard-top car like everyone else, with safety catches on the doors so the kids won't fall out. But one thing for sure – just as her folks did thirty-two years before – we'll leave on our honeymoon in the Jordan Playboy.

TRUCKS

Stephen King

The theme of vehicles with characters of their own is taken further in this next grim yarn, by Stephen King (1946–   ), the acknowledged best-selling modern writer of horror and fantasy fiction. Since his stunning debut with the story of a psychic child, 'Carrie', in 1974, Stephen has written one hugely successful book after another and has already had over a dozen films based on his work

As I mentioned in the earlier introduction, King's novel of a demonic car, 'Christine', was filmed in 1983 by John Carpenter and described by one critic as portraying 'America's love affair with the automobile'. Be that as it may, considering what happens, the story of the maladjusted teenager and the blazing red 1958 Plymouth Fury which he restores and in so doing unleashes a trail of destruction, was not the first motoring movie of its kind, but it is certainly among the most stunning to date. Interestingly, Stephen King decided to make the Fury the hero of his story 'because they were the most mundane Fifties car I could remember – and I didn't want a car that already had a legend attached to it like the Fifties Thunderbird or the Ford Galaxy'.

In 'Trucks', Stephen takes another 'mundane' vehicle as the focus of his tale and – as you will discover – endows it with equally sinister qualities. After reading the story, I doubt if you will ever again look at a haulage vehicle in quite the same way . . .

The guy's name was Snodgrass and I could see him getting ready to do something crazy. His eyes had got bigger, showing a lot of the whites, like a dog getting ready to fight. The two kids who had come skidding into the parking lot in the old Fury were trying to talk to him, but his head was cocked as though he was hearing other voices. He had a tight little potbelly encased in a good suit that was getting a little shiny in the seat. He was a salesman and he kept his display bag close to him, like a pet dog that had gone to sleep.

'Try the radio again,' the truck driver at the counter said.

The short-order cook shrugged and turned it on. He flipped it across the band and got nothing but static.

'You went too fast,' the trucker protested. 'You might have missed something.'

'Hell,' the short-order cook said. He was an elderly black man with a smile of gold and he wasn't looking at the trucker. He was looking through the diner-length picture window at the parking lot.

Seven or eight heavy trucks were out there, engines rumbling in low, idling roars that sounded like big cats purring. There were a couple of Macks, a Hemingway, and four or five Reos. Trailer trucks, interstate haulers with a lot of licence plates and CB whip antennas on the back.

The kids' Fury was lying on its roof at the end of long, looping skid marks in the loose crushed rock of the parking lot. It had been battered into senseless junk. At the entrance to the truck stop's turnaround, there was a blasted Cadillac. Its owner stared out of the star-shattered windshield like a gutted fish. Horn-rimmed glasses hung from one ear.

Halfway across the lot from it lay the body of a girl in a pink dress. She had jumped from the Caddy when she saw it wasn't going to make it. She had hit running but never had a chance. She was the worst, even though she was face down. There were flies around her in clouds.

Across the road an old Ford station wagon had been slammed through the guardrails. That had happened an hour ago. No one had been by since then. You couldn't see the turnpike from the window and the phone was out.

'You went too fast,' the trucker was protesting. 'You oughta –'

That was when Snodgrass bolted. He turned the table over getting up, smashing coffee cups and sending sugar in a wild spray. His eyes were wilder than ever, and his mouth hung loosely and he was blabbering: 'We gotta get outta here we gotta getouttahere wegottagetouttahere –'

The kid shouted and his girlfriend screamed.

I was on the stool closest to the door and I got a handful of his shirt, but he tore loose. He was cranked up all the way. He would have gone through a bank-vault door.

He slammed out the door and then he was sprinting across the gravel towards the drainage ditch on the left. Two of the trucks lunged after him, smokestacks blowing diesel exhaust dark brown against the sky, huge rear wheels machine-gunning gravel up in sprays.

He couldn't have been any more than five or six running steps from the edge of the flat parking lot when he turned back to look, fear scrawled on his face. His feet tangled each other and he faltered and almost fell down. He got his balance again, but it was too late.

One of the trucks gave way and the other charged down, huge front grille glittering savagely in the sun. Snodgrass screamed, the sound high and thin, nearly lost under the Reo's heavy diesel roar.

It didn't drag him under. As things turned out, it would have been better if it had. Instead it drove him up and out, the way a punter kicks a football. For a moment he was silhouetted against the hot afternoon sky like a crippled scarecrow, and then he was gone into the drainage ditch.

The big truck's brakes hissed like dragon's breath, its front wheels locked, digging, grooves into the gravel skin of the lot, and it stopped inches from jack-knifing in. The bastard.

The girl in the booth screamed. Both hands were clamped into her cheeks, dragging the flesh down, turning it into a witch's mask.

Glass broke. I turned my head and saw that the trucker had squeezed his glass hard enough to break it. I don't think he knew it yet. Milk and a few drops of blood fell onto the counter.

The black counterman was frozen by the radio, a dishcloth in hand, looking amazed. His teeth glittered. For a moment there was no sound but the buzzing Westclox and the rumbling of the Reo's engine as it returned to its fellows. Then the girl began to cry and it was all right – or at least better.

My own car was around the side, also battered to junk. It was a 1971 Camaro and I had still been paying on it, but I didn't suppose that mattered now.

There was no one in the trucks.

The sun glittered and flashed on empty cabs. The wheels turned themselves. You couldn't think about it too much. You'd go insane if you thought about it too much. Like Snodgrass.

Two hours passed. The sun began to go down. Outside, the trucks patrolled in slow circles and figure eights. Their parking lights and running lights had come on.

I walked the length of the counter twice to get the kinks out of my legs and then sat in a booth by the long front window. It was a standard truck stop, close to the major through-way, a complete service facility out back, gas and diesel fuel both. The truckers came here for coffee and pie.

'Mister?' The voice was hesitant.

I looked around. It was the two kids from the Fury. The boy looked about nineteen. He had long hair and a beard that was just starting to take hold. His girl looked younger.

'Yeah?'

'What happened to you?'

I shrugged. 'I was coming up the interstate to Pelson,' I said. 'A truck came up behind me – I could see it in the mirror a long way off – really highballing. You could hear it a mile down the road. It whipped out around a VW Beetle and just snapped it off the road with the whiplash of the trailer, the way you'd snap a ball of paper off a table with your finger. I thought the truck would go, too. No driver could have held it with the trailer whipping that way. But it didn't go. The VW flopped over six or seven times and exploded. And the truck got the next one coming up the same way. It was coming up on me and I took the exit ramp in a hurry.' I laughed but my heart wasn't in it. 'Right into a truck stop, of all places. From the frying pan into the fire.'

The girl swallowed. 'We saw a Greyhound going north in the southbound lane. It was . . . ploughing . . . through cars. It exploded and burned but before it did . . . slaughter.'

A Greyhound bus. That was something new. And bad.

Outside, all the headlights suddenly popped on in unison, bathing the lot in an eerie, depthless glare. Growling, they cruised back and forth. The headlights seemed to give them eyes, and in the growing gloom, the dark trailer boxes looked like the hunched, squared-off shoulders of prehistoric giants.

The counterman said, 'Is it safe to turn on the lights?'

'Do it,' I said, 'and find out.'

He flipped the switches and a series of flyspecked globes overhead came on. At the same time a neon sign out front stuttered into life: 'Conant's Truck Stop & Diner – Good Eats.' Nothing happened. The trucks continued their patrol.

'I can't understand it,' the trucker said. He had got down from his stool and was walking around, his hand wrapped in a red engineer's bandanna. 'I ain't had no problems with my rig. She's a good old girl. I pulled in here a little past one for a spaghetti dinner and this happens.' He waved his arms and the bandanna flapped. 'My own rig's out there right now, the one with the weak left tail-light. Been driving her for six years. But if I stepped out that door –'

'It's just starting,' the counterman said. His eyes were hooded and obsidian. 'It must be bad if that radio's gone. It's just starting.'

The girl had drained as pale as milk. 'Never mind that,' I said to the counterman. 'Not yet.'

'What would do it?' The trucker was worrying. 'Electrical storms in the atmosphere? Nuclear testing? What?'

'Maybe they're mad,' I said.

Around seven o'clock I walked over to the counterman. 'How are we fixed here? I mean, if we have to stay a while?'

His brow wrinkled. 'Not so bad. Yest'y was delivery day. We got two-three hunnert hamburg patties, canned fruit and vegetables, dry cereal, aigs . . . no more milk than what's in the cooler, but the water's from the well. If we had to, the five of us cud get on for a month or more.'

The trucker came over and blinked at us. 'I'm dead out of cigarettes. Now that cigarette machine . . .'

'It ain't my machine,' the counterman said. 'No sir.'

The trucker had a steel pinch bar he'd gotten in the supply room out back. He went to work on the machine.

The kid went down to where the jukebox glittered and flashed and plugged in a quarter. John Fogarty began to sing about being born on the bayou.

I sat down and looked out the window. I saw something I didn't like right away. A Chevy light pickup had joined the patrol, like a Shetland pony amid Percherons. I watched it until it rolled impartially over the body of the girl from the Caddy and then I looked away.

'We *made* them!' the girl cried out with sudden wretchedness. 'They *can't!*'

Her boyfriend told her to hush. The trucker got the cigarette machine open and helped himself to six or eight packs of Viceroys. He put them in different pockets and then ripped one pack open. From the intent expression on his face, I wasn't sure if he was going to smoke them or eat them up.

Another record came on the juke. It was eight o'clock.

At eight-thirty the power went off.

When the lights went, the girl screamed, a cry that stopped suddenly, as if her boyfriend had put his hand over her mouth. The jukebox died with a deepening, unwinding sound.

'What the *Christ!*' the trucker said.

'Counterman!' I called. 'You got any candles?'

'I think so. Wait . . . yeah. Here's a few.'

I got up and took them. We lit them and started placing them around. 'Be careful,' I said. 'If we burn the place down there's the devil to pay.'

He chuckled morosely. 'You know it.'

When we were done placing the candles, the kid and his girl were huddled together and the trucker was by the back door, watching six more heavy trucks weaving in and out between the concrete fuel islands. 'This changes things, doesn't it?' I said.

'Damn right, if the power's gone for good.'

'How bad?'

'Hamburg'll go over in three days. Rest of the meat and aigs'll go by about as quick. The cans will be okay, an' the dry stuff. But that ain't the worst. We ain't gonna have no water without the pump.'

'How long?'

'Without no water? A week.'

'Fill every empty jug you've got. Fill them till you can't draw anything but air. Where are the toilets? There's good water in the tanks.'

'Employees' res'room is in the back. But you have to go outside to get to the ladies' and gents'.'

'Across to the service building?' I wasn't ready for that. Not yet.

'No. Out the side door an' up a ways.'

'Give me a couple of buckets.'

He found two galvanised pails. The kid strolled up.

'What are you doing?'
'We have to have water. All we can get.'
'Give me a bucket then.'
I handed him one.
'Jerry!' the girl cried. 'You –'
He looked at her and she didn't say anything else, but she picked up a napkin and began to tear at the corners. The trucker was smoking another cigarette and grinning at the floor. He didn't speak up.
We walked over to the side door where I'd come in that afternoon and stood there for a second, watching the shadows wax and wane as the trucks went back and forth.
'Now?' the kid said. His arm brushed mine and the muscles were jumping and humming like wires. If anyone bumped him he'd go straight up to heaven.
'Relax,' I said.
He smiled a little. It was a sick smile, but better than none.
'Okay.'
We slipped out.
The night air had cooled. Crickets chirred in the grass, and frogs thumped and croaked in the drainage ditch. Out here the rumble of the trucks was louder, more menacing, the sound of beasts. From inside it was a movie. Out here it was real, you could get killed.
We slid along the tiled outer wall. A slight overhang gave us some shadow. My Camaro was huddled against the cyclone fence across from us, and faint light from the roadside sign glinted on broken metal and puddles of gas and oil.
'You take the ladies',' I whispered. 'Fill your bucket from the toilet tank and wait.'
Steady diesel rumblings. It was tricky; you thought they were coming, but it was only echoes bouncing off the building's odd corners. It was only twenty feet, but it seemed much farther.
He opened the ladies'-room door and went in. I went past and then I was inside the gents'. I could feel my muscles loosen and a breath whistled out of me. I caught a glimpse of myself in the mirror, strained white face with dark eyes.
I got the porcelain tank cover off and dunked the bucket full. I poured a little back to keep from sloshing and went to the door. 'Hey?'
'Yeah,' he breathed.
'You ready?'

'Yeah.'

We went out again. We got maybe six steps before lights blared in our faces. It had crept up, big wheels barely turning on the gravel. It had been lying in wait and now it leaped at us, electric headlamps glowing in savage circles, the huge chrome grille seeming to snarl.

The kid froze, his face stamped with horror, his eyes blank, the pupils dilated down to pinpricks. I gave him a hard shove, spilling half his water.

'Go!'

The thunder of that diesel engine rose to a shriek. I reached over the kid's shoulder to yank the door open, but before I could it was shoved from inside. The kid lunged in and I dodged after him. I looked back to see the truck – a big cab-over Peterbilt – kiss off the tiled outside wall, peeling away jagged hunks of tile. There was an ear-grinding squealing noise, like gigantic fingers scraping a blackboard. Then the right mud-guard and the corners of the grille smashed into the still-open door, sending glass in a crystal spray and snapping the door's steel-gauge hinges like tissue paper. The door flew into the night like something out of a Dali painting and the truck accelerated towards the front parking lot, its exhaust racketing like machine-gun fire. It had a disappointed, angry sound.

The kid put his bucket down and collapsed into the girl's arms, shuddering.

My heart was thudding heavily in my chest and my calves felt like water. And speaking of water, we had brought back about a bucket and a quarter between us. It hardly seemed worth it.

'I want to block up that doorway.' I said to the counterman. 'What will do the trick?'

'Well –'

The trucker broke in: 'Why? One of those big trucks couldn't get a wheel in through there.'

'It's not the big trucks I'm worried about.'

The trucker began hunting for a smoke.

'We got some sheet sidin' out in the supply room,' The counterman said. 'Boss was gonna put up a shed to store butane gas.'

'We'll put them across and prop them with a couple of booths.'

'It'll help,' the trucker said.

It took about an hour and by the end we'd all got into the act, even the girl. It was fairly solid. Of course, fairly solid wasn't going to be good enough, not if something hit it at full speed. I think they all knew that.

There were still three booths ranged along the big glass picture window and I sat down in one of them. The clock behind the counter had stopped at 8.32, but it felt like ten. Outside the truck prowled and growled. Some left, hurrying off to unknown missions, and others came. There were three pickup trucks now, circling importantly amid their bigger brothers.

I was starting to doze, and instead of counting sheep I counted trucks. How many in the state, how many in America? Trailer trucks, pickup trucks, flatbeds, day-haulers, three-quarter-tons, army convoy trucks by the tens of thousands, and buses. Nightmare vision of a city bus, two wheels in the gutter and two wheels on the pavement, roaring along and ploughing through screaming pedestrians like ninepins.

I shook it off and fell into a light, troubled sleep.

It must have been early morning when Snodgrass began to scream. A thin new moon had risen and was shining icily through a high scud of cloud. A new clattering note had been added, counterpointing the throaty, idling roar of the big rigs. I looked for it and saw a hay baler circling out by the darkened sign. The moonlight glanced off the sharp, turning spokes of its packer.

The scream came again, unmistakably from the drainage ditch: 'Help . . . *meeeee* . . .'

'What was that?' It was the girl. In the shadows her eyes were wide and she looked horribly frightened.

'Nothing,' I said.

'Help . . . *meeeee* . . .'

'He's alive,' she whispered. 'Oh, God. *Alive*.'

I didn't have to see him. I could imagine it all too well. Snodgrass lying half in and half out of the drainage ditch, back and legs broken, carefully pressed suit caked with mud, white, gasping face turned up to the indifferent moon . . .

'I don't hear anything,' I said. 'Do you?'

She looked at me. 'How can you? How?'

'Now if you woke him up,' I said, jerking a thumb at the kid, '*he* might hear something. He might go out there. Would you like that?'

Her face began to twitch and pull as if stitched by invisible needles. 'Nothing,' she whispered. 'Nothing out there.'

She went back to her boyfriend and pressed her head against his chest. His arms came up around her in his sleep.

No one else woke up. Snodgrass cried and wept and screamed for a long time, and then he stopped.

Dawn.

Another truck had arrived, this one a flatbed with a giant rack for hauling cars. It was joined by a bulldozer. That scared me.

The trucker came over and twitched my arm. 'Come on back,' he whispered excitedly. The others were still sleeping. 'Come look at this.'

I followed him back to the supply room. About ten trucks were patrolling out there. At first I didn't see anything new.

'See?' he said, and pointed. 'Right there.'

Then I saw. One of the pickups was stopped dead. It was sitting there like a lump, all of the menace gone out of it.

'Out of gas?'

'That's right, buddy. *And they can't pump their own*. We got it knocked. All we have to do is wait.' He smiled and fumbled for a cigarette.

It was about nine o'clock and I was eating a piece of yesterday's pie for breakfast when the air horn began – long, rolling blasts that rattled your skull. We went over to the windows and looked out. The trucks were sitting still, idling. One trailer truck, a huge Reo with a red cab, had pulled up almost to the narrow verge of grass between the restaurant and the parking lot. At this distance the square grille was huge and murderous. The tyres would stand to a man's chest cavity.

The horn began to blare again; hard, hungry blasts that travelled off in straight, flat lines and echoed back. There was a pattern. Shorts and longs in some kind of rhythm.

'That's Morse!' the kid, Jerry, suddenly exclaimed.

The trucker looked at him. 'How would you know?'

The kid went a little red. 'I learned it in the Boy Scouts.'

'You?' the trucker said. '*You?* Wow.' He shook his head.

'Never mind,' I said. 'Do you remember enough to –'

'Sure. Let me listen. Got a pencil?'

The counterman gave him one, and the kid began to write letters on a napkin. After a while he stopped. 'It's just saying "Attention" over and over again. Wait.'

We waited. The air horn beat its longs and shorts into the still morning air. Then the pattern changed and the kid started to write again. We hung over his shoulders and watched the message form. 'Someone must pump fuel. Someone will not be harmed. All fuel must be pumped. This shall be done now. Now someone will pump fuel.'

The air blasts kept up, but the kid stopped writing. 'It's just repeating "Attention" again,' he said.

The truck repeated its message again and again. I didn't like the look of the words, printed on the napkin in block style. They looked machine-like, ruthless. There would be no compromise with those words. You did or you didn't.

'Well,' the kid said, 'what do we do?'

'Nothing,' the trucker said. His face was excited and working. 'All we have to do is wait. They must all be low on fuel. One of the little ones out back has already stopped. All we have to do –'

The air horn stopped. The truck backed up and joined its fellows. They waited in a semicircle, headlights pointed in towards us.

'There's a bulldozer out there,' I said.

Jerry looked at me. 'You think they'll rip the place down?'

'Yes.'

He looked at the counterman. 'They couldn't do that, could they?'

The counterman shrugged.

'We oughta vote,' the trucker said. 'No blackmail, damn it. All we gotta do is wait.' He had repeated it three times now, like a charm.

'Okay,' I said. 'Vote.'

'Wait,' the trucker said immediately.

'I think we ought to fuel them,' I said. 'We can wait for a better chance to get away. Counterman?'

'Stay in here,' he said. 'You want to be their slaves? That's what it'll come to. You want to spend the rest of your life changin' oil filters every time one of those . . . *things* blats its horn? Not me.' He looked darkly out the window. 'Let them starve.'

I looked at the kid and the girl.

'I think he's right,' he said. 'That's the only way to stop them. If someone was going to rescue us, they would have. God knows what's going on in other places.' And the girl, with Snodgrass in her eyes, nodded and stepped closer to him.

'That's it then,' I said.

I went over to the cigarette machine and got a pack without

looking at the brand. I'd stopped smoking a year ago, but this seemed like a good time to start again. The smoke rasped harsh in my lungs.

Twenty minutes crawled by. The trucks out front waited. Behind, they were lining up at the pumps.

'I think it was all a bluff,' the trucker said. 'Just –'

Then there was a louder, harsher, choppier note, the sound of an engine revving up and falling off, then revving up again. The bulldozer.

It glittered like a yellowjacket in the sun, a Caterpillar with clattering steel treads. Black smoke belched from its short stack as it wheeled around to face us.

'It's going to charge,' the trucker said. There was a look of utter surprise on his face. 'It's going to charge!'

'Get back,' I said. 'Behind the counter.'

The bulldozer was still revving. Gear-shift levers moved themselves. Heat shimmer hung over its smoking stack. Suddenly the dozer blade lifted, a heavy steel curve clotted with dried dirt. Then, with a screaming howl of power, it roared straight at us.

'The *counter!*' I gave the trucker a shove, and that started them.

There was a small concrete verge between the parking lot and the grass. The dozer charged over it, blade lifting for a moment, and then it rammed the front wall head on. Glass exploded inward with a heavy, coughing roar and the wood frame crashed into splinters. One of the overhead light globes fell, splashing more glass. Crockery fell from the shelves. The girl was screaming but the sound was almost lost beneath the steady, pounding roar of the Cat's engine.

It reversed, clanked across the chewed strip of lawn, and lunged forward again, sending the remaining booths crashing and spinning. The pie case fell off the counter, sending pie wedges skidding across the floor.

The counterman was crouching with his eyes shut, and the kid was holding his girl. The trucker was wall-eyed with fear.

'We gotta stop it,' he gibbered. 'Tell 'em we'll do it, we'll do anything –'

'A little late, isn't it?'

The Cat reversed and got ready for another charge. New nicks in its blade glittered and heliographed in the sun. It lurched forward with a bellowing roar and this time it took down the main support to the left of what had been the window. That section of the roof fell in with a grinding crash. Plaster dust billowed up.

The dozer pulled free. Beyond it I could see the group of trucks, waiting.

I grabbed the counterman. 'Where are the oil drums?' The cookstoves ran on butane gas, but I had seen vents for a warm-air furnace.

'Back of the storage room,' he said.

I grabbed the kid. 'Come on.'

We got up and ran into the storage room. The bulldozer hit again and the building trembled. Two or three more hits and it would be able to come right up to the counter for a cup of coffee.

There were two large fifty-gallon drums with feeds to the furnace and turn spigots. There was a carton of empty ketchup bottles near the back door. 'Get those, Jerry.'

While he did, I pulled off my shirt and yanked it to rags. The dozer hit again and again, and each hit was accompanied by the sound of more breakage.

I filled four of the ketchup bottles from the spigots, and he stuffed rags into them. 'You play football?' I asked him.

'In high school.'

'Okay. Pretend you're going in from the five.'

We went out into the restaurant. The whole front wall was open to the sky. Sprays of glass glittered like diamonds. One heavy beam had fallen diagonally across the opening. The dozer was backing up to take it out and I thought that this time it would keep coming, ripping through the stools and then demolishing the counter itself.

We knelt down and thrust the bottles out. 'Light them up,' I said to the trucker.

He got his matches out, but his hands were shaking too badly and he dropped them. The counterman picked them up, struck one, and the hunks of shirt blazed greasily alight.

'Quick,' I said.

We ran, the kid a little in the lead. Glass crunched and gritted underfoot. There was a hot, oily smell in the air. Everything was very loud, very bright.

The dozer charged.

The kid dodged out under the beam and stood silhouetted in front of that heavy tempered steel blade. I went out to the right. The kid's first throw fell short. His second hit the blade and the flame splashed harmlessly.

He tried to turn and then it was on him, a rolling juggernaut, four tons of steel. His hands flew up and then he was gone, chewed under.

I buttonhooked around and lobbed one bottle into the open cab and the second right into the works. They exploded together in a leaping shout of flame.

For a moment the dozer's engine rose in an almost human squeal of rage and pain. It wheeled in a maddened half-circle, ripping out the left corner of the diner, and rolled drunkenly towards the drainage ditch.

The steel treads were streaked and dotted with gore and where the kid had been there was something that looked like a crumpled towel.

The dozer got almost to the ditch, flames boiling from under its cowling and from the cockpit, and then it exploded in a geyser.

I stumbled backward and almost fell over a pile of rubble. There was a hot smell that wasn't just oil. It was burning hair. I was on fire.

I grabbed a tablecloth, jammed it on my head, ran behind the counter, and plunged my head into the sink hard enough to crack it on the bottom. The girl was screaming Jerry's name over and over in a shrieking insane litany.

I turned around and saw the huge car-carrier slowly rolling towards the defenceless front of the diner.

The trucker screamed and broke for the side door.

'Don't!' the counterman cried. 'Don't do that –'

But he was out and sprinting for the drainage ditch and the open field beyond.

The truck must have been standing sentry just out of sight of that side door – a small panel job with 'Wong's Cash-and-Carry Laundry' written on the side. It ran him down almost before you could see it happen. Then it was gone and only the trucker was left, twisted into the gravel. He had been knocked out of his shoes.

The car-carrier rolled slowly over the concrete verge, onto the grass, over the kid's remains, and stopped with its huge snout poking into the diner.

Its air horn let out a sudden, shattering honk, followed by another, and another.

'Stop!' the girl whimpered. 'Stop, oh stop, please –'

But the honks went on a long time. It took only a minute to pick up the pattern. It was the same as before. It wanted someone to feed it and the others.

'I'll go,' I said. 'Are the pumps unlocked?'

The counterman nodded. He had aged fifty years.

'No!' the girl screamed. She threw herself at me. 'You've got to stop them! Beat them, burn them, break them –' Her voice wavered and broke into a harsh bray of grief and loss.

The counterman held her. I went around the corner of the counter, picking my way through the rubble, and out through the supply room. My heart was thudding heavily when I stepped out into the warm sun. I wanted another cigarette, but you don't smoke around fuel islands.

The trucks were still lined up. The laundry truck was crouched across the gravel from me like a hound dog, growling and rasping. A funny move and it would cream me. The sun glittered on its blank windshield and I shuddered. It was like looking into the face of an idiot.

I switched the pump to 'on' and pulled out the nozzle; unscrewed the first gas cap and began to pump fuel.

It took me half an hour to pump the first tank dry and then I moved on to the second island. I was alternating between gas and diesel. Trucks marched by endlessly. I was beginning to understand now. I was beginning to see. People were doing this all over the country or they were lying dead like the trucker, knocked out of their boots with heavy treadmarks mashed across their guts.

The second tank was dry then and I went to the third. The sun was like a hammer and my head was starting to ache with the fumes. There were blisters in the soft webbing between thumb and index finger. But they wouldn't know about that. They would know about leaky manifolds and bad gaskets and frozen universal joints, but not about blisters or sunstroke or the need to scream. They needed to know only one thing about their late masters, and they knew it. We bleed.

The last tank was sucked dry and I threw the nozzle on the ground. Still there were more trucks, lined up around the corner. I twisted my head to relieve a crick in my neck and stared. The line went out of the front parking lot and up the road and out of sight, two and three lanes deep. It was like a nightmare of the Los Angeles Freeway at rush hour. The horizon shimmered and danced with their exhaust; the air stank of carburisation.

'No,' I said. 'Out of gas. All gone, fellas.'

And there was a heavier rumble, a bass note that shook the teeth. A huge silvery truck was pulling up, a tanker. Written on the side was: 'Fill Up with Phillips 66 – The Jetport Fuel'!

A heavy hose dropped out of the rear.

I went over, took it, flipped up the feeder plate on the first tank, and attached the hose. The truck began to pump. The stench of petroleum sank into me – the same stink that the dinosaurs must have died smelling as they went down into the tar pits. I filled the other two tanks and then went back to work.

Consciousness twinkled away to a point where I lost track of time and trucks. I unscrewed, rammed the nozzle into the hole, pumped until the hot, heavy liquid splurted out, then replaced the cap. My blisters broke, trickling pus down to my wrists. My head was pounding like a rotted tooth and my stomach rolled helplessly with the stench of hydrocarbons.

I was going to faint. I was going to faint and that would be the end of it. I would pump until I dropped.

Then there were hands on my shoulders, the dark hands of the counterman. 'Go in,' he said. 'Rest yourself. I'll take over till dark. Try to sleep.'

I handed him the pump.

But I can't sleep.

The girl is sleeping. She's sprawled over in the corner with her head on a tablecloth and her face won't unknot itself even in sleep. It's the timeless, ageless face of the warhag. I'm going to get her up pretty quick. It's twilight, and the counterman has been out there for five hours.

Still they keep coming. I look out through the wrecked window and their headlights stretch for a mile or better, twinkling like yellow sapphires in the growing darkness. They must be backed up all the way to the turnpike, maybe further.

The girl will have to take her turn. I can show her how. She'll say she can't, but she will. She wants to live.

You want to be their slaves? the counterman had said. *That's what it'll come to. You want to spend the rest of your life changin' oil filters every time one of those things blats its horn?*

We could run, maybe. It would be easy to make the drainage ditch now, the way they're stacked up. Run through the fields, through the marshy places where trucks would bog down like mastodons and go –

– back to the caves.

Drawing pictures in charcoal. This is the moon god. This is a tree. This is a Mack semi overwhelming a hunter.

Not even that. So much of the world is paved now. Even the playgrounds are paved. And for the fields and marshes and deep woods there are tanks, half-tracks, flatbeds equipped with lasers, masers, heat-seeking radar. And little by little, they can make it into the world they want.

I can see great convoys of trucks filling the Okefenokee Swamp with sand, the bulldozers ripping through the national parks and wildlands, grading the earth flat, stamping it into one great flat plain. And then the hot-top trucks arriving.

But they're machines. No matter what's happened to them, what mass consciousness we've given them, *they can't reproduce*. In fifty or sixty years they'll be rusting hulks with all menace gone out of them, moveless carcasses for free men to stone and spit at.

And if I close my eyes I can see the production lines in Detroit and Dearborn and Youngstown and Mackinac, new trucks being put together by blue-collars who no longer even punch a clock but only drop and are replaced.

The counterman is staggering a little now. He's an old bastard, too. I've got to wake the girl.

Two planes are leaving silver contrails etched across the darkening eastern horizon.

I wish I could believe there are people in them.

THE HITCH-HIKER

Roald Dahl

If Britain has an equal to Stephen King in the field of macabre fiction, then it is surely Roald Dahl (1916–) whose various books for both children and adults have earned him universal praise. The best of his short stories have, of course, recently been used as the basis for one of television's most successful series, 'Tales of the Unexpected'. And as a writer, he can take the simplest of situations and the most ordinary of people and use them as the basis for the most spellbinding mysteries.

Indeed, what more commonplace sight can there be than a hitch-hiker? Every motorist has seen one and probably occasionally picked one up, though sometimes misgivings can intrude about such a kindly act – particularly in the light of some of the terrible acts committed over the years by evil-intentioned hitch-hikers. And, of course, there is a fairly long-standing tradition about phantom hitch-hikers, strange passengers who have been picked up at remote localities, and later learned to have been persons who died years before. There are quite a number of such cases on record, I believe, and not so long ago a book about this phenomenon was published.

The hitch-hiker in Roald Dahl's story is no phantom, however, but he is a very strange man possessed of curious powers. The tale is every bit as effective, I think, as his other excellent motoring story, 'The Man From The South', about a boy who bets his car for fingers! For any reader who only knows Dahl through his screenplay for that delightful motoring film, 'Chitty, Chitty, Bang, Bang' I advise caution regarding the next few pages. And when you reach the end, Happy Motoring – and may the only mystery you have to face hereafter be the reason why your car won't start!

I had a new car. It was an exciting toy, a big BMW 3.3 Li, which means 3.3 litre, long wheelbase, fuel injection. It had a top speed of 129 m.p.h. and terrific acceleration. The body was pale blue. The seats inside were darker blue and they were made of leather, genuine soft leather of the finest quality. The windows were electrically operated and so was the sun-roof. The radio aerial popped up when I switched on the radio, and disappeared when I switched it off. The powerful engine growled and grunted impatiently at slow speeds, but at sixty miles an hour the growling stopped and the motor began to purr with pleasure.

I was driving up to London by myself. It was a lovely June day. They were haymaking in the fields and there were buttercups along both sides of the road. I was whispering along at seventy miles an hour, leaning back comfortably in my seat, with no more than a couple of fingers resting lightly on the wheel to keep her steady. Ahead of me I saw a man thumbing a lift. I touched the footbrake and brought the car to a stop beside him. I always stopped for hitch-hikers. I knew just how it used to feel to be standing on the side of a country road watching the cars go by. I hated the drivers for pretending they didn't see me, especially the ones in big cars with three empty seats. The large expensive cars seldom stopped. It was always the smaller ones that offered you a lift, or the old rusty ones, or the ones that were already crammed full of children and the driver would say, 'I think we can squeeze in one more.'

The hitch-hiker poked his head through the open window and said, 'Going to London, guv'nor?'

'Yes,' I said, 'Jump in.'

He got in and I drove on.

He was a small ratty-faced man with grey teeth. His eyes were dark and quick and clever, like a rat's eyes, and his ears were slightly pointed at the top. He had a cloth cap on his head and he was wearing a greyish-coloured jacket with enormous pockets. The grey jacket, together with the quick eyes and the pointed ears, made him look more than anything like some sort of a huge human rat.

'What part of London are you headed for?' I asked him.

'I'm goin' right through London and out the other side,' he said. 'I'm goin' to Epsom, for the races. It's Derby Day today.'

'So it is,' I said. 'I wish I were going with you. I love betting on horses.'

'I never bet on horses,' he said. 'I don't even watch 'em run. That's a stupid silly business.'

'Then why do you go?' I asked.

He didn't seem to like that question. His little ratty face went absolutely blank and he sat there staring straight ahead at the road, saying nothing.

'I expect you help to work the betting machines or something like that,' I said.

'That's even sillier,' he answered. 'There's no fun working them lousy machines and selling tickets to mugs. Any fool could do that.'

There was a long silence. I decided not to question him any more. I remembered how irritated I used to get in my hitch-hiking days when drivers kept asking *me* questions. Where are you going? Why are you going there? What's your job? Are you married? Do you have a girl-friend? What's her name? How old are you? And so on and so forth. I used to hate it.

'I'm sorry,' I said. 'It's none of my business what you do. The trouble is, I'm a writer, and most writers are terrible nosy parkers.'

'You write books?' he asked.

'Yes.'

'Writin' books is okay,' he said. 'It's what I call a skilled trade. I'm in a skilled trade too. The folks I despise is them that spend all their lives doin' crummy old routine jobs with no skill in 'em at all. You see what I mean?'

'Yes.'

'The secret of life,' he said, 'is to become very very good at somethin' that's very very 'ard to do.'

'Like you,' I said.

'Exactly. You and me both.'

'What makes you think that *I'm* any good at my job?' I asked. 'There's an awful lot of bad writers around.'

'You wouldn't be drivin' about in a car like this if you weren't no good at it,' he answered. 'It must've cost a tidy packet, this little job.'

'It wasn't cheap.'

'What can she do flat out?' he asked.

'One hundred and twenty-nine miles an hour,' I told him.

'I'll bet she won't do it.'

'I'll bet she will.'

'All car makers is liars,' he said. 'You can buy any car you like and it'll never do what the makers say it will in the ads.'

'This one will.'

'Open 'er up then and prove it,' he said. 'Go on, guv'nor, open 'er right up and let's see what she'll do.'

There is a roundabout at Chalfont St Peter and immediately beyond it there's a long straight section of dual carriageway. We came out of the roundabout on to the carriageway and I pressed my foot down on the accelerator. The big car leaped forward as though she'd been stung. In ten seconds or so, we were doing ninety.

'Lovely!' he cried. 'Beautiful! Keep goin'!'

I had the accelerator jammed right down against the floor and I held it there.

'One hundred!' he shouted . . . 'A hundred and five! . . . A hundred and ten! . . . A hundred and fifteen! Go on! Don't slack off!'

I was in the outside lane and we flashed past several cars as though they were standing still – a green Mini, a big cream-coloured Citroën, a white Land-Rover, a huge truck with a container on the back, an orange-coloured Volkswagen Minibus . . .

'A hundred and twenty!' my passenger shouted, jumping up and down. 'Go on! Go on! Get 'er up to one-two-nine!'

At that moment, I heard the scream of a police siren. It was so loud it seemed to be right inside the car, and then a policeman on a motor-cycle loomed up alongside us on the inside lane and went past us and raised a hand for us to stop.

'Oh, my sainted aunt!' I said. 'That's torn it!'

The policeman must have been doing about a hundred and thirty when he passed us, and he took plenty of time slowing down. Finally, he pulled into the side of the road and I pulled in behind him. 'I didn't know police motor-cycles could go as fast as that,' I said rather lamely.

'That one can,' my passenger said. 'It's the same make as yours. It's a BMW R90S. Fastest bike on the road. That's what they're usin' nowadays.'

The policeman got off his motor-cycle and leaned the machine sideways on to its prop stand. Then he took off his gloves and placed them carefully on the seat. He was in no hurry now. He had us where he wanted us and he knew it.

'This is real trouble,' I said. 'I don't like it one bit.'

'Don't talk to 'im any more than is necessary, you understand,' my companion said. 'Just sit tight and keep mum.'

Like an executioner approaching his victim, the policeman came strolling slowly towards us. He was a big meaty man with a belly, and his blue breeches were skintight around his enormous thighs. His goggles were pulled up on to the helmet, showing a smouldering red face with wide cheeks.

We sat there like guilty schoolboys, waiting for him to arrive.

'Watch out for this man,' my passenger whispered. "Ee looks mean as the devil.'

The policeman came round to my open window and placed one meaty hand on the sill. 'What's the hurry?' he said.

'No hurry, officer,' I answered.

'Perhaps there's a woman in the back having a baby and you're rushing her to hospital? Is that it?'

'No, officer.'

'Or perhaps your house is on fire and you're dashing home to rescue the family from upstairs?' His voice was dangerously soft and mocking.

'My house isn't on fire, officer.'

'In that case,' he said, 'you've got yourself into a nasty mess, haven't you? Do you know what the speed limit is in this country?'

'Seventy,' I said.

'And do you mind telling me exactly what speed you were doing just now?'

I shrugged and didn't say anything.

When he spoke next, he raised his voice so loud that I jumped. *'One hundred and twenty miles per hour!'* he barked. 'That's *fifty* miles an hour over the limit!'

He turned his head and spat out a big gob of spit. It landed on the wing of my car and started sliding down over my beautiful blue paint. Then he turned back again and stared hard at my passenger. 'And who are you?' he asked sharply.

'He's a hitch-hiker,' I said. 'I'm giving him a lift.'

'I didn't ask you,' he said. 'I asked him.'

"Ave I done somethin' wrong?' my passenger asked. His voice was as soft and oily as haircream.

'That's more than likely,' the policeman answered. 'Anyway, you're a witness. I'll deal with you in a minute. Driving-licence,' he snapped, holding out his hand.

I gave him my driving-licence.

He unbuttoned the left-hand breast-pocket of his tunic and

brought out the dreaded books of tickets. Carefully, he copied the name and address from my licence. Then he gave it back to me. He strolled round to the front of the car and read the number from the number-plate and wrote that down as well. He filled in the date, the time and the details of my offence. Then he tore out the top copy of the ticket. But before handing it to me, he checked that all the information had come through clearly on his own carbon copy. Finally, he replaced the book in his tunic pocket and fastened the button.

'Now you,' he said to my passenger, and he walked around to the other side of the car. From the other breast-pocket he produced a small black notebook. 'Name?' he snapped.

'Michael Fish,' my passenger said.

'Address?'

'Fourteen, Windsor Lane, Luton.'

'Show me something to prove this is your real name and address,' the policeman said.

My passenger fished in his pockets and came out with a driving-licence of his own. The policeman checked the name and address and handed it back to him. 'What's your job? he asked sharply.

'I'm an 'od carrier.'

'A *what*?'

'An 'od carrier.'

'Spell it.'

'H-O-D C-A- . . .'

'That'll do. And what's a hod carrier, may I ask?'

'An 'od carrier, officer, is a person 'oo carries the cement up the ladder to the bricklayer. And the 'od is what 'e carries it in. It's got a long 'andle, and on the top you've got two bits of wood set at an angle . . .'

'All right, all right. Who's your employer?'

'Don't 'ave one. I'm unemployed.'

The policeman wrote all this down in the black notebook. Then he returned the book to its pocket and did up the button.

'When I get back to the station I'm going to do a little checking up on you,' he said to my passenger.

'Me? What've I done wrong?' the rat-faced man asked.

'I don't like your face, that's all,' the policeman said. 'And we just might have a picture of it somewhere in our files.' He strolled round the car and returned to my window.

'I suppose you know you're in serious trouble,' he said to me.

'Yes, officer.'

'You won't be driving this fancy car of yours again for a very long time, not after *we've* finished with you. You won't be driving *any* car again come to that for several years. And a good thing, too. I hope they lock you up for a spell into the bargain.'

'You mean prison?' I asked, alarmed.

'Absolutely,' he said, smacking his lips. 'In the clink. Behind the bars. Along with all the other criminals who break the law. *And* a hefty fine into the bargain. Nobody will be more pleased about that than me. I'll see you in court, both of you. You'll be getting a summons to appear.'

He turned away and walked over to his motor-cycle. He flipped the prop stand back into position with his foot and swung his leg over the saddle. Then he kicked the starter and roared off up the road out of sight.

'Phew!' I gasped. 'That's done it.'

'We was caught,' my passenger said. 'We was caught good and proper.'

'I was caught, you mean.'

'That's right,' he said. 'What you goin' to do now, guv'nor?'

'I'm going straight up to London to talk to my solicitor,' I said. I started the car and drove on.

'You mustn't believe what 'e said to you about goin' to prison,' my passenger said. 'They don't put nobody in the clink just for speedin'.'

'Are you sure of that?' I asked.

'I'm positive,' he answered. 'They can take your licence away and they can give you a whoppin' big fine, but that'll be the end of it.'

I felt tremendously relieved.

'By the way,' I said, 'why did you lie to him?'

'Who, me?' he said. 'What makes you think I lied?'

'You told him you were an unemployed hod carrier. But you told *me* you were in a highly skilled trade.'

'So I am,' he said. 'But it don't pay to tell everythin' to a copper.'

'So what *do* you do?' I asked him.

'Ah,' he said slyly. 'That'd be tellin', wouldn't it?'

'Is it something you're ashamed of?'

'Ashamed?' he cried. 'Me, ashamed of my job? I'm about as proud of it as anybody could be in the entire world!'

'Then why won't you tell me?'

'You writers really is nosy parkers, aren't you?' he said. 'And you ain't goin' to be 'appy, I don't think, until you've found out exactly what the answer is?'

'I don't really care one way or the other,' I told him, lying.

He gave me a crafty litle ratty look out of the sides of his eyes. 'I think you do care,' he said. 'I can see it on your face that you think I'm in some kind of a very peculiar trade and you're just achin' to know what it is.'

I didn't like the way he read my thoughts. I kept quiet and stared at the road ahead.

'You'd be right, too,' he went on. 'I *am* in a very peculiar trade. I'm in the queerest peculiar trade of 'em all.'

I waited for him to go on.

'That's why I 'as to be extra careful 'oo I'm talkin' to, you see. 'Ow am I to know, for instance, you're not another copper in plain clothes?'

'Do I look like a copper?'

'No,' he said. 'You don't. And you ain't. Any fool could tell that.'

He took from his pocket a tin of tobacco and a packet of cigarette papers and started to roll a cigarette. I was watching him out of the corner of one eye, and the speed with which he performed this rather difficult operation was incredible. The cigarette was rolled and ready in about five seconds. He ran his tongue along the edge of the paper, stuck it down and popped the cigarette between his lips. Then, as if from nowhere, a lighter appeared in his hand. The lighter flamed. The cigarette was lit. The lighter disappeared. It was altogether a remarkable performance.

'I've never seen anyone roll a cigarette as fast as that,' I said.

'Ah,' he said, taking a deep suck of smoke. 'So you noticed.'

'Of course I noticed. It was quite fantastic.'

He sat back and smiled. It pleased him very much that I had noticed how quickly he could roll a cigarette. 'You want to know what makes me able to do it?' he asked.

'Go on then.'

'It's because I've got fantastic fingers. These fingers of mine,' he said, holding up both hands high in front of him, 'are quicker and cleverer than the fingers of the best piano player in the world!'

'Are you a piano player?'

'Don't be daft,' he said. 'Do I look like a piano player?'

I glanced at his fingers. They were so beautifully shaped, so slim and long and elegant, they didn't seem to belong to the rest of him at all. They looked more like the fingers of a brain surgeon or a watchmaker.

'My job,' he went on, 'is a hundred times more difficult than playin' the piano. Any twerp can learn to do that. There's titchy little kids learnin' to play the piano in almost any 'ouse you go into these days. That's right, ain't it?'

'More or less,' I said.

'Of course it's right. But there's not one person in ten million can learn to do what I do. Not one in ten million! 'Ow about that?'

'Amazing,' I said.

'You're darn right it's amazin',' he said.

'I think I know what you do,' I said. 'You do conjuring tricks. You're a conjuror.'

'Me?' he snorted. 'A conjuror? Can you picture me goin' round crummy kids' parties makin' rabbits come out of top 'ats?'

'Then you're a card player. You get people into card games and deal yourself marvellous hands.'

'Me! A rotten card-sharper!' he cried. 'That's a miserable racket if ever there was one.'

'All right. I give up.'

I was taking the car along slowly now, at no more than forty miles an hour, to make quite sure I wasn't stopped again. We had come on to the main London–Oxford road and were running down the hill towards Denham.

Suddenly, my passenger was holding up a black leather belt in his hand. 'Ever seen this before?' he asked. The belt had a brass buckle of unusual design.

'Hey!' I said. 'That's mine, isn't it? It *is* mine! Where did you get it?'

He grinned and waved the belt gently from side to side. 'Where d'you think I got it?' he said. 'Off the top of your trousers, of course.'

I reached down and felt for my belt. It was gone.

'You mean you took it off me while we've been driving along?' I asked, flabbergasted.

He nodded, watching me all the time with those little black ratty eyes.

'That's impossible,' I said. 'You'd have had to undo the buckle and slide the whole thing out through the loops all the way round. I'd have seen you doing it. And even if I hadn't see you, I'd have felt it.'

'Ah, but you didn't, did you?' he said, triumphant. He dropped the belt on his lap, and now all at once there was a brown shoelace dangling from his fingers. 'And what about this, then?' he exclaimed, waving the shoelace.

'What about it?' I said.

'Anyone around 'ere missin' a shoelace?' he asked, grinning.

I glanced down at my shoes. The lace of one of them was missing. 'Good grief!' I said. 'How did you do that? I never saw you bending down.'

'You never saw nothin',' he said proudly. 'You never even saw me move an inch. And you know why?'

'Yes,' I said, 'Becaue you've got fantastic fingers.'

'Exactly right!' he cried. 'You catch on pretty quick, don't you?' He sat back and sucked away at his home-made cigarette, blowing the smoke out in a thin stream against the windshield. He knew he had impressed me greatly with those two tricks, and this made him very happy. 'I don't want to be late,' he said. 'What time is it?'

'There's a clock in front of you,' I told him.

'I don't trust car clocks,' he said. 'What does your watch say?'

I hitched up my sleeve to look at the watch on my wrist. It wasn't there. I looked at the man. He looked back at me, grinning.

'You've taken that, too,' I said.

He held out his hand and there was my watch lying in his palm. 'Nice bit of stuff, this,' he said, 'Superior quality. Eighteen-carat gold. Easy to flog, too. It's never any trouble gettin' rid of quality goods.'

'I'd like it back, if you don't mind,' I said rather huffily.

He placed the watch carefully on the leather tray in front of him. 'I wouldn't nick anything from you, guv'nor,' he said. 'You're my pal. You're giving me a lift.'

'I'm glad to hear it,' I said.

'All I'm doin' is answerin' your questions,' he went on. 'You asked me what I did for a livin' and I'm showin' you.'

'What else have you got of mine?'

He smiled again, and now he started to take from the pocket of his jacket one thing after another that belonged to me – my driving-licence, a key-ring with four keys on it, some pound notes, a few coins, a letter from my publishers, my diary, a stubby old pencil, a cigarette-lighter, and last of all, a beautiful old sapphire ring with pearls around it belonging to my wife. I was taking the ring up to the jeweller in London because one of the pearls was missing.

'Now *there's* another lovely piece of goods,' he said, turning the ring over in his fingers. 'That's eighteenth century, if I'm not mistaken, from the reign of King George the Third.'

'You're right,' I said, impressed. 'You're absolutely right.'

He put the ring on the leather tray with the other items.

'So you're a pickpocket,' I said.

'I don't like that word,' he answered. 'It's a coarse and vulgar word. Pickpockets is coarse and vulgar people who only do easy little amateur jobs. They lift money from blind old ladies.'

'What do you call yourself, then?'

'Me? I'm a fingersmith. I'm a professional fingersmith.' He spoke the words solemnly and proudly, as though he were telling me he was the President of the Royal College of Surgeons or the Archbishop of Canterbury.

'I've never heard that word before,' I said. 'Did you invent it?'

'Of course I didn't invent it,' he replied. 'It's the name given to them who's risen to the very top of the profession. You've 'eard of a goldsmith and a silversmith, for instance. They're experts with gold and silver. I'm an expert with my fingers, so I'm a fingersmith.'

'It must be an interesting job.'

'It's a marvellous job,' he answered. 'It's lovely.'

'And that's why you go to the races?'

'Race meetings is easy meat,' he said. 'You just stand around after the race, watchin' for the lucky ones to queue up and draw their money. And when you see someone collectin' a big bundle of notes, you simply follows after 'im and 'elps yourself. But don't get me wrong, guv'nor. I never takes nothin' from a loser. Nor from poor people neither. I only go after them as can afford it, the winners and the rich.'

'That's very thoughtful of you,' I said. 'How often do you get caught?'

'Caught?' he cried, disgusted. '*Me* get caught! It's only pickpockets get caught. Fingersmiths never. Listen, I could take the false teeth out of your mouth if I wanted to and you wouldn't even catch me!'

'I don't have false teeth,' I said.

'I know you don't,' he answered. 'Otherwise I'd 'ave 'ad 'em out long ago!'

I believed him. Those long slim fingers of his seemed able to do anything.

We drove on for a while without talking.

'That policeman's going to check up on you pretty thoroughly,' I said. 'Doesn't that worry you a bit?'

'Nobody's checkin' up on me,' he said.

'Of course they are. He's got your name and address written down most carefully in his black book.'

The man gave me another of his sly, ratty little smiles. 'Ah,' he said. 'So 'e 'as. But I'll bet 'e ain't got it all written down in 'is memory as well. I've never known a copper yet with a decent memory. Some of 'em can't even remember their own names.'

'What's memory got to do with it?' I asked. 'It's written down in his book, isn't it?'

'Yes, guv'nor, it is. But the trouble is, 'e lost the book. 'E's lost both books, the one with my name in it *and* the one with yours.'

In the long delicate fingers of his right hand, the man was holding up in triumph the two books he had taken from the policeman's pockets. 'Easiest job I ever done,' he announced proudly.

I nearly swerved the car into a milk-truck, I was so excited.

'That copper's got nothin' on either of us now,' he said.

'You're a genius!' I cried.

''E's got no names, no addresses, no car number, no nothin',' he said.

'You're brilliant!'

'I think you'd better pull in off this main road as soon as possible,' he said. 'Then we'd better build a little bonfire and burn these books.'

'You're a fantastic fellow,' I exclaimed.

'Thank you, guv'nor,' he said. 'It's always nice to be appreciated.'

Acknowledgements

The editor wishes to thank the following authors, their agents or executors, for permission to include copyright material in this collection:

A. P. Watt Ltd for 'The Dust-Cloud' by E. F. Benson from *The Room in the Tower*.
The estate of Archie Binns for 'The Last Trip'.
Jonathan Cape Ltd for 'The Demon Lover' by Elizabeth Bowen from *The Demon Lover & Other Stories*. Also 'The Hitch-Hiker' by Roald Dahl from *The Wonderful Story of Henry Sugar*.
The executors of H. Russell Wakefield for 'Jay Walkers' from *The Clock Strikes Twelve*.
Arthur Emmons for 'The Ghost of the Model T' by Betsy Emmons.
Good Story Magazine Co. for 'The Ghost Car' by Ken Batten.
The Estate of L. T. C. Rolt for 'New Corner' from *Sleep No More*.
The author for 'Just Like Wild Bob' by William F. Nolan.
A. D. Peters Literary Agency for 'Auto Suggestion' by Charles Beaumont.
Don Congdon Literary Agency for 'Duel' by Richard Matheson.
Holt, Rinehart Inc for 'Second Chance' by Jack Finney from *The Third Level*.
New English Library Ltd for 'Trucks' by Stephen King from *Night Shift*.

Every effort has been made to trace the copyright holders of the stories in this book. The editor offers his apologies in the event of any acknowledgement being accidentally omitted.